TWO
BROKEN
GIRLS

BOOKS BY HELEN PHIFER

STANDALONES

Lakeview House

TWO
BROKEN
GIRLS

HELEN PHIFER

bookouture

Published by Bookouture in 2024

An imprint of Storyfire Ltd.
Carmelite House
50 Victoria Embankment
London EC4Y 0DZ

www.bookouture.com

Storyfire Ltd's authorised representative in the EEA is Hachette Ireland
8 Castlecourt Centre
Castleknock Road
Castleknock
Dublin 15, D15 YF6A
Ireland

ISBN: 978-1-83790-380-1
eBook ISBN: 978-1-83790-379-5

1

Little did she know that this morning would be the last time she would look in the mirror. It was the last time she'd spend thirty minutes agonising over the shade of her lipstick, the style of her hair and whether she should wear the boots or the trainers to college. If she knew that this was going to be her choice of clothes for all of eternity, would she have chosen differently?

He looked down at what he was wearing, in contrast. He would be quite happy if he died now and had to haunt the world dressed like this. It would, he supposed, be quite fitting for a man like him. She was rushing around her bedroom now, curtains open wide, Taylor Swift loudly filtering down onto the street through the open window. Everyone listened to Swift's music – he didn't see the attraction, but he wasn't a woman and didn't appreciate the lyrics. His stepdaughter listened to her too, as well as his ex who he thought had got her courage and inspiration to end their relationship from one of her many songs. He wasn't too sad when his ex had found the strength to tell him it was over, as it had been coming to an end anyway. She was just a good person to hide behind; loud, funny, friendly. He supposed she had taken him under her wing and tried to bring out the best in him, and she had succeeded for a little while. If he was honest with himself, he was somewhat relieved that she had called it a day. He felt as if he could breathe again, was free to take up where he'd abruptly left off. The thing was, he thought, you can't keep who you really are bottled up like a jar of ketchup at the back of the store cupboard. He was now, and always had been, a bit of a predator, collecting girlfriends – then victims – like trophies.

He looked across at the small wooden box in which he kept his little keepsakes, and he smiled; the engraved lid had the name *Sarah* faintly written on it. Sarah had been his first. Whenever anyone asked about it, he told them it belonged to his gran, end of that story and no further questions asked. He loved collecting little trinkets that fit inside of his box. What could he add to them? He hoped she was wearing the small gold cross today. It would be a fitting reminder of his time with her; and it would make an excellent addition to his collection.

He looked at his watch. He had all the time in the world.

She would leave the house at some point, there was no hurry. Her mum had left the house to go to work, and he knew she wouldn't be back until at least four, maybe even later. Her mum worked full time so that gave him at least six glorious hours of not worrying about anyone coming back.

He had the car window down, and the spring air was warm today. It was heating up nicely after the miserable wet winter they'd suffered through. He closed his eyes, the warmth from the sun relaxing him nicely. He wouldn't fall asleep, though; he was just resting them, as his old dad used to say. He was alert to everything, the traffic, the sound of a lawnmower a street away, the music coming from her bedroom. He had to be careful, as he could be lulled into a false sense of security, and he knew that it would be a fatal mistake if he did fall asleep. He was too tightly wound for what he was about to do: sleep was not an option. He was merely trying to keep his blood pressure down and keep calm – he had to pull this off with no mistakes.

He was a little rusty, but he was sure it was like riding a bicycle. Once he got back in the saddle he would be right back where he left off. He reached out one hand and trailed his fingers across the old, worn rope that had served him well. He didn't do knives or blood, not in large amounts as he couldn't bear the mess. What he liked was a nice, clean kill with no fuss. Once you started using weapons it began to get very messy. Besides he hated the smell of blood, that coppery tang turned his stomach. Choking someone to death took a little more strength. It was more intimate too because you had to get really close to them. And he enjoyed the smell of fear that would seep from the pores of his victims too much to spoil it by tainting it with the stench of blood.

Lost in his thoughts it took him a moment to realise the music had stopped. He opened his eyes, pushed the rope into his pocket and tucked the small wooden box underneath the front seat of the car. He popped the button for the engine and then jumped out of the car. Lifting the bonnet, he stood there staring down into the engine. Just in time, too, as the door to her house slammed shut. She walked past him, headphones on, backpack slung over her shoulder, then paused and turned back. 'Oh hi, is everything okay?' She pointed to his car, and he shrugged.

'Hi, Melody, it's making a funny noise but I'm not sure what it is. I don't know anything about cars.'

She shrugged. 'Me either, sorry.'

When she smiled at him, it was such a beautiful smile it made him feel a little sad that out of all the people he could have chosen he had chosen her. Then he pushed his fingers into his pocket and felt the rough hemp rope, and his sadness lifted.

He grinned back at her. 'Don't worry. Do you want a lift to college? Well, I can't guarantee we'll get there on time if it breaks down, but I'm heading that way.'

She didn't even pause, which made him even sadder. She turned around and walked towards the front seat of the car. 'Yes please, I hate the bus.'

He stayed hidden behind the bonnet of the car so she couldn't see the gleeful expression that had spread across his face. Sucking in a deep breath he stopped smiling to himself and slammed the bonnet down. The voice inside his head repeatedly whispering *keep it cool, keep it cool*, he got inside the car, pressed the button and the engine turned over as smoothly as always.

Melody slipped her headphones around her neck. 'Sounds okay to me.'

He nodded. 'It does when I first turn it on, then after a couple of miles it starts to make a funny clunking sound. But let's see how far we get. Don't let me stop your entertainment, are you a Swiftie too?' He pointed to the Beats headphones, and she smiled at him.

'I'm listening to an audiobook, I love them. It's a cool way to start the day, getting an extra hit of education, but yes, I do love her as well.'

'Well, I'd be a fool to say if it isn't.'

She slid the headphones back onto her ears and stared out of the window as he drove out of the street. Damn if he didn't have even more regrets about what he was going to do to her very soon, but it was too late – he had set it in motion and couldn't back down. If he let her go and she told anyone about his broken-down car, they could tie his modus operandi to the last woman he had strangled and dumped in woodland. He hoped they wouldn't, that their bodies were far enough away, but he knew that the team here in Rydal Falls was very good, they had more experience with murders than most inner-city cops. He wasn't prepared to get caught before he'd finished what he wanted to accomplish, even though the older he got the worse he felt about it. He glanced at his eyes in the rear-view mirror and scolded himself. He had a plan, and he had to stick to it.

2

Detective Constable Morgan Brookes had decided to walk to work this morning, much to Ben's amusement.

'Are you feeling ill, do you need to go see a doctor?' he'd said. As her partner and work colleague, he knew first-hand that this was a very rare occurrence.

'What, because I want to walk to work? Don't be so cheeky. It's a gorgeous morning and I want to start exercising a little bit. I hate the gym. I equally hate running too, but walking doesn't seem too bad. Why don't you walk with me?'

He paused as if thinking about it, then shook his head. 'Absolutely not, Brookes, I hate walking as much as you hate running.'

'Suit yourself.'

'You haven't made some crazy bet with Cain again, have you? Because we know how that one ended. He got himself stabbed to get out of it.'

Morgan's eyes almost popped out of her head in horror. Cain had been stabbed and left bleeding at the bottom of a staircase when they were hunting for the guy who'd killed Cora

Dalton, leaving her body at Castlerigg Stone Circle. 'You did not just say that.'

'I did.'

He was grinning at her, and she loved it when he grinned. His eyes crinkled and his whole face lit up, sending a rush of overpowering love straight to her heart like a direct dopamine hit. She decided there and then that she needed to make him laugh a lot more. He was so serious a lot of the time because of the high pressures from his job. Seeing him relaxed as he wandered around in his Calvins and a washed-out T-shirt had her questioning whether she should spend the twenty minutes it would take her to walk to work in the bedroom instead.

'Well, good luck, I'll see you on the other side when you're all sweaty. Make sure you have a tin of deodorant in your bag.'

And with that statement every ounce of passion she'd been feeling seconds ago was wiped clean. 'Bugger off, I will not. See you at work.'

She grabbed her backpack, turned on the *outside walk* mode on her watch and watched the green numbers count down then give a little beep.

'See you soon, I love you. Are you stopping off for coffee on the way?'

She turned around and gave him the middle finger, which made him laugh even louder. Then she was out of the front door, slamming it shut behind her loudly for effect.

She had no idea why it amused everyone whenever she tried a different method of exercise, and then she smiled to herself. Actually, she did. She complained about it nonstop. Today, she had on a pair of trainers but had left a pair of Docs in her locker at work ready to change into. Her trusty Docs were a part of her identity and had saved her arse on more than a few occasions. The spring sunshine felt good as it warmed her face, and it wasn't hot enough to burn her fair skin yet. Her copper-coloured hair was in a high ponytail and she wondered if she should have put it in a messy bun instead, but she wasn't planning on getting all sweaty like Ben had mentioned – it would ruin her perfect winged eyeliner – she was merely taking a brisk walk to work.

She ducked past Mrs Walker's bay window, not wanting to get caught up in a conversation about the rising crime rates before the start of her shift, or what the man a couple of doors down had been up to. Morgan didn't like that kind of gossip, purely because she wasn't interested. Work gossip was far more entertaining and a bit of fun. Cain would be a great match for Mrs Walker; he was her constant source of who was having an affair, who had got themselves in trouble, who was up to what at work. As she reached the high street and saw The Coffee Pot, the lure of a latte was too much. Deciding that she wasn't carrying a tray of coffees to work but could treat herself to one, she popped inside.

She was surprised to find it so quiet, considering it was almost lunchtime – she must have beat the rush. Jade was smiling at her from behind the counter.

'How many?'

'Just one, please.'

'Oh, are you not at work? Should I put it in a cup, and you can sit down at a table like a civilised customer and not rush out with it?'

Morgan laughed. 'I hate to ruin your day, but I'm definitely not civilised, unhinged more like.'

Jade shook her head. 'You are most certainly not unhinged. Have you seen my two o'clock customers? There's three of them come in every day and not one of them can speak a word of sense, but they turn up rain or shine and I love them dearly for that.'

Morgan snorted with laughter. 'You're just trying to make me feel better.'

She shrugged. 'Come back at two, that will definitely make you feel better.'

She passed a pink cardboard cup across the counter towards Morgan. 'Cake?'

Morgan surveyed the cake cabinet. There were tray bakes of every flavour, cupcakes, brownies and cookies. She let out a sigh. 'My heart says one of each, my trousers are saying not today, Satan.'

Jade crossed her arms. 'I think you should follow your heart because those trousers are lying to you.'

'I'm okay, thanks, I've got myself a little packed lunch for when I get to work.'

Morgan double-clicked the side button on her phone to pay for the coffee, and Jade shook her head. 'This one's on the house. I couldn't do what you do for all the money in the world.'

Morgan felt her cheeks burning; she wasn't good at taking kindness and compliments.

'Are you sure?'

'One hundred per cent.'

'Thank you so much, that's really kind of you.'

She left the café feeling a little overwhelmed; random acts of kindness were so lovely. She would be sure to pay it forward at some point today.

Her phone began to vibrate, and she saw Ben's face. Taking a sip of her coffee, she slid her finger across the screen. 'What's up, bragging you got to work first.'

'No, just checking you don't want picking up?'

'I'm good, thanks. See you soon.'

She hung up. She was going to sip her coffee and enjoy the walk before the stress of whatever was waiting for her at the station took over.

She heard the sirens before she saw them, and felt her heart skip a beat. There were multiple sirens, meaning multiple vans off to an IR: an immediate response.

It was too nice a day to have to deal with death and sadness right at the beginning of her shift, and surely, they had to catch a break at some point. She was still having nightmares about High Wraith Cottage and seeing Margery's body swaying from the tree in the middle of a raging storm.

3

Arthur Brown walked his dog by the riverside at the same time each day, and he had since he'd got the little pug as a puppy. He had never thought he'd take to owning a dog, but his daughter had turned up with it a month after his wife had died and told him it was his. She had brought everything a dog needed, plus more teddy bears than it knew what to do with, and then she'd left. Leaving him staring at the tiny puppy sitting in the cardboard box. It had stared right back at him, and once he'd got over the initial shock of how ugly it was, combined with the shock that his daughter had done this to him, he had fallen in love with it.

Scooping its trembling body into his arms he'd cradled it, stroking it and talking to it. Wrapping it in a soft blanket to keep it warm, he had marvelled at how soft it was and how he now had to be responsible for the small animal, which was huge for Arthur because he'd never owned a dog in his life. The first thing he had done was to think of a name for it. He had placed it on the floor and the poor thing had tried to run after him, but ended up rolling around on its belly, which had made him laugh so much that tears had trickled down his cheeks and he decided that Tumbles was the perfect name.

Now as Tumbles sniffed and grunted his way along the riverbank, Arthur unclipped the lead from his harness and let him off to have a run around. He wouldn't go far, he never did – always having to keep Arthur in his line of sight – but Tumbles took off running towards the wooded area, which puzzled him. Arthur thought nothing of it until he heard the familiar bark of his dog, and he picked up his pace, calling his name repeatedly, but he didn't come running back like he usually did. Getting annoyed, Arthur made his way through the small patch of oak trees and stopped in his tracks, not sure what he was looking at.

Lying on the floor, curled up at the base of the tree nearest to the riverbank, was a woman. He blinked and told himself it must be one of those shop mannequin things; there was no reason for a woman to be lying in the woods. For one thing it wasn't warm enough and well, it wasn't that kind of place. The dog was standing near to her, still barking, and reluctantly he forced his feet to move towards whatever it was.

'Hello, are you okay?'

There was no movement, no sign of life.

'Tumbles, come here now.'

The dog looked at him then turned back to the woman and carried on barking. As Arthur got nearer, he could see she had something around her neck, and he realised it was a pair of those oversized headphones all the kids were using nowadays. He saw her hands, they were folded neatly across her stomach, and she had a dazzling, glittery shade of sky-blue nail varnish on her nails. Her head was turned away from him, exposing an angry red mark on the skin around her neck underneath the headphones.

Arthur wanted to get out of there, afraid that she might turn her head and scream as if he had done this to her. His hands shaking, he felt in his pocket for the phone he rarely used and remembered he had left if charging on the kitchen side. *Damn you, Arthur, all you had to do was unplug it.*

He heard his dead wife's voice inside his head, and he pleaded with her what to do. *Go make sure she doesn't need your help is what you should do.* He looked around, feeling somewhat like a voyeur, walking towards a young, very dead woman. He bent towards her and pushed his finger against her shoulder, which was hard to the touch, and then he started screaming.

4

Morgan walked to the main entrance of the Rydal Falls police station and slipped past the people waiting to be seen through the double doors into the glass atrium of the open-plan ground floor. There was, of all things, a tree planted smack bang in the middle that had seen better days, its leaves were turning brown at the ends, and she was curious to know if anyone watered it. Brenda appeared with a jug of water, as if she'd summoned her out of the small kitchen area, and walked towards her.

'Morning, I wouldn't take your coat off if I were you.'

'Why?'

'Some hysterical guy phoned up screaming down the phone and talking gibberish.'

'Is that where the vans were going?'

Brenda nodded as she poured the water around the base of the tree. 'Yep, poor bugger must be bad to make him scream like that. We could still hear him in the background as Control passed the job over on the radio.'

Morgan felt her heart sink. She had only been inside the station for three minutes and already she wanted to turn around and walk back out, make the start of her shift a better one without anyone suffering distress or trauma.

'Thanks.'

Brenda looked up at her. 'Sorry to be the bearer of bad news, love. Thought I'd better warn you, that's all.'

'It's okay, I appreciate it.'

The woman who had worked for Cumbria Constabulary for what seemed like forever winked at her. 'It could be worse.'

'How?'

'If you'd have been here a few minutes earlier you'd have got dragged off with the inspector. Poor Amy's face was a picture as she followed him out. You had a lucky escape.'

Morgan smiled. 'Where's Ben?'

'Custody, last I heard, had to go speak to someone who got arrested last night, and give them a bollocking.'

'Where's the duty sergeant?'

'Mads couldn't do it, said it was his son's friend so asked Ben.'

'Ah, okay. See you later.'

Morgan headed towards the lift; she'd done her exercise for the day, and she wasn't going to finish herself off going up the stairs. She turned back to Brenda. 'I think that tree needs some plant food or something, it looks like it's dying.'

Brenda laughed. 'Don't we all? What it needs is some sunlight and to be planted outside. Who in their right mind thought this was a suitable environment for a tree?'

Morgan shrugged and stepped into the lift, wondering what had made a guy phone up screaming. It must be bad if Marc had dragged himself out of his cosy little office, taking Amy along for the ride. Their CID office was empty, and Cain was nowhere to be seen.

She didn't bother shrugging off her coat but sat down and logged on to the computer to read the incident log and find out what was happening. When she saw the location, her heart almost jumped out of her chest. There was little information on the log: it said *dead body by the riverside. No further information at present, caller too upset.* She closed her eyes. The banks of the River Rothay had been the hunting ground for the Riverside Rapist when she was a child; he also just happened to be her murderous, biological father. She hadn't thought about Gary Marks for some time. The riverbank was also where Milly Blake had been abducted. For such a beautiful place it had witnessed a lot of tragic events.

Ben pushed the door open a little too energetically with one hand, sending it crashing into the wall and making her jump out of her skin. In his other he balanced a mug.

'Sorry, what's got you all jumpy? Did something happen on your walk?'

'No, it was nice. Have you heard about the guy screaming by the river?'

His eyes narrowed as he said, 'What?' He came towards her, sloshing coffee all down himself, muttering, 'Shit, that's hot.' Then slammed the dripping mug down on her desk. He leaned over her shoulder, and she relished the warmth and the comforting scent of his aftershave. He stood up and picked up her radio, which was on the desk, turning it on. 'I missed this, I was in custody.' When the radio finally connected to the network he asked. 'Control, have we got an update from the scene?'

Marc answered.

'Amy is with the guy, I'm just about to clear it. Ben, I'm going to need you down here, full scene. Deceased female aged around eighteen to twenty, suspicious.'

Both Morgan and Ben were heading out of the door. 'Can someone get CSI travelling with a tent ASAP, and we better have paramedics too. Call it, Control.'

As they climbed into the car, Morgan whispered, 'I hate that river with a passion.'

Ben reached out his hand and squeezed her knee gently. He didn't have to answer because she knew he felt the same way: for a beauty spot, it had an awful lot of death and painful memories attached to it.

5

Morgan was relieved to see the incident wasn't near to Milly Blake's parents' house. They had suffered enough without dredging up painful memories for them all over again. They must feel as if they were living some kind of never-ending nightmare, and she wondered if Milly might leave the area and make a fresh start someplace new. But no, they were far from her house. This scene was half a mile down the road, away from the tourist area where the huge flat boulders that had been placed there as stepping stones led across from one side of the river to the other, an area that was popular with families coming to picnic on a warm day.

There were a few people gathering though; dog walkers and hikers all standing watching the circus further down. Amber was in the middle of the path to divert anyone who wandered that way. Ben parked next to a police van with its lights still flashing. Amy was inside with an older man, who was sitting with a brindle pug on his lap. Ben got out and pointed to the light rack, and Amy, who knew his thoughts on turning crime scenes into beacons, leaned forward to switch them off. Morgan thought it was amusing how much it annoyed him. It was one of his few pet hates, and he was constantly reminding patrol officers that they served a job and that was fine, but what was the point of blinding everyone in the vicinity to announce something terrible had gone down? The van was a clear enough indication of that without the light show. Marc was already suited and booted.

Ben whispered, 'He came prepared, he's getting used to this place.'

Morgan gave him a small smile; she didn't want to go and see who this poor woman was but knew that she must. It was what she did so well, assessing crime scenes, looking for vital clues that might tell them why the victim had been murdered. Her favourite part was hunting the killer down and putting an end to their reign of violence before anyone else got hurt. The River Rothay was fast flowing today, the water was dark and turbulent, and it seemed appropriate for what she was about to do and matched her mood perfectly. Her insides felt dark and turbulent too, despite the warmth from the spring sun and the dramatic backdrop of the fields on the opposite side, where deer often grazed and Loughrigg Fell looked down onto it. There was a large house not too far away that had been turned into three holiday homes, all of them had patios that looked out onto the river, but she didn't think they would be able to see through the copse of trees to where the body lay, as she couldn't see it from where she stood.

A warm hand on her shoulder brought her mind back to the open packet of crime-scene coveralls she was clutching.

'Are you going to put those on or tuck them under your arm like a new Louis Vuitton clutch?' Wendy was smiling at her.

'I was miles away.'

'I guessed that, is everything okay? You and Ben are still fine?'

Morgan frowned, wondering why she'd ask such a strange question. 'Yep, we're good, thanks. You?'

Wendy shrugged. 'Same shit, different day, and I mean no disrespect to whoever has been murdered, but you know.'

Morgan nodded. She did know, she knew all too well because that was exactly how she was feeling. Sad at the fact that people were killed without a second thought; sad that she had to deal with their loved ones and tell them the devastating news that would forever change their lives; and sad that humanity was in such a mess.

'Blimey, what a pair we are today, feeling sorry for ourselves.'

Morgan deftly pulled on the white suit, slipped some boot covers on and thanked her lucky stars that the ground was dry, otherwise she'd be slipping and sliding around like she was on roller skates. Wendy took a stack of metal plates from the van, heading in the direction of the trees to place them down and create a path for them to walk on that would minimise contaminating the scene. Ben was talking to Marc, and she realised she was going to have to join them to find out what the plan was. Marc nodded at her, and she nodded back.

'I guess you should both go take a look. I asked Wendy to put a tent over, but as she so rightly pointed out, there is not enough room for a full-size tent with the trees being so close together. She's got a four foot one instead on its way. Joe had it in his van. It will keep the victim out of sight and dry until the pathologist can get here. Unlike the last crime scene.'

Morgan glanced at Ben; the inspector was never getting over the mess that happened when they were sent to deal with Margery Lancaster. Ben didn't show any emotion. He was managing to keep his cool and not rise to the inspector's comment. They had done what they had under difficult circumstances, but Marc could not let it go.

'There are a lot of walkers around, it's a nice day.'

Marc looked at her. 'Meaning?'

'They may have seen someone; wouldn't it be worthwhile

putting something in the press to ask anyone who may have been in the vicinity earlier to get in touch?'

Ben smiled at her. 'Yes, we will do that.'

Marc's phone began to ring, and he turned to walk away from them as he clamped it to his ear.

Morgan whispered, 'Who rattled Marc this morning?'

'Maybe his ex-wife. At least it wasn't us. He was in a bad mood before we turned up.'

Morgan didn't know an awful lot about their boss, but she knew he was having a tough time with his divorce and that his wife wanted everything he owned, including not letting him see his teenage daughters.

They waited for Wendy to give them a thumbs up, and walked along the metal plates going a little way into the trees where it was much darker. The earthy smell combined with a hint of pine and wild garlic filled Morgan's nostrils. It smelled like a walk through the woods should, and she was relieved the air wasn't tainted with the smell of decay and decomposition. The fast-flowing river could be heard gurgling not too far away as it bubbled and frothed with the water that ran down from the mountains and fells – all the recent rainfall making it much higher than usual. If it wasn't for the pit of dread in her stomach this would be a pleasant way to spend her morning. Would she ever again be able to enjoy the beauty of the Lake District without seeing mutilated, dead bodies where she should be able to sit and take in the views?

A flash of clothing through the trees made Morgan pause. Ben turned back to her.

'Everything okay?'

She nodded, gave him a small smile and carried on walking towards the crime scene. It was Ben's turn: he stopped so abruptly, she walked into the back of him, almost pushing him off the metal plates onto the woodland floor.

'Sorry.'

'My fault.'

They both stared at the body lying at the base of the tree, and Morgan felt an overwhelming sense of sadness and a strong desire to shrug off her jacket to cover the girl up. She felt like she needed to keep her warm and give her some dignity. Morgan's fingers were clenching, she was so angry with the person who had done this. The woman looked as if she had been thrown to the ground, discarded like a piece of rubbish.

'Jesus,' whispered Ben. 'I don't think I'll ever understand how people's minds work.'

Morgan was trying to control the wave of anger that was rising inside of her. She was sure if it was a cold day there would actually be steam coming out of her ears like some cartoon character.

'It looks to me like he was in a rush. Look at the way the body has been thrown. It's not been placed carefully like bodies often are. Do you think he got startled?'

Ben said, 'Maybe. Perhaps he picked this area so she'd be found quickly, but underestimated just how busy it is. There are a lot of dog walkers here.'

She nodded. 'Yes, he definitely wanted her found, or wasn't scared of her being discovered. That poor bloke talking to Amy will never get her image out of his mind.'

Ben had crouched down to take a closer look at the body and pointed to her neck area.

'The only sign of injury is the red groove around her neck.'

He stood up, and they stood there both of them stunned by what they were seeing, taking in the scene around them.

'Got the tent.'

Joe's voice came out of nowhere making both of them jump.

Morgan clutched at her heart. 'Where did you come from?'

They hadn't heard him approaching and he'd startled them both.

'Bowness, was on a job there.'

Morgan shook her head. 'No, I mean how did you get here so quietly?'

'Ah, I'm like a silent Ninja, I'm good at not making any noise. Used to spend hours playing army in the park with my mates, hiding out so they couldn't find me.'

He was smiling at her, and she couldn't help but smile back. Then he looked past Ben's shoulder and let out a small, painful sound.

'Oh, man,' he said, clutching his stomach. 'That's bad, oh my God... I know her, it's Melody Carrick. Oh, I'm sorry, I can't do this.'

His hands were shaking, and he'd dropped the bag with the tent inside onto the floor by his feet. His eyes were bulging out of his head and his skin was clammy. He looked as if he was going to be sick or maybe faint, possibly both. Morgan grabbed his arm, gently turning him away from the body, and began to push him back to where Wendy and Marc were standing, her hands firmly gripping his arms to propel him forward away from the scene.

'I'm sorry, I'm so sorry,' was all he kept repeating, and Morgan felt terrible for him. She knew how awful the shock was of seeing someone dead who you knew, and everyone dealt with it differently. For her it was more of an internal shock to her system. She was trying to think if she knew the name, but she didn't. As they reached the small clearing through the trees where Wendy and Marc were talking, they both turned to the pair of them. Joe stepped off the plates and ran towards where the van was parked. Going behind it they heard him start to retch.

Wendy lifted her hands up. 'What's up with him?'

'He knows the victim.'

At this she paled a little. Wendy had attended a crime scene where her own gran had been found battered and bloody, killed by a vicious killer and left discarded on the street in a pool of her own blood.

'Oh no, poor guy.'

Marc looked mildly annoyed. 'Name of victim then if he knows her?'

Morgan glared at him. 'Melody Carrick.'

'Means nothing to me. How does he know her? Are they friends?'

She couldn't stop what was about to spill out of her mouth even if she wanted to.

'Why would it? You haven't been here long enough to know everyone in the station let alone all of Rydal Falls. You barely remember our names. He probably knows her from around the town or college, or maybe he just knows of her.'

He was about to reply then thought better and went to the van to retrieve his radio; he asked the control room operator to do a search for any Carricks in the area.

There was one address, which they passed over, and Morgan scribbled it on the back of the blue glove she had on, then she headed back towards Ben. Having a positive ID would make their life a little easier, but it would also mean that Melody's parents and family's lives were about to come crashing down around them, changed forever at the loss of their loved one. It saddened her beyond belief to know that she would be the person to do this to them.

6

Home Office Forensic Pathologist Declan Donnelly headed towards her, his footsteps so heavy they made the metal plates underneath their feet vibrate. He was tall and looked so imposing that for one moment a cold chill washed over Morgan's whole body, making her shudder. As he reached her, he nodded and removed one of his gloves. He pressed his fingers against her forehead. 'Are you well, Morgan? You don't look it.'

'I'm cold.'

He nodded. 'You look a little peaky, maybe you should go sit in the van for a while.'

'I'm okay but thank you. How are you?'

This little greeting seemed strange even to her – he didn't seem his usual self. He shrugged. 'I'd be a lot better if you could all stop finding bodies for me to examine.'

She smiled and it hit her that he didn't relish the thought of dealing with another murder victim so soon. 'Wouldn't we all.'

They did a funny little dance as he tried to step around her, and she almost lost her balance falling off the walkway. He grabbed her to steady her and somehow, they had swapped places. He winked at her and headed towards the body; a low whistle as he pursed his lips filled the air.

'For the love of God, why? Just why did whoever do this think it was okay to dump her here in public, where anyone could find her?'

Morgan could hear the horror in his voice, at the indignity of what had been done to Melody, and she realised that he was as tired of the senseless violence they dealt with far too regularly as she was. He was already bending down next to Melody.

'She hasn't been dead long, there's rigor setting in but early stages and it's not complete.'

Ben asked. 'How long?'

'Couple of hours maybe.'

With his gloved fingers he gently picked up her hand and sighed. 'Doesn't look as if she put up a fight, there are no defence wounds. That's a nasty wound around her neck, so whoever did this is strong; it's a deep groove.'

'How did he manage to strangle her without her putting up a fight?'

'Drugs or alcohol would be my guess. Those edibles laced with cannabis are getting quite popular, and you can buy them with melatonin added to help aid sleep. I thought I would try some, purely for research purposes, and I don't know how they're allowed to sell them over the counter. I had two before bed and was so out of it I woke up in my pants and had been sick all down myself. I didn't even realise. I could have choked on my own vomit. A couple of those would have a sedative effect.'

'Enough to let someone strangle you without a fight?'

Declan nodded. 'Those ones I tried, I had no idea what I was doing so I'd say yeah.'

Morgan smiled at him. 'I didn't get you as the edible taking kind of guy.'

He shook his head. 'I'm not, I don't do drugs, well not since my early days in med school, and boy could I tell you some tales. That was more of a social experiment and the fact that the guy I was seeing raved about them and begged me to take two. He said it would enhance—' He stopped. 'Wrong time, wrong place for this conversation.'

He went on. 'Then there are your run-of-the-mill date rape drugs. As we both know, they can be bought relatively easily, and we've seen them used in the past. Obviously, I'm not saying this is the case here because I'd need the toxicology results for that, but it's just some ideas for you to peruse at your leisure. Or he could have just been so strong and overpowered her pretty quickly, so quick she might not have had time to fight back if she wasn't expecting it, and he whipped the rope around her neck so fast she couldn't do anything about it.' Declan saw a glint of something yellow caught up in the victim's hair and bent down to retrieve it with a pair of tweezers. He lifted it up to study it and showed it to Morgan.

'It looks as if she's missing a necklace, this is the catch off a gold chain, the killer must have ripped it off unless it snapped in the struggle, it might be underneath her. Tell CSI to double check. This makes me so sad,' he added, 'seeing a bright young woman with her whole future ahead of her stripped of her life and her dignity. Please find the vile person who did this sooner rather than later, because I get this awful gnawing feeling in my gut that she won't be the last. I don't know what it is, but around here there is never just one victim, one is never the magic number. They are always greedy for more.'

Morgan glanced back at the body, there was something so cold and calculated about her killing. It was bold, it was a statement. She was sure she'd listened to an unsolved case on a podcast just recently about a killer some time around 2008 to 2010 who had never been caught, who'd left two female victims dumped in wooded areas, both causes of death strangulation. A deep-seated feeling of unease was niggling away inside of her, but that was just a coincidence, surely? Had the killer heard the episode, too, and after all this time decided to take up killing again, or had it inspired a copycat? Perhaps she was reading too much into it, which in all probability was the real answer. Those victims hadn't been killed in the Lake District. If they had been, she would have asked Ben if she could look into the cold cases.

Morgan turned away from the scene, her shoulders slumped, and walked back to the van where Joe was sitting inside on his own. He looked so young, so vulnerable. She hadn't realised he was probably around her age. She had lost that fresh-faced youthfulness that had rounded her face a little when she'd first joined the police force almost immediately after being thrust into her role helping CID. Now, she felt ancient, way older beyond her years because of the terrible crimes she'd witnessed, and regardless of the toll they took on her she knew she was helpless to stop doing what she did. She knocked on the van window, jolting him out of whatever place he'd been to in his mind. He opened the door. The sun was still warm, but there was a distinct chill that had settled upon her shoulders.

'Hey, how are you?'

Joe turned to her, his face still pale and his skin looked clammy. He shrugged, not speaking.

'It's hard, too hard this job at times. We get sent to deal with the aftermath of brutal, terrible crimes yet nobody cares about us and how we're coping with the situation. I'm sorry for your loss, Joe. It's bad when it's someone we know.'

He blinked a couple of times, clearing the tears that were threatening to fall. His voice was low, his throat dry as he mumbled, 'Thanks.' Then coughed to clear it.

'Did you know Melody very well?'

He shrugged. 'Kind of, we hung around in the same circles at school, then college. She's a couple of years younger than me.'

'I know it's painful, but can you tell me where she worked,

lived, who she hung around with, what she liked? When was the last time you saw her?'

'Not for ages,' he confirmed. 'I don't know her that well, I couldn't tell you who her friends are. She works in a café on the high street. We weren't best friends or anything, but I always liked her. No, it was more than that, I always fancied her but was never brave enough to ask her out on a proper date. She was well out of my league.' His voice cracked as he tried to swallow the sob that was threatening to break it and whispered, 'I'll never get the chance now.'

If Morgan hadn't already felt sad for Joe, now she wanted to bawl like a baby. She let out a long, drawn-out sigh. She reached out her hand for his, and she squeezed it. 'Life is truly shit at times.'

Joe nodded.

'I bet if you'd asked her, she'd have said yes in a heartbeat. There is no way she would have turned you down.'

He stared into her eyes as if gauging to see if she was just being nice to him. 'You think so?'

'I do, I honestly do, why wouldn't she? I mean I wouldn't say no if I wasn't already with Ben.'

Which wasn't strictly true, but she was doing her best to make him feel better and little white lies didn't hurt if they were used to do something good.

He gave her the saddest smile she'd ever seen.

'Thanks, you're kind. I'm going to spend the rest of my life wondering if I could have stopped this. How, if I'd been brave enough to ask her out, it could have changed things. Would she have been with me instead of on her own? Would she still be alive? Her mum is going to be devastated; it was just the two of them. She's going to have to close the café because she won't want to keep it open when she's had her whole life ripped to shreds in front of her.'

Icy fingers of fear began to creep softly up the back of

Morgan's neck, softly caressing the skin leaving a trail of goose-bumps. 'What café?' She already knew what he was going to say, because now he'd mentioned a café she saw an image of a bubbly Melody waiting tables at The Coffee Pot on the week-ends and in the school holidays when tourist season was in full swing. For a split second she prayed that she was wrong. She almost didn't want Joe to answer her because she didn't think she could bear the weight of the grief for her mum, Jade, who had served her a free latte with a warm smile on her lips, less than an hour ago, while her daughter was lying dead, thrown into a copse of trees like a sack of rubbish.

'The Coffee Pot.'

Morgan's voice was much quieter. 'Is her mum Jade?' A voice inside her head was whispering *please say no, please say no*.

He nodded, and it was her turn to blink away the tears desperately trying to pool in the corners of her eyes. She turned away from him and stared into the trees, where she saw flashes of white moving between them from Wendy's suit as she moved around, and she knew she couldn't do this. She couldn't go and tell the kindly woman who always had a smile on her face that her daughter was dead, and for once Morgan wished that she could go home, grab her passport and drive to Manchester airport, get on the first flight to anywhere that was as far away from here as possible. Morgan had never once thought about running away from anything, but this was too much. She had been chatting with Melody's mum less than an hour before, and the woman had been so kind as to give her a free coffee and now she was about to go and ruin her life, bring her world crashing down around her. Jade didn't deserve this, nobody deserved this, but it was always the good people, and life was too cruel to repay someone's kindness in the worst possible way. Her fingers touched her chest, and she gently rubbed at the dull ache that had settled inside of her heart that she knew wouldn't go away until this was over. She thought there was a possibility that it might not ever be over.

Joe got out of the van, sucked in a deep breath and nodded at Morgan.

'I'm good, I want to do this. I can't sit here and watch Wendy do all the work. I want to be the one doing something to help catch whoever did this. It's all I can do for Melody now.'

Morgan nodded, she knew the feeling of helplessness that came along with the shock and the grief, then the cold, hard determination to make a difference. 'Check with Ben that you're okay to carry on, Joe. He will be glad you are, but will want to make sure you're good.'

He walked in Ben's direction, and she watched him, his head held high. He was determined and that was a good thing; it would help him for the next few hours. It wouldn't help him later on when he was on his own reliving everything though. Those thoughts would creep in when he least expected them, but for now work would keep them at bay.

Declan had finished and was on his way back, stopping to talk to Ben and Marc. She turned to look back down the river-bank, horrified to see the small crowd of people that had formed outside the taped-off area. Amber was doing a great job of keeping them contained, but the audacity of some people who thrived from someone else's tragedy never ceased to amaze her. Inside the paper suit she felt beads of perspiration trickling down the back of her neck. The warmth from the spring sun was drawing people to the river; the killer had thrown in some free entertainment for them all. No doubt this was all over Facebook already, and then it hit her: they needed to tell Jade before someone else did.

She made her way to where Ben and Marc were standing. 'Declan found a piece of broken necklace. If the rest of it isn't under the body, then the killer must have taken it. I don't want to do this, but we need to go let her mum know. Have you seen the crowd?'

Both men turned at the same time, and she heard Ben's astounded voice.

'Bloody hell, where did they come from?'

She shrugged. Marc headed in Amber's direction, and Ben whispered, 'Come on, let's go do this before she hears about it off social media.'

7

Paige Evans could hear her mum sobbing from upstairs in her bedroom as she was brushing her hair. It had been two days now and she hadn't stopped. It wasn't as if the creep had died. He'd moved out, at her mum's insistence, and now she was regretting it big time. Unlike Paige who had never felt happier. The whole house had a different vibe without him there, at least it would when her mum stopped crying. She picked up her phone and opened the Snapchat Alisa had sent her. It was a picture of a lot of police vans by the riverside, and officers in those white suits that they wear on all the television dramas. A bad feeling enveloped her body from her head to her toes, wrapping her in some kind of bubble of doom. She messaged Alisa back.

What's going on?

Someone said they found a body.

Who?

I dunno, I'm not a copper, but is now a good time?

Paige thought about *him* and where he might be, if he was still in the area or had gone to see his brother to stay with him like he'd said he would when he took his stuff. Her mum had gone out after the fight of all fights, leaving her here with him while he threw his stuff into the boot of his car. Scared to death, she had taken out the big kitchen knife she kept under her mattress – and had done since he'd moved in – and sat on the chair she had wedged underneath her bedroom door handle, gripping the handle of the knife so tight she thought her fingers were going to drop off with the numbness that had spread through them. She couldn't believe that her mum had fucked off out and left her alone with him after telling him to leave. She hadn't cared that she'd left her only teenage daughter in a house with a man whose favourite hobby was watching serial killer documentaries, commenting throughout how he would have done it better; and his idea of a family day out was driving them around the sites of local murders to take their photographs in the exact spots he'd memorised after devouring the news articles about them. Some mother she was; she could have come back to find Paige murdered in her own bedroom. Paige liked true crime as much as everyone else, she loved listening to podcasts and watching YouTube documentaries about serial killers from the seventies and eighties, but she didn't enjoy being made to stand in the same places where bodies had been discovered. That, in her opinion, was taking it too far. It was more than a weird obsession – making his girlfriend's kid sit on top of a rock where a woman was found with her throat slashed was just sick.

Her long hair tied up in a messy bun, she grabbed her phone and backpack then went down to see what was going on. Her mum was on the sofa, box of tissues next to her, large glass of white wine in one hand and a photo album in the other. She was flicking through the said pictures taken by Alan. Paige tutted in disgust not realising just how loud it had sounded.

'Why are you crying over him, Susan? You were the one to throw him out.'

Her mum sniffed, took a gulp of wine, the whole time glaring at her with her glazed, red and puffy eyes, and Paige knew then what she was going to say. Would have bet a year's worth of her wages working in Bargain Booze every weekend on what her reply was going to be.

'This is your fault.' She jabbed her finger in the air in her direction. 'You hated him, you made life so difficult that we did nothing but argue over you. What's the matter, were you jealous of us because you can't get a boyfriend of your own?'

Paige stared at her. 'I knew you'd blame me. How about the fact that he cheated on you almost every other week with your friends, or that he wouldn't let you have a life of your own and was a control freak whose only enjoyment was watching stuff about women getting tortured and killed. I mean, did that not ring any alarm bells with you, Susan?'

'Don't call me Susan.'

Paige didn't have the energy to argue with her, and she shrugged. 'It's your name.'

'And I'm your mum, have you got no respect?'

'You told him to leave because Jackie told you she'd slept with him after one too many glasses of wine; you didn't tell him to leave because I hated him. I told you from day one he was a weirdo, and you didn't listen to me, so don't go blaming me. I had to sit there scared stiff in my bedroom with a knife in case he decided to come and kill me to get his own back on you. You walked out and left me with a raving lunatic, so don't go pretending that you did it for me. You did it because Jackie has a big mouth, and finally you couldn't take the shame.'

Paige ducked as the wine glass flew in her direction, just missing the top of her head. It smashed into a million pieces, leaving a damp patch of wine running down the matt putty-coloured wall, and glass sprinkled around the laminate floor like confetti. She lifted a finger to her cheek and pressed it against the skin, it was covered in blood. Her mum started sobbing again, and Paige shook her head.

'It's eleven a.m. and you're drunk. You're a violent drunk too, sort yourself out.'

Paige went into the kitchen and tore a piece of kitchen roll to dab at the fine cut. She wasn't staying here when her mum was like this. It was never-ending, the chaos and uncertainty. The only good thing was Alan hadn't come back begging for forgiveness – at least not yet and, if he did, she was out of here for good. She couldn't live in the same house as him. She'd ask Alisa if she could stay with her or one of her other friends until she could find somewhere else. Alan scared the shit out of her, and he had done since the day she met him. She thought that both of them had been relatively lucky to escape him unharmed.

8

Morgan reversed the car into a space opposite The Coffee Pot – no breaking the rules and parking on double yellows while she ran in for a coffee this time. She had no idea how long they would be here. Ben had been on the phone to Claire Williams the entire short journey. Based in Carlisle, Claire was the DCI of the Murder Investigation Team and already up to her neck in a murder-suicide on the Botchergate estate. Morgan thought in a way she was lucky, at least she knew who the killer was, and he was already stuffed into a body bag on his way to the mortuary. He wasn't killing anyone ever again, unlike theirs who could be Melody's boyfriend, ex-boyfriend, jealous stalker even. What she hoped was that this was just that, and not the start of a series of murders.

The whole way Melody's murder had been orchestrated made her blood run cold. She knew that whoever it was, they wouldn't stop at Melody. The high he would be on after getting away with killing her and leaving her body like that would be hard to let go of, and he would want more: they always wanted more.

Ben was getting out of the car, tucking his phone into his

pocket. He leaned in and gently placed a hand on her shoulder. The warmth from his skin felt good because her entire body was cold, despite it being a warm day.

'Are you okay with this?'

She shook her head. 'I am not and never will be okay with doing this, with telling someone something so horrific that their life will be forever changed. How is anyone okay with it?'

He sighed. 'They're not, I'm not, you're not. I was just asking, it's what I do. I can do this on my own if you'd rather stay in the car, Morgan.'

Her cheeks flushed red. She was taking her frustration out on him and that wasn't fair.

'Sorry, yes, I'm okay to do this. I wouldn't let you do it on your own, that's not fair either. You shouldn't have to carry the burden of this alone.'

He shut the door, and she squeezed her eyes shut for a moment, picturing Jade's happy, smiling face less than an hour ago. Another tiny piece of her heart tore off. What would happen when she had no more pieces of heart left to break? She got out of the car; Ben was already across the road standing outside the café. A group of walkers came out of the door, four women in hiking boots all laughing at something. They were oblivious of what was about to happen, and she envied that, hoped they had made Jade smile when she served them, and been kind to her. The last one held the door open for Ben; she gave him a big grin.

'Thank you, have a good day, ladies.'

They giggled again and the blonde who had held the door said. 'We'll try to. Are you busy? You could join us and make it even better.'

Ben shook his head. 'I'm working but thank you.'

She winked at him, and Morgan smiled as his cheeks turned even redder than hers had minutes ago. She caught up to him, and he rolled his eyes at her as if to say *what just happened?* She knew what had happened, he'd just been hit on, and she guessed he wasn't used to it or was plain oblivious to his charm. He looked so dashing standing there in his navy pinstripe suit and white shirt. His tie, which had been hastily put back on in the car, was a little crooked but it somehow made him look a little less formal, and she thought that might be a good thing.

They stepped inside. The café was in mid swing of the dinner time rush and there was only one table where the women who had just left had vacated. Two teenage girls ducked behind them and scooted to the table, sitting down before either of them could, but they didn't need it. They could hardly tell Jade in front of a café full of customers, though. There was a teenage boy taking orders and another woman making coffees. That was good, at least Jade wasn't on her own. Ben hesitated as if he didn't want to do this, but they had no choice. Soon it was going to be public knowledge that a body had been found by the river, and it wouldn't take long for someone to figure out who it was. They owed it to Jade to tell her before she heard it third or fourth hand.

Morgan smiled at the teenager. 'Is Jade around?'

He nodded.

'Can you go get her, please?'

He looked at her, then he looked at Ben, and she knew that he knew something bad was going to happen, it was written all over his face, but he disappeared through a doorway and came back with Jade.

She grinned at Morgan. 'Morgan, twice in one day. What a pleasure.'

Morgan's heart was racing so fast she worried what her blood pressure would be.

'Hi, Jade, do you have somewhere a little more private we can have a chat?'

Jade's eyes narrowed; she frowned, and a row of deep creases across her brow made Morgan realise she was older than she'd first thought. Jade nodded and pointed to the doorway she'd come out of. The teenager was looking at the woman by the coffee machine with raised eyebrows, and Morgan saw him mouth the word 'cops' to her. Morgan smiled at them both before ducking through into the kitchen prep room area. There was another door with a small space that was just big enough for the desk and chair that filled it.

'Was my coffee that bad? Have you come to arrest me for it?'

Jade was laughing at her own joke, and Morgan felt her insides turn to ice. 'No, it was very good. In fact, it was the best I've had. We're not here about that.'

'Thank God, I thought you were going to tell me you found something awful in it. Can I get you guys a drink, something to eat?'

Ben shook his head. 'No, thank you.' He pointed to the chair. 'Would you like to sit down.'

Jade's head tilted a little as she took in his face, trying to figure out where this was going, and Morgan wished she could turn around and leave. Jade saw the seriousness in Ben's face and sat down.

'Okay, now what? Am I under arrest or something? I don't understand why you're here.'

'No, you're definitely not, Jade, you're not in any kind of trouble. I'm afraid we have some bad news for you and I'm so sorry to have to be the one to tell you this.'

She stared at Morgan, her blue eyes questioning without moving her lips.

Morgan glanced at Ben, who nodded for her to continue.

'Jade, a body has been found by the riverside. It is a teenage girl, and we believe it's Melody. I'm so, so, sorry.'

Jade opened her mouth, closed it then shook her head. 'What? You found a body, like a dead body by the river and you think it's Melody. Why do you think it's her?'

Morgan nodded. 'One of our crime-scene technicians is friends with your daughter and he recognised her straight away.'

'No, that's rubbish. She's at college. She goes in late on a Wednesday. She's doing another course, hairdressing, because she wasn't sure about going to uni just yet and thought it's better than sitting at home doing nothing.' Jade looked at her watch. 'Actually, she's probably in the canteen with her friends. I'll ring her and you can talk to her yourself.'

She pulled her phone out of her pocket, pressed her finger against Melody's name and smiled at the picture of the beautiful young woman on the screen smiling back at her. The phone rang and rang until voicemail kicked in.

'Melody, ring me back, sweetie, as soon as you get this. It's important.'

Jade's fingers were trembling as she jabbed at the *end call* button, but couldn't seem to press it hard enough. She finally did and put the phone on the desk, staring at the screen, willing it to ring so she could hear her daughter's voice telling her not to worry, she was fine.

Her voice was a whisper. 'She always answers the phone to me and if she can't she messages straight away. Any second now she'll message back. She's fine, this is a mix-up. What friend said it was her? They must be mistaken.'

Morgan found herself staring at the phone too, praying for a message to ping on the screen. She would much rather be mistaken and Jade's daughter still be alive than the dead silence that filled the room.

Ben reached out for Jade's hand. 'I wish we were; I would give anything that we were, Jade, but her friend is a colleague of ours and he was certain about who she was. We believe that it's Melody. We need a formal ID to confirm it. Would you be able to do that or is there someone else we can contact to come and be with you so they could do it?'

Jade was shaking her head. 'No, it's just me and Mel. I don't understand, how has this happened? I spoke to her before I left to open up. She was eating breakfast and trying to finish an essay at the kitchen table. She had a bowl of Shreddies, she loves them, and a chocolate twist with extra icing sugar on top. She has such a sweet tooth. I have no idea how she keeps her figure. If I ate as much chocolate as she did, I'd never get through the door.'

'I'm so sorry, Jade.'

Jade was staring at Morgan, unblinking. Her eyes had glazed over. 'Please, Morgan, tell me this isn't real, that it's some kind of nightmare.'

Morgan reached out and squeezed her fingers. 'I would give anything for this not to be real, Jade. We found a piece of broken chain next to the body. Did Melody wear a gold chain?'

Jade nodded, her fingers reaching up to her neck, she pulled a dainty, gold cross from underneath her T-shirt. 'We have matching necklaces, she never took it off.' Then she opened her mouth and began to wail.

9

Alisa didn't reply to any of Paige's messages, and she knew what she had to do – she just didn't want to do it. She sat on the bench outside the McDonald's watching the world go by and counted to three before sending one last message.

Last chance, if you don't reply I'm going to report you missing to the police. Please Alisa I'm worried about you.

She waited but the message wasn't delivered. Her friend's phone must be off, and she felt bad. No not bad, worried. Alan had a bit of a thing for her friend and would fuss over her as if she was royalty when she was at hers. He would try and make stupid jokes that she found revolting, but Alisa was too polite and would always laugh and tell him how funny he was. But she had seen the way he watched her from behind, had caught him eyeing her up the way a serpent watches its prey before it strikes, and she thought that he was very much like a tightly coiled spring, ready to let go and pounce on his victim the moment he thought he could get away with it. Now that he was away from her mum, he was behaving himself, wasn't he? Or could he have done something to Alisa?

Paige did the unthinkable and phoned Alisa's house phone, waiting for one of her parents to answer it, or her annoying little brother. It rang and rang until she hung up. She stood up as the bus approached and stuck out her hand to wave at the driver. The bus pulled over and she got on, flashing her student bus pass at the driver who nodded her on. She took a seat, it would take around forty-five minutes to get to Rydal Falls, then she'd have to walk to Alisa's house which was another ten. Then if she really couldn't get hold of her, she'd have to walk to the police station too. She opened Snapchat and swiped down from the camera to access the map, zooming in to see if Alisa's Bitmoji was on the screen. It usually was but she couldn't find her today. She could see where Jemma and Dan were, they were together in the park; Maddie was at college, but there was no sign of Alisa which was worrying. She always shared her location with Paige, and she did the same. Either Alisa had gone into Ghost Mode, or something was wrong and, judging by the heaviness and nausea she felt in her stomach, she was sure it was something bad.

She knocked on Alisa's door much louder than she usually would, but her parents' cars weren't on the driveway, and her friend's pastel pink bicycle that she rode everywhere was leaning against the garage door. She hammered even louder, and the neighbour from the semi next door looked out of the window, shaking her head. Paige tutted, *what was that supposed to mean?* Then the front door opened, and the woman smiled at her.

'You've had a wasted journey; they went out an hour ago.'

Paige felt a sigh of relief escape her lips. Thank God for that, maybe her phone had died, or they were in a place with no signal. It was like that in the Lake District; great views, crappy mobile phone coverage. You could take the most breathtaking photos, only you couldn't share them with anyone unless you were close to one of the little towns where the signal was better.

'Alisa went with them?'

'No, I haven't seen her since she left the house earlier. I meant her parents and brother.'

She felt that sinking feeling in the pit of her stomach again. 'Oh, what time was that?'

'Just after six. I was opening my curtains and saw her walking down the drive. She got into a white car. I didn't see who was driving it because it was early and I'd just woken up, and I didn't have my glasses on.'

Paige smiled at her. 'Thanks.'

'Is something wrong?'

'No, we were supposed to meet, and I was late, so I thought I'd come here.'

'Oh, well you missed them all.'

She turned to walk away; her heart was hammering against her ribcage. Alan drove a white car. She began to walk in the direction of the police station. She would rather report him and look like a dick than risk the chance of anything happening to Alisa. She looked at Snapchat again, and Alisa still wasn't online, but she'd messaged her over an hour ago. So she was okay then. But if she got into a white car at six, and it was now almost three, it didn't make sense unless her phone had died, which was the most likely answer and she was panicking over nothing. Paige still couldn't shrug off the creeping feeling that something bad had happened to her though, or was about to happen to her, so she carried on walking towards the police station. There was only one person there who she wanted to speak to, and she had no idea if she was even on duty, but she owed it to Alisa to give it her best shot.

10

Morgan didn't speak until they got into the car. She glanced at Ben's washed-out face. It looked a little grey and she felt a wave of concern for him.

'Are you okay? You don't look too good.'

He shook his head. 'I feel terrible, not ill terrible, just plain old terrible inside. That poor woman.'

Morgan nodded. She had ushered the customers out of the café, and Mandy, who had been making coffees, had gone to help Jade. The teenage boy who had been serving had given the customers takeout containers to scrape their food in and take-away cups for their drinks. No one complained, they knew something terrible had happened. They all left in stunned silence, except for one guy who had been genuinely concerned and asked if there was anything he could do to help. He was a locum at the health centre covering for one of the doctors. Morgan had taken him back to see Jade, and he'd gone over to the health centre and brought back some lorazepam, giving the distraught woman one to help calm her down. By the time they were leaving, she had been much calmer, crying but no longer so violently, and Morgan had hugged her fiercely before they had left. Mandy had promised she would phone Stu, Jade's ex-husband to come and help as they were still friends. Melody's dad was a different matter, he had moved to Germany when she was a baby after Jade and he split up and hadn't been around for years. The doctor had stayed too, holding Jade's hand and talking to her. Morgan had been so impressed with him she knew she would ask for him if she ever needed to go there. He had insisted they all call him Steve and promised them he would make sure Jade was settled before he left.

'We could go back and ask Steve to check you out, you know, make sure you're okay.'

'We could, but we're not. I'm fine. Have you looked at yourself?'

She turned down the sun visor; her face was ashen, too, almost as grey as Ben's. 'I guess it's the shock and the stress, I'll let you off.'

He smiled at her. 'That was tough, wasn't it?'

She nodded. 'Terrible.'

Her phone rang. 'Brookes.'

'*Morgan love, it's Brenda. There's a young lady at the front desk asking to speak to you. I told her you were very busy, but she said it's okay she's going to wait for you. I thought she might leave after half an hour, but she's still there.*'

'It's okay, we're heading back now. I won't be long; did she say what it was about?'

'*She's concerned about her friend; she can't get hold of her. I told her an officer could take the details, but she asked for you by name.*'

'See you soon, Brenda.'

Ben was searching his pockets for something, and he pulled out a packet of soft mints. 'Here, suck on one of these, the sugar will do you good.'

She looked at them in disgust. 'Well, there's an offer I can't refuse. I thought you were going to pull a chocolate bar out or something worthwhile eating.'

He laughed and passed the packet to her. 'Be thankful for what you get, Brookes.'

She unpeeled the green metallic paper and popped one into her mouth. 'I'm going to need more than a chewy mint to make me feel better.'

He nodded. 'Me too.'

When he pulled over at the security gates to swipe his pass so he could drive through into the back yard to park the car, she jumped out.

'I'll go speak to this girl and see what's wrong.'

The gates clanked open slowly, and he muttered, 'Another hour and these will be broken again, they never work.'

Waving at him, she strode towards the front entrance. As she walked in the only seat taken had a teenage girl sitting on it, staring at her phone. All the others were empty. Brenda pointed to the girl, and Morgan smiled her thanks.

'Hi, I'm Morgan, can I help you?'

The girl looked up at her. They had similar messy copper-coloured buns and were both dressed from head to toe in black, they even had matching black Dr Marten boots on. There was a small cut on her cheek which looked fresh. Morgan's winged eyeliner was a little more subtle than the girl's staring at her, but that was about the only difference. It was like meeting her doppelganger.

'Hi.' Was all the girl managed to say back.

'Should we go into a side room, and you can tell me what brought you here?'

She nodded. Morgan looked at Brenda who winked at her. Once they were both seated at the table she tried again.

'Can I get you a drink? Tea, coffee, water?'

'No, thanks, I'm okay.'

Morgan relaxed her shoulders and sat back a little, so she didn't come across too stiff and intimidating. 'What's your name?'

'Paige Evans.'

'Well, Paige, I'm Morgan Brookes, but you already know that because Brenda said you asked for me by my name. So how can I help you today?'

Paige's cheeks turned a little pinker than they had been seconds ago.

'I think my mum's ex-boyfriend has abducted my friend.'

Morgan's mouth dropped open, and she had to shut it again.

'That's quite some statement. What makes you think that he has?'

'I can't get hold of Alisa, and he's a real creep. My mum finally threw him out two days ago, and now you have a dead girl by the riverside and my friend is missing.'

'How do you know about the body by the riverside?'

'Alisa sent me a Snapchat of the coppers in white suits down there a couple of hours ago. Everybody knows about it.'

Morgan frowned; bloody social media was a pain in the arse at times. 'If you heard from Alisa a couple of hours ago, why are reporting her missing?'

Paige stared at Morgan. 'Isn't it obvious?'

She shook her head.

'I thought you were a shit hot detective.'

This made Morgan smile. 'I don't know who told you that. I am a detective, but I don't believe that I'm shit hot at it, nor do I pretend to be.'

'Well, the papers make you out to be.'

She sighed. 'The papers make a lot of stuff out that's not necessarily true. Why do you think your mum's partner has taken Alisa? Being a creep doesn't cut it. I need more than that.

I need cold, hard facts, evidence that would suggest he may have taken your friend.'

This time Paige smiled at her. 'But he is though. I'll tell you what I think. I think that the body you have by the riverside was put there by Alan. Then, I think, he decided that now he's provided you guys with a big enough distraction, it left him free to take Alisa, and God knows what he's going to do with her. It freaks me out thinking about it, but she's so gullible and thinks he's an okay guy.'

'Why does she think he's okay if you've told her he's not? And I assume that you have talked about Alan to her a lot.'

'Whenever she's at my house he's all over her, and it makes me feel sick inside. He's always joking with her and touching her. I've seen him staring at her when she wasn't looking, as if he wanted to eat her. He's disgusting, he flirts with her and she's seventeen. It's weird, he's weird.'

'How do you get on with Alan? How did you get that cut on your cheek?'

'I can't stand him. He's mean to my mum and me, he's always cheating on her with her friends, and he thinks the perfect day out is visiting all the places where other women have been killed. I cut it on a piece of broken glass.'

Morgan felt her spine straighten as she sat up. Now they were getting somewhere.

'You're not just jealous of the attention he gives Alisa? Or the fact that your mum spends more time with him than you?'

Paige laughed loudly. 'I'd rather spend time in a cell with Richard Ramirez than one of Alan's family days out. He makes me pose in the same places where bodies have been found. Don't you think that's weird?'

Morgan nodded. 'It's weird, of course it is, but some people are really into true crime. It doesn't make them killers.'

'Yeah, I suppose not. But he is obsessed; all he watches is Discovery Channel and the crime channels on Sky.'

'How do you know about Richard Ramirez, he's way before your time?'

'We had a Vampire of Sacramento themed night, we watched documentaries and some crappy film about him. Alan has this small box and inside it are odd, broken pieces of jewellery, broken necklaces, a bracelet that's snapped and odd earrings that don't match. He said it's precious to him and it belonged to his nan. He was furious when I found it and asked him about it. I told my mum it was really weird; I mean, didn't his nan have anything that she could actually wear? But Mum went mad with me too and told me I had no right going through his things. She said I was hateful and trying to cause trouble. I wasn't. I saw him staring at it one day when he thought he was alone in the house, but I'd come back to change my clothes, and he jumped up as if he'd been burned and shoved it behind the cushion on the sofa.'

Alarm bells were ringing inside Morgan's head. She watched Paige to see if she was displaying any signs that she was making this up, but she was holding Morgan's gaze as still as a picture.

'Where do you live?'

'We moved to Keswick recently but used to live in Lancaster. I know Alisa through college; we both go to Kendal college.'

'Why did you not go to the police there? What made you come all the way here?'

The girl leaned forward, elbows on the table, and pointed at Morgan. 'You are the reason I got the bus and walked for another twenty minutes, first to Alisa's house to check if she was there and then to here.'

'Me?'

She gave her a slow nod. 'You are the only person who can figure this out and find him before he hurts her, although I don't know how long he keeps them for or how he kills them, but he's gonna and you know your stuff.'

'How old are you?'

'Old enough to be here telling you this stuff.'

'I need your date of birth.'

'I'm seventeen.' She fished her small plastic provisional driving licence out of her pocket and passed it to Morgan, who felt relieved she hadn't just spoken to a minor without a consenting adult present.

'Thank you, I had to make sure, otherwise none of this would be admissible in court.'

'You're taking me seriously then?'

'I think that you have made some interesting points and yes, I will take a look at your stepdad.'

'He's not my stepdad.' Then she placed her hands together in the prayer position and looked up at the ceiling. 'Praise the Lord.'

'You said your mum threw him out. When was this?'

'Two days ago, and the only things he took were a backpack full of clothes and the jewellery box.'

'Is he familiar with this area?'

She rolled her eyes. 'It's the Lake District, who isn't?'

'No, Paige, I need to know if he ever brought you up here for days out. Did he come here walking before you moved here?'

'Yes, he brought me and mum back here lots of times to look at the police station and also, I told you, to go to the sites where previous bodies had been discovered. He called it the murder, mystery tour.'

Paige pulled an envelope out of her pocket and passed it across the plastic-coated table. Morgan picked it up, and sliding the photographs out she looked at the first one and felt fingers of ice begin to snake around the back of her neck. The first one was of Castlerigg Stone Circle, which was a hugely popular tourist spot; but Paige was standing in a pair of hot pants and a cropped T-shirt on the exact stone that Cora Dalton's body had been discovered. Morgan looked at the next, a photograph of Paige sitting on the drystone wall at the lay-by looking down onto Thirlmere where Jasmine Armer's body had been found in her car. Morgan looked at Paige who had her arms crossed and was looking back at her, as if to say *told you so*. Morgan examined the next photograph, which was of Paige again, standing under the shelter in the park where they had not too long ago found Lexie's body. Morgan felt her throat go dry and found it hard to speak.

'I need his full name, address, phone number, anything else you can tell me about him so I can look into him and see if he's on our system. Have you got any pictures of him?'

Paige was smiling at her. 'He's scary, huh? He's scared me since the day he moved in. I'm worried he might hurt Alisa and then come back for me.' She passed one last photo to Morgan. It was of a man in his forties maybe. He was tall, lean, athletic looking; he had a pair of glasses on, but it was his eyes that drew her in. They were an icy-blue colour that seemed to be burning holes into the back of her mind, his gaze was so intense.

Morgan nodded. 'We'll put some measures in place to make sure you're protected.'

'Alan Cooper, I think he's forty-seven, but he might be older. My mum will know for sure. He lived with us for two years in Lancaster before we moved to 6 Meadowfield View in Keswick. I don't know where he was before that or anything. He never talks about it, at least he doesn't to me. You need to speak to my mum, but she's pissed so you won't get much out of her at the moment.'

'Why is she angry, because you've come here?'

Paige laughed. 'Not pissed as in angry, pissed as in drunk as a skunk; she's been on the wine since she woke up.'

'Oh.'

'Yes, oh. She's regretting throwing him out now because she hates to be alone.'

'I need to speak to my boss; can you wait here?'

She shrugged. 'Yeah.'

Morgan left Paige sitting there scrolling on her phone and hurried to speak to Ben.

11

The office was empty. *They must all be in the blue room for the briefing*, Morgan thought. The aroma of freshly brewed coffee lingered in the air, and it smelled so good. She had bought a filter coffee machine after being caught out in the storm of the year out on the fells, but nobody remembered to fill it up and clean it out except for her and occasionally Cain. He must have known it was going to be a long shift and she could squeeze him she was so grateful.

Heading towards the blue room she hesitated outside the door. Marc was in full swing, and she knew he wouldn't be pleased if she interrupted him, but she also knew that Paige was a teenage girl who wouldn't sit around forever waiting for her. She walked in and every head turned her way then quickly turned back to Marc who nodded at her and carried on issuing orders to everyone. She looked at Ben, her head doing a little nod in the direction of the door, and he shook his at her. Opening her eyes wide she silently pleaded with him to follow her.

'Have you got a tic, Morgan, or developed Tourette's? What's the matter with you?'

'No, sir. Sorry, I need to borrow the boss for a moment.'

Marc paused, looking from her to Ben. 'Is it important? We're in the middle of a briefing.'

'I would say so, yes.'

He looked at Ben and lifted his hand in Morgan's direction. Ben's cheeks were burning, and he looked mortified, but he stood up and followed her out of the door. Neither of them spoke until they were walking down the stairs out of earshot of everyone in the room.

'What the hell, Morgan?'

'You need to speak to this girl; she might have a suspect for us.'

'Let me guess, her dad or her ex-boyfriend?'

'Close, her mum's ex-boyfriend.' He had the audacity to roll his eyes at her, and she felt a little spark of anger flicker inside of her chest.

'I wouldn't have dragged you away if I didn't think it was relevant to Melody Carrick.'

She opened the door and felt relieved to see Paige still sitting there; it would have been embarrassing if she'd left and she'd pulled him out of the briefing for nothing.

'Paige, this is my boss, Ben Matthews. Could you tell him what you told me?'

'What, like all of it?'

Morgan nodded, and Paige sighed. 'My mum's ex-boyfriend is a murder freak; he takes us to visit all the sites bodies have been found. He has a thing for my best friend, is always perving over her and now I can't get hold of her, and I think he could have taken her. I also think he killed whoever's body you found earlier.'

Ben sat down beside Morgan. 'Why do you think your friend is missing?' he asked. 'How long has it been since you last spoke to her?'

'A couple of hours, and I went to her house before I came

here. Beryl, her nosey neighbour, told me she left about six a.m. this morning and got in a white car. Alan drives a white car.'

He stole a glance at Morgan; he wasn't convinced.

'Paige, show him those photographs.'

Paige pushed the pictures towards him, and he picked them up, slowly looking at each one. He didn't need telling the locations where they had been taken, he had dealt with the bodies and like Morgan those memories were permanently imprinted into his brain.

'Can we keep these?'

She shrugged. 'If you want.'

'Have you given Morgan all your details?'

She nodded.

'We need your friend's address, phone number, names of her mum, dad, family, Alan's full name and date of birth, his address, make and model of car.'

Paige stared at him. 'Is that it? Thought you might ask me to go look for the pair of them myself.' She rhymed off everything he'd asked for. 'I don't know what number Alisa lives at, I just know the house, and I don't know where Alan is now. Probably shacked up with my mum's friend Jackie, who he has been sleeping around with and, before you ask, I have no idea where she lives.'

He studied her face. 'Have you spoken to your friends' parents? Are they concerned?'

'No, they went out for the day with her bratty little brother. I don't know where they are.'

'Paige, are you mad with Alan and trying to make him look like a suspect? This is a murder investigation and up to now you have taken up the time of two of the key detectives. I need to know that this is not some angry cry for help or some way to get your revenge on him. Any moment we spend chasing the wrong leads puts other women in danger.'

She leaned forward, her arms crossed and a fire in her eyes that told Morgan she was angry.

'I came here because I want to help. He has a treasure box full of broken jewellery; he does nothing but talk about murder, especially local ones; he's a weird guy and I think he is a killer. I think he's killed in the past and when you do find him and do a DNA test on him you'll discover he's linked to cold cases that have lain unsolved for years. But that's just my teenage girl opinion and I could be full of shit and attention seeking, but you won't know unless you take me seriously and look for him, will you?'

She stood up. 'Morgan knows where to find me, if he doesn't come looking for me first.'

She walked out of the door, letting it slam for effect, leaving Ben and Morgan staring at each other. She was annoyed with Ben; he had just treated Paige as if she was some kind of suspect. He held up his hands, palms facing towards her.

'I know, and before you say I'm a dick, I know I am. But, come on, how many people have gone to Castlerigg Stone Circle and have unknowingly stood on the exact same stone we found Cora Dalton's body draped across? How many people park in the lay-by to look at the view down onto Thirlmere? I'm sorry, I need more than that. You can go speak to her friend's parents and see if they're concerned about their daughter, and do the relevant searches on this guy who sounds like a creep. If anything interesting shows up then we'll step it up and focus on him more.'

She nodded, unable to speak she was so annoyed with him; he had brushed Paige off and annoyed her in the process. He walked out of the room leaving her wondering if she should try and catch up with Paige, and she realised she didn't even have a clue about which was Alisa's house.

Morgan shot out of the room and legged it out of the front doors looking for her, but she had gone. At least she had Paige's address, and she could look Alisa's parents up on the quick address system – it just depended upon how long they had lived there and if it had been updated. She would give Paige time to get home then go and see her and her mum, who would hope-fully be sober enough to answer her questions.

12

The blue room was empty now, and the only thing left to remind Morgan of the briefing she'd missed was an empty coffee mug and some discarded sheets of paper. She recognised Ben's chipped *I can't believe I work with these idiots* mug and picked it up, gathered the pieces of paper that had doodles on the other side and took them to the recycling bin. She stared out of the small window down onto the rear car park that was overshadowed by the snow-topped peaks of Helvellyn. If this heat carried on, the snow would be gone soon from the mountain, and as much as she was an autumn girl, Morgan was ready for some warm sunshine on her pale face and not having to work outside in the middle of fierce storms. A fleeting image of Melody's still body flickered across her mind, and she blinked it away. She had to focus, she couldn't let Melody or her mum, Jade, down. She should have asked Paige if she knew Melody; *bloody hell* she muttered under her breath.

'Talking to yourself already? It's not a good sign at your age.'

She turned to see Cain's huge frame leaning against the doorway, his arms crossed.

'Yes, I am. I'm fed up, Cain, tired of all this death that seems to follow me around, well not just me, all of us, I suppose.'

He walked towards her. 'Do you need a hug?'

She grinned at him and nodded, and he pulled her close and gave her the biggest squeeze ever. His bear hugs were legendary, and it had been a while since she'd had one. When he finally let her go, she sighed. 'Man, that was good.'

'Better than sex?'

Her cheeks turned pink. 'Erm there's no comparison to that, they're on a different level.'

He laughed.

She changed the subject. 'How are things with Angela?'

'Good, she's like the coolest woman I've ever talked to. After you, of course, Morgan, you're pretty cool too.'

She smiled. 'That's great, I'm so happy you're both getting along.'

'Why did I never date an older woman before? It's like there's none of that jealous, self-loathing stuff going on with her like the other women I've been out with, no insecurities. I don't get why you women are so hard on yourselves. It's really sad. But Angela isn't like that. It's like she's just happy being Angela. They should teach that to everyone in school and colleges; focus more on loving yourself and being at peace with who you are instead of all the pressure there is to be like some stupid celebrity who only looks the way they do because of the whole team of people that make them look like that.'

'Wow, that's deep, Cain, you been reading self-help books?'

He shrugged. 'It's right though. Why can't people just be themselves? It's sad.'

'We always want more, always comparing ourselves, and you're right it is sad. I gave up on that in my last year at school. I was never going to fit in with the popular girls despite hanging around with them, they just weren't my vibe, and it got harder to try and fit in, so I decided to just do my own thing.'

'You're not like that though, are you? I mean you're the only Goth copper I've ever met, and you have never changed yourself to conform to the rules, which is why I love you so much.'

Morgan laughed. 'Goth copper?'

'You know what I mean, you wear your eyeliner, always dress in black, are rarely seen without your Dr Marten boots on. You have cool tattoos, and if you were in a lineup, I'd never pick you out as a detective, that's for sure.'

'Oh, wow, thanks. Are you saying I look like a criminal?'

'No, I'm saying you are just yourself and I think that it's a brilliant thing. You're amazing at your job too, pretty crap at running but a good detective.'

'Yeah, exercise and me, it's not a good thing. I hate it, I don't mind walking but anything else is just—'

She didn't finish her sentence because Marc was standing at the door.

'What is this, some kind of therapy session?'

Cain had his back to him and rolled his eyes at Morgan, and then he turned slowly.

'No, sir, it's a make your colleague feel better session. I believe they are free and should be initiated as and when needed.'

Marc smiled. 'Very good, remind me next time I'm having a bad day to come have a chat with you, Cain. Have you ever considered a career as a psychotherapist?'

'Maybe when this gets too much, but for now I'm happy where I am. What about you?'

'Same. Morgan, why did you take Ben out of the briefing?'

'A possible lead came in, and I thought he should hear about it.'

'Oh, that's good. Are you following up on this lead? What is it?'

'A teenage girl thinks her mum's ex-boyfriend might have abducted her friend and could be responsible for the murder.'

'Are you looking into this? Is it true? Do you think there are any grounds to it?'

'Just waiting for Ben's approval to go and find out.'

'Go, I'll tell him where you are.'

She was surprised; it was usually Marc who put the stop on things, and she didn't feel comfortable walking out of the station before speaking to Ben.

'Thanks, I just need to grab my jacket.'

He nodded and strolled away. Cain let out a low whistle.

'Is he trying to cause trouble or being nice?'

'Probably being nice, but if I disappear without Ben's approval it doesn't seem right.'

'No, you better clear it with the boss first or it's going to cause trouble at home later.'

'What did you come back for?'

He pointed to the screwed-up papers in her hands. 'My artwork. I thought I'd better remove it, but you saved me the bother. Come on, Brookes, let's go tell the teacher first before Marc does.'

They headed in the direction of the CID office, hoping to beat the inspector there, and the relief that they did wasn't lost on Morgan. Ben was busy writing on the knackered old white-board that he had fought tooth and nail to save when they came to install a new smart board for them. The smartboard was next to it, but all of them preferred to be able to stick the pictures of victims and suspects with a blob of ancient Blu-Tack on the old one, and list their actions for each case. There were still faint traces of green and blue marker below a new purple one. Morgan had bought a set of brightly coloured pens on her last stationery haul when they'd gone shopping to Liverpool, along with notebooks, Post-it notes, page markers for the books she was reading – anything that she wanted to remember, she used those little sticky tabs so she could find it again without having to crease the corner of the page.

'The boss told me to go and speak to Paige's mum and then check on Alisa.'

Ben turned to her; his eyes wide in surprise. 'He did?'

She nodded.

'When you come back, can you join in with the house to house by the scene? I want everyone speaking to anyone who could have been out walking their dog, and every property checking for video doorbells, dashcams, you know the score.'

'I do.'

'Amy will come to the post-mortem with me.'

Morgan bit her tongue, relieved to not have to go, but at the same time she got the distinct impression Ben was angry with her. She didn't know why, all she was doing was following leads like any detective would. In the early days when she had been put on an attachment to CID, he always told her to follow her nose, and she didn't understand why he was so against it now.

She sat down and logged on to the quick address system to double check the house number for the street Paige lived in, just in case she was leading them on a wild-goose chase. She would leave him to it, let him take Amy to the post-mortem, and maybe she could find this guy who was raising all the red flags and bring him in for a voluntary interview. It would be such a relief if he was their person of interest.

13

He had thought long and hard about the possibility of copying previous murderers, those who had killed at his favourite locations, but there was nothing clever about that. It was almost an insult to his own intelligence really, the more he thought about it. Copying what another killer had done didn't show very much initiative; it was lazy and not very exciting for anyone. It was far better to be his own kind of killer. He chuckled out loud to himself.

He was giving himself a pep talk, maybe he could write the first motivational book for other killers, become the Oprah of the sick and twisted and reap the royalties so he could live out the rest of his life in comfort and never have to work another day again.

He glanced in the rear-view mirror. It had been risky, probably too risky and too soon to take another girl, but the opportunity had presented itself and now there she was, lying on the back seat, hog-tied so she couldn't move, a thick gag in her mouth and her eyes wide with fear. He could smell it emanating from her pores; it was a cold, sweet smell not too dissimilar to the sweetness of death on the breath of someone who had taken their last breaths as their heart stopped beating.

The police were busy at the crime scene down by the riverside, and there weren't enough of them to be stopping vehicles, or so he hoped. He wasn't sure how he would get out of this particular predicament should a cop pull him over. How do you explain a trussed-up teenager in the back seat? His gaze fell on the speedometer, and he released his foot off the accelerator a little, so that he stayed under the 40 mph speed limit on this road.

He had no plan, no idea what to do with her and wished that for moment he had resisted the urge to do what he had, as this was going to cause him problems. He didn't know her, had never set eyes on her before. He could let her go, *should* let her go so he didn't fuck everything up. He realised the burning sensation inside of his stomach was anger: he was so mad at himself. Yes, she would go to the police but what were the chances of them being able to find him? It would be far better to take the chance and let her out than to rush things. She wasn't who he wanted anyway.

He carried on driving until he found a secluded bit of road. Pulling into the overgrown entrance to a field, he drew the baseball cap low over his eyes and jumped out of the car. As he opened the passenger door, she began to whimper the best that she could, and he lifted his finger to shush her.

'This is your lucky day, be quiet and I won't have to hurt you. All you must do is sit here like a good girl and give me a few minutes to drive away before you try and call for help. It's up to you, you can do as I ask and get to live out the rest of your life like God thinks you should, or you can start to scream like there's no tomorrow and cause a fuss. If I don't get to drive a safe distance before you do decide to start screaming, and I get stopped by the cops, I will come back for you, do you understand that? And if I can't come back to finish what I should then my friend who is even scarier than me will. Do I make myself clear?'

She nodded at him, her head furiously bobbing up and down.

He snapped on a pair of rubber gloves and untied the rope from her feet then grabbed hold of her arms and dragged her out of the back seat and into the long grass. The only sounds were the birds singing in the trees above them and the laboured breaths she was taking through the gag in her mouth. He pushed her shoulders so she was facing away from him and began to loosen the ropes around her wrists. He wasn't making it too easy for her; if she still had to struggle to get loose it would buy him some time to make a clean escape. Should he just kill her and be done with it? It was risky, she was going to talk to the cops, but what could she tell them? In all reality she didn't know anything. He continued working his slender fingers at the ropes, impressed with how tight his knots were. She would never escape out of these without a little help.

The sound of a car in the distance made him freeze for a second then he pulled her close to him and wrapped his arms around her in some kind of hug, squeezing her body against his so if the driver glanced at them, it looked as if they were a couple of lovers making out. The car sped past doing way more than forty, and he didn't think they even glanced their way. He pushed her away from him, and the terror in her eyes almost made him feel bad for what he was putting her through.

'Sit down.' He pointed to the floor, and she dropped like a rock to the ground.

He nodded. 'Good, now you are going to sit there until I have driven away. You may try to untie yourself once I'm out of sight. If you even try to move before then, I will turn around and mow you down, okay?'

She nodded.

Despite his internal voice telling him to kill her, he

managed to get back in and drive away. In his mirror he saw that she hadn't stepped onto the road yet. Good, that was good. He glanced at her phone on the seat next to him, wiped it against his trousers, then, using his sleeve to grab it, launched it out of his window into the bushes at the side of the road. Then he put his foot down on the accelerator and this time, he did break the speed limit. He had to get out of here before someone called the cops.

14

Morgan was on her way to Keswick to speak to Paige's mum, and then she was going to locate Alisa's parents or even better Alisa herself. The hire car she was driving had a radio and it was almost hard to believe she was working. As her fingers tapped in time to music, she sang along to 'Stop', her favourite out of the Spice Girls songs, at the same time she was admiring the views to the right of her. The lush green valley that dipped down onto Thirlmere was stunning, there was no getting away from it despite the horrors of the lay-by she had passed a few minutes ago, and the memories of Jasmine Armer's dead face that were forever frozen in time in her mind.

From the corner of her eye, she caught sight of the girl who stumbled from out of nowhere on the opposite side into the middle of the road as if she was drunk, and swerved to avoid her, hitting the brake too hard. The car skidded and she felt it swerve a little too fast as it ploughed into the drystone wall with a loud screaming crunch of metal. The airbag deployed, and she felt herself thrown into it at full force, her ears popping at the high-pitched scream that had come out of her own mouth as she jolted forward then back, slamming into the seat. Finding it hard to breathe, she unbuckled the seat belt and tried to open her door which was wedged too close to the damn wall, making her scramble out of the passenger door. Morgan grabbed her radio that had been flung down into the footwell of the car and looked around for the girl. Had she just imagined her? She turned around to see her crouched down behind the car, hands tied with rope and hiding her face as she cowered.

'Hey, are you okay?'

The girl was sobbing. Morgan glanced at the state of the brand-new hire car that Mads had told her had been dropped off at the station about an hour before she had booked it out and muttered, 'Oh fuck.'

She jogged towards the girl. 'It's okay, I'm a police officer, you're okay now. Did I hit you?'

The girl looked up at Morgan and she knew she was trying to imagine if this woman in front of her was a copper. The girl shook her head and pointed to her face. 'You're bleeding.'

'I am?'

She nodded.

Morgan lifted her fingers and began to prod at her face until she found a large gash above her eyebrow and grimaced as her fingers touched the warm, sticky blood.

'What happened to you?'

'Can you call the police? Some guy grabbed me off the street.' She drew in a breath and let out a loud sob. 'I thought he was going to kill me but then he pulled over and dragged me out of the car and left me here.'

Morgan's mind was working overtime. 'I am the police. How long ago? What kind of car?' Before the girl could answer, she lifted the radio. 'Control, I've had a road traffic accident, single vehicle.'

'*Morgan, are you okay?*'

'Slight injury to my head, but I'm okay.'

She turned to look at the car which was most definitely not

okay. 'The car's a mess, can you send patrols? I swerved to avoid a girl as she ran across the road, who is claiming she was abducted, and you better send a supervisor about the car and a recovery truck.'

Mads's voice crackled over the radio handset.

'Brookes, you did not just crash that car?'

She shrugged, what was she going to say? That she was winding him up. 'Erm that's confirmed, sir.'

He let out a low whistle.

'On my way.'

Ben hadn't answered. *Was he so angry that Marc had given her permission to go to Keswick that he didn't care?* Her phone was vibrating from the footwell of the car, but she didn't have time to go pick it up.

'Did you see the car?'

The girl nodded. 'It was a white SUV type, but I didn't see the make.'

'What's your name?'

Morgan thought she was going to say Alisa.

'Chloe Smith.'

There was a gag tied around the girl's mouth but despite how scared she looked she was able to talk freely.

'You need to wipe your face or get something to press against that cut.'

Morgan nodded; shock was a great pain reliever. She went to the car to see if she could find a first aid kit in the boot and pulled out a small black bag. Unzipping it she took out a small bandage and ripped open the plastic, pushing it onto the cut on her forehead. She grimaced at how painful it was.

'I'm going to take some photographs of your hands, Chloe, and the ropes then I'll untie you.'

Chloe nodded; she was now sitting on the floor, her hands in front of her.

'Are you in a lot of trouble about the car? It's brand new.'

Morgan looked at it and shrugged. 'It's only a car, better to have damaged that than run you over.'

'Sorry.'

'Hey, it wasn't your fault, don't be sorry. I'm just glad you're okay. Are you okay? Did he hurt you?'

She shook her head. 'I thought he was going to kill me; he had the scariest eyes, they were so blue, and then he just stopped the car and dragged me out of it. He pointed something into my back and told me it was a gun, but I don't know if it was. I didn't see one, but I was too busy crying to take any notice.'

Morgan sat down on the gravelly verge next to her. 'I'd have been crying too.'

Chloe looked at her then shook her head. 'I don't think you would, you're bleeding all down the side of your face and you haven't even flinched.'

She laughed. 'That's because I can't see how bad it is. Did you recognise him, Chloe? Can you give me a description?'

'Never seen him before in my life and I hope I never see him again. He had a black baseball cap pulled low, but I could still see his eyes; he is white, taller than you but not a lot.' She squeezed her eyes shut. 'I think he had a pale blue shirt on and blue jeans, trainers but no idea what make. I was so scared, I only glanced at him. All I kept thinking was I would never see my mum again.' She began to sniffle, trying to stem the tears that were pooling in the corners of her eyes.

Morgan spoke into the radio. 'Can patrols be on the lookout for a white SUV travelling in the direction of Ambleside, lone male driver. The person who abducted the victim is driving one. White male around five feet ten, blue shirt, blue jeans, trainers and black baseball cap.'

Sirens echoed around the valley, and Morgan was glad to hear them even though Mads would be pissed with her about the car. This had to be one of the strangest situations she had ever been in. Crashing a car to avoid running over a kidnap victim who had escaped and then sitting together waiting to be rescued by the cops was a pretty surreal situation.

The van that screeched to a halt first had an angry-looking Mads in the passenger seat. He jumped out, took one look at the car, then at Morgan and Chloe, and then he spoke.

'Why am I not surprised? You need an ambulance, Brookes?'

She shook her head. 'No, just a plaster.'

He snorted. 'You're going to need more than a plaster for that head.'

He turned to Chloe. 'I'm Sergeant Paul Madden, what happened to you?'

Chloe held up her arms. 'Someone took me, then let me go and I ran into the road. It wasn't her fault she crashed the car: it was totally mine.'

Then she let out a loud sob as the shock of what had happened to her wore off and the realisation of how grave her situation could have been kicked in.

15

It was chaos at the scene of the accident, there was no other way to describe it. Someone had called an ambulance, which turned up, but it couldn't get near because Mads had insisted the road be shut off in both directions until CSI had been to see if they could get any forensics from where Chloe had been dragged out of the car. Wendy, who had not long resumed from the crime scene where Melody's body had been found, had got changed and come straight out, photographing Chloe and the ropes before cutting them off and leaving the knot intact. She had then passed her a white paper suit and asked her if she could have her clothes. Chloe was wearing an oversized white Gymshark T-shirt and running leggings. Wendy had told her she didn't think there would be anything of forensic value on them, but she still had to try. Chloe had got changed in the back of her van, dropping all of her outer clothing and shoes into the brown paper sack Wendy had given her. While they were waiting for Chloe, Wendy had peered at the cut on Morgan's eyebrow.

'You better go get checked out. The airbag deployed, so you know, better safe than sorry.'

'I'd rather not.'

Wendy shrugged. 'Ben will be mad if you don't, and I'm not being mean but Mads isn't going to let you take another hire car out after this. Where were you heading anyway? I thought you'd have been going to the post-mortem with Ben?'

'I think he's officially seen his arse with me.'

Wendy arched an eyebrow at her. 'Who, Ben or Mads?'

Morgan grinned; it wasn't funny but what was a dire situation if you couldn't at least have a laugh about it? 'Both of them.'

Wendy let out a loud laugh that made Mads turn and glare at the pair of them, which made them both laugh even more. Wendy lowered her voice. 'He's upset about the paperwork.'

He came striding towards them holding Morgan's phone in his hand. 'You better phone Ben back, you have like ten missed calls from him.'

She nodded and took the phone off him.

'What are you two laughing at?'

'Life,' replied Wendy.

'Yeah, it's hilarious. Get her into that ambulance and out of my way, can you, please? I don't want Ben racing here and getting all upset over her.'

Wendy shook her head at him. 'Morgan is her own person.'

'Tell me about it, she's a walking disaster magnet. Not only does she write-off a brand-new car, but she also finds kidnapped victims in the middle of nowhere. I mean, what other copper does that?'

Morgan clamped the phone to her ear and walked towards the waiting ambulance, to Mads giving her a round of applause. She was tempted to turn back and give him the middle finger, but decided not to make him even angrier than he already was.

'What's going on, Morgan, are you hurt?'

Ben's voice was concerned, so maybe he wasn't angry with her after all.

'I'm fine, just a small cut on my head. I'm better than the car, that's for sure.'

'*Only you could find a missing girl moments after her disappearance is reported!*' He exclaimed. '*Was it the girl who Paige had reported missing?*'

'Sadly not.'

Ben let out a sigh.

'*What the hell is going on? We have one dead girl, one apparently missing and one that was abducted but was let go. Is this the work of the same guy, do you think?*'

The paramedic took her arm and helped her into the back of the ambulance, and she smiled at Nick, as it had been some time since she'd last been attended to by him. He looked tanned and happy, and she noticed he was now wearing a wedding ring. She pointed to it. 'Congratulations,' she whispered, as he pointed at her head and shook his head.

'*Congratulations to who?*'

'Oh, Nick the paramedic.'

'*I'm confused.*'

'I don't know if it's the same guy, but I'm hoping so; otherwise we have a huge problem on our hands if there are three separate mad men running around this area.'

'*What was the guy called who Paige reported?*'

'Alan Cooper.'

'*Right, well we better find him ASAP just in case. Seriously, are you okay? I'm sorry for sending you out alone.*'

'I'm fine and you weren't to know what was going to happen, nobody did.'

'*No, except for the guy who killed Melody and took that girl.*'

'Do you think it's a distraction? Make us run around chasing our tails all day and getting nowhere fast.'

Nick leaned in with antiseptic on some gauze, pressing it to the open wound, making her hiss between her teeth.

'*What's up?*'

'Nothing, it just stings a bit.'

'Ring me as soon as you're back at the station. I want you to go back and grab Cain. I do not and I repeat this, do not want you out there looking for Alan Cooper on your own, and besides, you shouldn't drive with a head injury anyway, but you know that, right?'

Morgan wanted to hang up. He was talking to her like some sulky teenager, not his colleague and life partner.

'Morgan.'

'Yeah, right. I will, boss.' She ended the call and looked at Nick. 'What's that? Acid?'

'Sorry, I know that you won't come back to the hospital with us, so I'm cleaning it extra hard to make sure it doesn't get infected.'

'Well thanks, I appreciate that, but if you could leave a little of my skin there to heal over it, I'd be grateful.'

'Still as grouchy as ever. You're not engaged or anything then?'

He had hold of her left hand, looking at her bare ring finger.

She shook her head. 'Way too young for that. How come you got married so quick?'

'Morgan, it's been four years since we first had the pleasure of each other's company, that's practically a lifetime, and besides she's very special. I would have married her after the third date if she'd said yes.'

She smiled at him. He was a good-looking guy and he'd asked her out multiple times over the course of the first few months of them meeting. She'd declined because she'd been too busy with working her first murder investigation, and pining over Ben who she hadn't believed would give her a second glance.

'I'm happy for you, that's great.'

'Thanks, I'd be happy for you too if you could manage to stop hurting yourself. Is that a new car you've totalled?'

She smirked. 'Yes, I believe it is, or it was.'

He shook his head. 'At least you only have a cut. I'll have this glued shut in no time.'

'Thank you, Nick. You've helped put me back together a few times. I appreciate it.'

'All part of the fabulous service from the NHS.'

'Brookes, you've totally blown it this time. Mads said you're not fit to let out on a BMX let alone a vehicle with an engine.'

She knew Cain was standing there the moment the light was blocked out by his huge broad shoulders and a dark shadow filled the back of the truck. 'What are you doing here?'

'Came to have a look for myself and to give you a ride back, boss's orders. I'm to babysit you for the rest of the day because you can't drive for shit.'

She didn't argue with him. She was glad to see him as it meant they could get to Keswick without any detours or time lost. She was desperate to find Alisa and track down Alan Cooper.

16

Ben was quiet. He was worried and felt terrible for leaving Morgan alone. As if to prove his worries right they'd only been apart an hour or so and already she'd crashed a car. Amy was used to him being quiet, so he didn't feel bad about that. Before Morgan had come along and roused him out of the walking depression that he'd been unable to shift since his wife had died, he would often go for hours without speaking to anyone in his team. Then again, back in the day, murders were the exception to the rule. They were few and far between, almost always a domestic gone wrong. They were nothing like the kinds of cases they dealt with now. Which, quite frankly, terrified him. It was like the 1970s had exploded back onto the scene. He remembered his mum talking about the volume of American serial killers back in the seventies and how she was glad they didn't live in the US, which used to make him smile when she'd be sitting chatting to his gran over a pot of tea and cakes on a Sunday afternoon. They had always lived in or near to the beautiful Lakeland village, which was more like a town due its ever-growing expansion of Rydal Falls. The top crimes had been stolen sheep and tractors when he was growing up. How had it come to this? It kept him awake at night, the pondering over the state of affairs and just how many violent deaths his team had dealt with the last four years.

'So, what's the plan, boss? Is the body here, did anyone release the scene?'

He looked at Amy and swore underneath his breath. 'Yes, of course, the scene was released. The body should be here waiting for us. Declan would have phoned if she hadn't been moved here.'

He sounded confident, but there was a niggling feeling in his gut that was making him doubt himself. Had he released the scene? He didn't think that he had, maybe Marc had. Why didn't he know this? His head was a mess today. He got out of the car, and Amy followed.

'We're here now, may as well go in.'

She side-eyed him. 'You didn't release the scene, did you?'

He couldn't lie, that wasn't his style. 'I don't know, I can't remember if I specifically did release it.'

'Are you losing it a little, boss? You've been acting weird all day, and now we're at the mortuary waiting for a post-mortem on a body that hasn't even been booked in.'

'I am not losing it; we went and delivered the death message, which was hard, and I assumed that we were good to go after Declan had done his initial examination.'

She shrugged. 'Nothing to do with me, it's all beyond my pay scale.'

They made it to the doors of the mortuary, which were unlocked. It made a change from having to ring the bell and wait out in the rain for someone, usually Susie, to answer it. There were three women and one man in the waiting area, all of them arguing quietly between themselves. They stopped when Ben glared at them. He wasn't in the mood; the last thing he wanted was a full-on domestic here. He didn't have the time or the energy for it. Susie appeared and he marvelled at her latest hair colour, which was half green and half black with a mixed green and black fringe. She smiled at him then turned her attention to the other people.

'If you're ready, we can go and see your dad.'

This stopped their bickering, as they all realised just how grave a situation they were in; their dad was dead, and they needed to put aside their differences and unite for the sake of their loved one.

Susie turned to Ben. 'Declan's in his office.'

He nodded and strode towards it, Amy behind him. He knocked on the door before opening it, to have a screwed-up ball of paper whoosh past his head and bounce off the wall.

'Sorry, sorry that's my bad. I'm practising my basketball skills and as you can tell, not improving much. So, why are you here, my friend, because your body hasn't arrived yet?'

Ben let out a sigh. 'I messed up, I thought we'd released the body. Let me phone the boss and clear it with him.'

Declan shrugged. 'That's all very decent of you, admitting you fucked up, Ben, but you know that it could be a couple of hours before it reaches here. Have you eaten today, are you dehydrated?' Declan turned to Amy. 'Do you want to go to the canteen and get us something to eat and drink, put it on my tab.'

She was about to argue with him, but he smiled at her, giving a gentle nod in Ben's direction and she shrugged, then turned to go find out if there was anything worth eating in the canteen.

As she closed the door, Declan waited for Ben to take a seat.

'Now, what's the matter, because I've never known you to make this kind of error of judgement.'

'I don't know, I feel tired, like drained kind of tired, and I was horrible to Morgan, sending her off to do house to house because she spoke to Marc about a job, and she only went and crashed the car.'

'Dear God, is the girl okay?'

'I think so, she said she had a small cut on her forehead. She swerved to avoid a kidnapping victim that had been thrown out of a car.'

Declan was shaking his head and lifted both hands to the side of it, miming his brain exploding. 'Mind blown, is there anything or anywhere that girl can go without this amount of drama?'

'It seems not.'

'Can you not get her a desk job? Can she not solve all these heinous crimes without leaving the safety of the station?'

'Good luck telling her that. I wouldn't dare.'

'Why were you mad at her talking to Marc? Were you feeling a little jealous that she's chatting to him?'

Ben laughed. 'No, she's never given me a reason to feel jealous, and I don't think the boss is her type, but she's got it in her head that she needs to guide him to work better with the team, and I don't want her getting too involved with him because he's an arse who has more mood swings than a perimenopausal woman.'

Declan had taken a long gulp from the bottle of water he'd picked up off his desk and he spat it all over himself and Ben, spraying him with spit and water. Ben grimaced.

'Thanks.'

Declan was laughing. 'Maybe it's time you took a career break, get yourself a gig at the comedy club that's opening in Ambleside. Your humour is better than your general knowledge. Speaking of, are you going to the quiz?'

He nodded. 'I can't see my stand-up routine being a big hit, but yes to the quiz as long as nothing else crops up.'

'I think I know what's wrong with you, my friend.'

'You do? You should be a doctor.'

Declan winked at him. 'I think you have a bit of seasonal depression brought on by the number of murders you deal with, plus you're thinking, at the back of your mind, will there be more murders this time?'

Before Ben could answer his phone began to vibrate, and he answered it.

'Ben, did you release the scene? I asked Control if you had, and they said they weren't aware of it, so I've done it and the undertakers have just arrived. Where are you?'

'At the mortuary and thanks, I got a bit sidetracked.'

Marc didn't answer for a few seconds.

'It's okay, I asked Morgan to go to the hospital to talk to the girl who is claiming she was abducted and get a statement from her, but she said she had to get to Keswick ASAP in case the guy the girl who turned up at the station about earlier was responsible for the murder and the abduction. I agreed as long as she went with Cain. If you're hanging around waiting for the body to arrive, is there any chance you can speak to the abduction victim? We need to know if she's telling the truth. Morgan got a first account from her, but I figured, seeing as you were there, you could speak to her and see if her story is the same. I mean it's a bit of a coincidence having a murder and an abduction in the same afternoon.'

Ben didn't tell him that it wasn't really, because this was Rydal Falls, where sleeping killers lay in wait to take their turn in the limelight, and that the things most people had nightmares about when the night was dark and the moon was full were very possible.

17

Meadowfield View was exactly that: there were six white new-build houses all with pale green doors; drystone walls enclosed the properties in a semicircle, and their fenced-off back gardens had once been part of the meadow that ran behind them. They looked expensive and a little out of place. She was surprised that the local planning department had agreed to let them build here. Morgan looked at Cain who gave a low whistle.

'Bet these cost a pretty penny. Which one are we going to?'

'Number six.'

She got out of the car and wondered if Paige was already home, and was Alan Cooper tall with the bluest of eyes? There was only one way to find out. The low hum of a lawn mower was the only sound in the entire area, and she looked around to see a tall guy in the garden at the opposite end busy mowing the lawn. His white pickup had *The Lawn Guy* emblazoned along one side. The house had a doorbell camera, which was good, as it meant they would have access to footage of anyone coming and going should they need it. Morgan pressed the button and waited; the camera had kicked in the moment they had got out of the car, and she could see the circular light was spinning.

There was no reply, so she walked down towards where the guy was mowing the lawn. He had stopped and was watching them. 'Hey, do you know the family that live in that house? Have you seen them?'

His face was tanned, and he looked as if he could be a model for some sports catalogue; he was handsome. He shook his head. 'I have no idea, I'm here to mow the lawns. They don't talk to me, I don't talk to them.'

She smiled at him, and he winked at her, mopped his brow with a piece of cloth he had hanging out of his back pocket then pointed to the lawn mower and began mowing again. She walked back to Cain who shook his head. 'You fancy him.'

'I do not; well, he's nice.'

'Oh, don't let the boss hear you talking like that.'

'I don't want to run away with him, Cain. He's obviously good looking. It's a fact, that's all.' Cain shook his head at her and leaned forward as he hammered against the composite door with his curled-up fist.

'She won't answer; she never does.'

Morgan turned to see Paige standing at the gate. 'If you'd said you were coming here, you could have given me a lift. Save me sitting on that bus that takes forever. I always get the same driver; they're never in a rush and just dawdle along the lanes without a care in the world.'

'You left before I had chance to tell you, and I was involved in an accident on the way here so probably better that you didn't.'

Paige pointed to the white strips taped across the skin above her eyebrow. 'You hurt yourself.' It wasn't a question it was a statement.

'A little. I'm a big girl, I'll be okay.' She didn't mention the blinding headache that was pulsating behind her eye.

Paige walked down the path and took out her key. 'I don't

know what kind of mood she's going to be in or how drunk she is, so don't be mad if she's no use and can't tell you anything.'

'I'm not here to get mad. I'm here to get answers.'

Paige nodded. 'She's going to be mad I went to you though; she doesn't like the police.'

'Does anyone?' replied Cain.

Paige glanced in his direction and shrugged. 'No, I don't know that they do.'

He smirked at her, and her cheeks turned pink. She opened the door and yelled, 'Mum, the police are here,' at the top of her voice.

A woman stumbled out of a doorway and stood clutching the architrave in the wide hall, staring at all three of them. She was older than Morgan had imagined with a very shiny frownline-free forehead. If she had to age her, she'd say mid-forties.

The woman turned to Paige. 'What have you done, you little shit?'

'Susan, I'm Detective Morgan Brookes and this is my colleague, Cain. Paige hasn't done anything except give us some information, and we'd like to have a chat with you about what she's told us, if that's okay.'

Susan screwed up her eyes so small it made her look like a mouse. 'I bet she has been talking crap again and making accusations that have no truth to them.' She was glaring at her daughter; Paige didn't look in the least bit bothered.

'Come in then.'

Susan pointed to the room behind her. It was a large, spacious and very beige lounge.

'Have a seat. Paige, you better tell me what the hell you've told these people.'

Susan didn't seem quite as drunk as she'd expected. Morgan said, 'Paige told us some concerns she had about your ex-partner Alan Cooper.'

Susan rolled her eyes. 'Jesus, did she tell you he's a serial killer with a trophy box of broken jewellery?'

Morgan's heart dropped. Was this a tale she'd told before? 'She talked about something like that. Do you want to tell us a little about it?'

There was an empty wine bottle on the table next to an empty glass and Susan stared at it longingly, no doubt wishing she had a full one to replace it and ease the pain of these questions. Morgan hoped her open question would help her unravel this strange family dynamic.

'My only concern with Alan was his inability to keep his trousers zippered shut. I do not believe he is a killer who collects victims' broken jewellery. He told me that stuff belonged to his nan. She listens to too many true crime podcasts,' Susan said, nodding her head in Paige's direction. 'She watches too many documentaries; it's not normal to have an interest in that kind of stuff.'

Paige was shaking her head ever so slightly. Morgan pondered what Susan would think about her and her obsession with true crime, although technically Morgan's could be classed as research now because of her role as a detective. Plus, that knowledge she was sure was the reason she was able to do her job as well as she did.

'Do you know where he is now?'

Susan shrugged. 'Probably with that old dog Jackie, but I don't know for sure, and I don't really care.'

'Where does Jackie live?'

'Rydal Falls, has a tiny flat that isn't big enough to swing a cat in above the Co-op, yet he'd rather live there than with us.'

'Does he work, have any friends in the area, any pubs he likes to frequent, and what kind of car does he drive?' Morgan gave Susan her best smile then added, 'You have a beautiful home.'

'Thank you, and before you ask what I do for a living, I was left some money when my mum died, and I used it to put a deposit down on this house. This has nothing to do with him, he didn't put a penny towards it. I work part time at Westmorland and Furness Council to pay the rest of the bills. He doesn't go out drinking unless we're together and I'm paying for it. He spends his time here watching those awful true crime documentaries that him and Paige are both obsessed with. He's between jobs too. He moved here and got a job as a delivery driver for the supermarket, but he got laid off a month ago. He drives a beaten old Nissan. Do you want his shoe size, inside leg measurements?'

'Not at the moment, but thank you. Did Alan's behaviour ever give you cause for concern? Did you not mind going to the local murder sites with him for days out?'

Susan paused, her eyes once more falling on her empty glass. She licked her lips a little and Morgan thought that maybe she was more dependent on alcohol than was good for her. Not that she was judging, if a bottle of wine got Susan through her day, who was she to comment? She couldn't live without caffeine and she was partial to a large glass of ice-cold rosé, if only she didn't get called out to serious crime scenes so much.

'I didn't enjoy those days out; I'm not interested in the macabre unlike Paige and Alan. They both have the same morbid interests. I don't know why she hates him so much, as they have a lot in common. I went along for the ride and to keep the peace. It was the only way we could spend time together without arguing over everything.' She glared at Paige again. 'You hated him the minute he walked through the door. Why are you doing this and causing a fuss? You've embarrassed yourself and me.'

'You said it was weird, don't go changing your mind because the cops are talking to you. Why are you trying to protect him? I can't get hold of Alisa and she left the house this morning to get in a white car with a man.'

Susan sat up straight. 'When was this?'

'Six a.m., the neighbour said.'

Morgan was watching the pair of them, and she could see Susan was thinking deeply about all of this.

'It doesn't mean it was Alan.'

'It doesn't mean it wasn't. He always acts like a creep around her. Touching her as often as he could get away with. Maybe he's not shacked up with Jackie at all; maybe he's killed that girl who was found earlier and now he's taken Alisa.'

Susan's eyes widened at the same time as her mouth. 'What girl, who was found earlier, what do you mean?'

A cold chill spread up Morgan's spine: a white SUV had been used to abduct Chloe Smith.

'The body of a teenage girl was discovered earlier on today. Do you have a recent photograph of Alan that I can keep hold of? And I need to speak to Alisa's parents; can you phone them for me, Paige?'

She nodded, took out her phone and then passed it to Morgan.

'Hello, is this Alisa's mum?'

'Yes, who is this? Why are you phoning off Paige's phone?'

'I'm a detective with Rydal Falls police. Paige was worried about Alisa. Is she with you by any chance?'

'No, she's not home. Why is Paige worried about her, has she not phoned her?'

'When was the last time you spoke to your daughter?'

There was a slight pause.

'Last night. We've been out all day but when we left, she was still in bed. I didn't bother to wake her because she was quite adamant she wasn't coming with us to Greenland's Farm in Carnforth. Said she'd rather stick a hot poker through her eyeball than spend a day on a farm that smelled of animals and bratty kids.'

'Please can you phone her, or try and locate her, then can

you call me back on this number?' Morgan recited her phone number to her.

'Yes, of course. Should I be worried?'

'The neighbour told Paige that she left with a man in a white car at six a.m.'

'She did? Oh, I had no idea. She comes and goes all the time as she pleases. I don't monitor what she does; she's almost eighteen. Her ex-boyfriend has a white car, it could have been his.'

'Mrs Halliday are you concerned for your daughter's whereabouts?'

'Not really. Look, I'll try and get hold of her then I'll speak to Joe, her ex, and see if he's seen her. I'll phone you back soon. Tell Paige to stop worrying about her; she's probably just forgot to charge her phone or not told her what she was doing today.'

She lowered her voice.

'I think sometimes Paige gets a little too involved or intense and sometimes Alisa has to pull back from her for a bit of breathing space, so maybe that's why she never told her what she was doing or hasn't answered her phone to her. She's a good kid but can be a little hard work at times.'

'Thank you, please call me as soon as you know where she is.'

'Absolutely.'

Susan passed Morgan a photograph, and she looked down at it; this one was different to the one Paige had shown her. Here, Susan was very smartly dressed, standing next to a guy wearing a pair of seventies-style sunglasses and sporting a bit of a beard; he was dressed in a white suit with a pink shirt. She gave an involuntary shudder. He looked like a throwback from the seventies, and he looked mean as hell behind his shades. He wasn't much taller than Susan who looked about five feet six; he didn't match the description that Chloe had given.

'Do you know if Alan has ever been in trouble with the

police in the past? Did he ever mention having a criminal record, being arrested?'

Susan looked even more horrified at Morgan's last questions than she already did, and she shook her head.

Morgan passed Paige's phone back to her. 'Her mum isn't overly worried about her. Hopefully she'll turn up soon.'

Paige didn't look convinced, and judging by the expression on Susan's face, neither did her mum.

18

Ben made his way to the A&E department; Amy still hadn't returned from the canteen and Declan had gone to speak to the bickering family to explain why their dad's sudden death would need a post-mortem. The guy at the reception desk had a weird smile on his face as if he was enjoying his job a little too much, something that Ben didn't see very often.

'Hi, I'm DS Ben Matthews from Rydal Falls police, can I speak to Chloe Smith, please?'

Ben pressed his warrant card against the plexiglass screen that had been put up at the beginning of the Covid pandemic and not removed. The guy nodded and pointed to the double doors further down that gave access to the unit. Ben met him as the doors opened, and he never said a word to him, just smiled then turned and led the way to a cubicle where the curtain was drawn across.

He spoke through the curtain. 'Chloe, it's Detective Matthews, I'm going to be in charge of the investigation regarding your case. Can I come in?'

The curtain was pushed back by Amber. Chloe was sitting cross-legged on the bed. Her messy bun had all but fallen out, and she looked far too young to be sitting in one of their crime scene coveralls.

'Hey, how are you holding up?'

'I'll be better when I can go home. I don't want to be stuck here.'

He nodded. 'No, I bet you don't, it's just a precaution. Are you injured?'

She shook her head. 'Just a little shaken. I did say I didn't want to come but this guy in a suit insisted I did.'

'Ah, my boss. He's a stickler for the rules. Is there anyone we can contact to come and rescue you?'

Chloe pointed at Amber. 'She let me phone my mum; she's on her way.'

'Good, that's good. Has anyone taken a statement from you?'

He was looking at Amber when he asked this, and she shrugged. 'The boss said to wait for one of you lot to do it. He doesn't trust us to do it properly, thinks we'll mess it up despite statement taking being one of our main tasks. We can do it with our eyes shut.'

Ben nodded. 'He wouldn't, he's a—' He stopped himself from saying arse out loud in front of Chloe. She was watching him with a smirk on her face, and he was glad he'd made her smile. 'So, can you tell me what happened?'

Chloe sucked in a deep breath. 'I was on my way to the shop for some chocolate, and this guy was parked in the middle of my road at the end of the street with his car bonnet up and trying to turn his engine, but straining to see under the bonnet at the same time.' She paused. 'I don't know why I did it, but he looked okay, you know, he looked normal, and I even thought to myself about Ted Bundy and his fake broken arm, trying to lure women into his van. I even shared the meme all over my Instagram, you know the one where it says *how to kidnap me* then it's a van full of books or puppies. Then I told myself I was being ridiculous; he looked more like someone's dad.'

Ben didn't do Instagram, but he knew the joke she was on about. Morgan would screenshot memes all the time and send them to him. She'd sent him the one with a van full of books. 'What did you do?'

'I asked if he needed help. He was so grateful and kept saying thank you, I really appreciate it, I'm late to pick my daughter up, so I walked over and asked what he wanted me to do. He pointed to the engine and said if he turned the car on could I see if the spark plugs were sparking. I mean I had no idea what he was talking about, but I'd got myself into this mess and it was not so easy to admit that I was full of shit and didn't have a clue.' She lifted a finger to her mouth and began to nibble at one of her nails.

'You were only being a good person, there's no crime in that, don't feel bad about it. Then what happened?' Ben's voice was gentle and coaxing.

She looked at him and gave him a sad smile. 'No, I don't suppose there is. I'll never offer to help anyone ever again after this. The engine started and I didn't hear him approach me. I was too busy staring down to see if I could figure out what a spark plug was. I didn't even look up. I felt a fast whoosh of air and the edge of the bonnet slammed into my head so hard it knocked me forwards. I felt a huge pain on my head and then he hit me with something else. I felt so dizzy I wasn't sure what was happening. Next thing he's dragging me into the back of the car. I was seeing double and still I thought he was helping me, that maybe I'd hit my head myself, because, you know, I'm a bit clumsy and always falling over my own two feet, but he tugged my hands behind my back and tied rope around them and my feet so I couldn't move, and then he pushed me onto the floor of the car and slammed the door shut. It felt like it took forever but it must have been a minute, maybe two then he was driving away, and I was wondering what had just happened to me.'

'You weren't going to the gym, Morgan said you were wearing gym gear?'

She laughed. 'No way. I wear the stuff, so I don't need to go; everyone wears it now.'

Ben smiled at her. 'You must have been so scared.'

She nodded. 'I was, like I said, he gave off all the Ted Bundy vibes and I still fell for it.'

'What made him let you go? Did he tell you that?'

'I felt the car stop and he dragged me out, told me to let him drive away or he'd come back and run me over. He seemed more panicked than before.'

Ben closed his eyes, trying to push down the anger that was rising inside of his chest at the audacity of this man who had thought he could do this to the girl sitting in front of him with no consequences. Had he heard that Melody's body had been found?

'Can you give me a detailed description? When you first saw him, you said he looked like someone's dad. Why did you think that?'

'He just did, he was wearing a pale blue shirt, blue jeans; and I think they were white trainers. In all the horror movies, the bad guys wear boiler suits or dirty red and green striped jumpers, hockey masks, horror masks. You don't expect them to be wearing a pair of blue jeans, shirt and a baseball cap, be standing in the middle of a street in broad daylight and pull some shit like that. I always thought the baddies came out at night, creeping around with butcher's knives or machetes when everyone was in bed.'

Ben reached out and squeezed her hand. 'You did amazing. Do you think you would recognise him again if you saw him?'

She nodded. 'He looked so normal it might be hard, but yeah probably. Oh, he had the bluest eyes I've ever seen.'

'What did he talk like, did he sound like he was from around here?'

She shook her head. 'No, he had a soft voice and a bit of an accent, but I don't know, it was kind of mixed. He sounded a bit Irish or maybe it was Welsh, could have been Geordie. I don't know, sorry.'

'That's fine, you're doing so well. When you're up to it, do you think you could come to the station, and we can see if we can identify the guy from our mug shots?'

A nurse stepped through the curtains. 'Your mum's here, Chloe. I'm just going to clean the graze on your scalp and once the doctor has seen you, we'll get you out of here.'

Ben stood up. 'What kind of car was it?'

She shrugged. 'A white four by four type, but I was so shocked he'd thrown me out I didn't take much notice.'

'Thank you, Chloe. Amber will stay with you and if you like she can drive you and your mum home.'

'I know, she told me that. Mum has some new clothes with her so you can keep those.'

'Thank you.'

'Do you think he'll come back for me?'

Ben shook his head. 'Honestly, I don't think he will, but I'm going to arrange to have an unmarked police car outside of your house for the next couple of days to make sure. If he let you go, he won't risk coming back for you. Did you tell him where you lived or your name?'

She shook her head.

'Good, well done for not giving him anything.'

'But he saw me walking along the street. He might have watched me leave the house.'

'We will be watching your address so try not to worry too much. I don't think he would come back, as it's far too risky. You saw his face, so you would recognise him.'

'How's the policewoman who crashed her car? Is she okay?'

Ben nodded. 'She's fine.'

'Can you tell her I'm sorry. I hope I didn't get her in any trouble.'

'Of course I will, and don't worry about her, you haven't got Morgan into any trouble.'

Amber sniggered. 'No, you don't have to, she is quite capable of doing that on her own.'

Ben dead-eyed her, and she stopped talking.

'Take care, Chloe, and if you get worried that the guy is nearby or you think you see him when you're out and about, phone 999. Okay? That's what we're here for.'

Tears sprang from her eyes and began to fall down her cheeks just as her mum rushed through the curtains and enveloped her daughter in a huge hug, covering her face with kisses.

Ben stepped out, his own eyes filling with tears, glad that this story was one with a happy ending. Sadly, it hadn't been that way for Melody Carrick.

19

Morgan scanned the living room and hallway on her way out, looking for any more photographs of Cooper. There weren't any and she supposed if Susan had thrown him out, she wouldn't be keeping his photo on display. She didn't find Susan the friendliest of people. Alan sounded like a creep that was for sure. She didn't know him, but she knew that she didn't like him one little bit. She didn't like the way he was with Alisa. She was trying not to judge him for his love of true crime, because she was equally as fascinated with it, but perhaps it was a worrying hobby too. She had left Paige and her mum having some kind of glaring contest. As they reached the door Paige called after them.

'Now what happens?'

'Can you ask your mum for Alan's date of birth, please? Does she know where he lived previously?'

Paige disappeared and came back. 'His date of birth is seventh of December 1981; and she said he's from Burnley or maybe Blackburn. She doesn't really know, as he never talked about his past.'

'Do you know Alan's registration plate?'

'COo PR.'

'Not hard to miss then? Thanks, we'll be in touch if we need to ask anything else and when we find Alisa. Paige, do you think Alan would come back here?'

Paige stared at her. 'He might, if Jackie throws him out and he has nowhere to go. Susan's definitely stupid enough to let him back in.'

'If he does, I want you to try and get out of the house and call the police. I'd rather be safe than sorry. Once we've checked his background on our databases, I'm sure he's fine, but you know.'

Paige nodded. 'Yeah, I know. Too many coincidences if you ask me, but who am I to tell you how to do your job?'

The door closed and Cain whistled through his teeth. 'She's a handful.'

'Maybe, but I think she's onto something and she knows it. I'd be angry too if nobody was listening to a word I said.'

They got back into the car, and Cain said. 'But you're listening to her, we're here now because of you. I think we need to find this creep regardless of whether he's involved or not, and have a little chat with him. What do you think?'

'I think so too. I thought so the moment she told me about him. I have a bad feeling about Alan Cooper. Did anyone ask Intel to do a deep dive into his records?'

He shrugged. 'It all got a bit chaotic. Should we go back and sort that out while we're waiting on news about the girl?'

Morgan agreed. She needed to find Cooper ASAP. 'We could always call at this Jackie's flat on the way in and see if he's there.'

'We could, why didn't I think of that? We could grab some coffee from The Coffee Pot.' He stopped and sighed. 'Oh boy, that's not going to be open for some time, is it? Not after this morning, it's so horrible.'

'No, it's not. It's tragic.' Morgan paused, she needed to

lighten the mood. 'You're going to have to either give in and go to Costa or make do with instant at the station, or clean the filter coffee machine if you're first in.'

'I think we should chip in and get a proper coffee machine. I can't drink that instant stuff, it gives me heartburn, and that filter coffee takes forever.'

'I guess we could. It would do us until Jade is feeling up to opening again. Then again, she might have to get someone in to run it for her, it's her business, she will need the money it brings in, won't she?'

They drove back to Rydal Falls in silence, both of them lost in their own thoughts. When Cain arrived on the main street, they both started looking around for a white 4x4. There were lots of white cars but none of them matched the description.

It wasn't there. Cain had to drive around a couple of times, up and down the back alleys and the main street to find somewhere to park. The downfall of not being in a marked police car was the inability to abandon the vehicle anywhere with no second thoughts. He finally squeezed into a space a short walk away. As they went down the small passage at the side of the Co-op, Cain stopped.

'Hey, his VRM matches the Co-op. What a guy, giving them all that free advertising, he must really like them.'

Morgan couldn't help it, she let out a loud laugh that echoed up and down the dark passageway. 'I wonder if he knows the irony of that.'

The passage opened onto a large courtyard filled with flower troughs and plant pots. There was a cast iron bistro set with a small vase of flowers on it; and it was sheltered and secluded.

'This is nice, I didn't expect this.'

'Me either, which flat are we going to?'

There were two sets of steps leading up to two floors, and

Morgan shrugged. 'She didn't know which one, just that she lived above the Co-op. Let's door knock and see who we find.'

She ran up the steps, Cain following behind, and knocked on the first door. There was no answer, but they heard a door open above them and footsteps coming down the steps. The guy looked surprised to see them standing there. Morgan recognised him from the photos she'd seen, and stepped towards him.

'Alan Cooper?'

He nodded. 'Yes, and you are?'

'We're detectives from Rydal Falls police. Can we have a word with you?'

A flash of panic crossed his eyes. He looked at the stairs leading down to the ground floor, then at Cain, and she knew he was deciding if he could make a run for it. She stepped closer, Cain was behind her and there wasn't much room for him to get past.

Alan smiled, took a step towards them, then took off running down the metal steps, the sound of his heavy footsteps vibrating off them loudly. Cain pushed Morgan to one side and took off after him. Morgan followed. She wasn't about to give chase, she couldn't run for shit, but Cain could.

'Patrols to the Co-op on main street, suspect has taken off on foot.'

Morgan ran down as best as she could and out of the passage onto the main street, where she saw Cain in hot pursuit of Alan. She got the sudden urge to cheer Cain on then remembered she was at work and not at a sports day. She began to jog in the same direction. Alan wasn't fit enough to outrun Cain, and his initial burst of energy was wearing off as he began to slow a little, allowing Cain with his long legs to catch up to him.

Morgan let out a loud 'Ouch' as Cain threw himself at Alan and took him down to the ground with a rugby tackle that would do a pro rugby player proud. The pair of them hit the cobbled street with a thud that she heard from a good distance away, and she heard a loud shout from Alan as Cain landed on top of him, winding him.

When she reached them, Cain was disentangling himself from Alan who was lying winded on the floor, his legs curled into his chest as he tried to breathe through the pain. She tugged out the handcuffs from her jacket pocket and winked at Cain, who was breathing heavy from the exertion.

'Good effort, Cain. Alan Cooper, I'm arresting you on suspicion of abduction and resisting arrest.' It was all she could think of because apart from him making a run for it they had no evidence really to take him in. She didn't want to let him know about the murder and give anything away, so that would do for now. She read him his rights, and when she'd finished, he was glaring at her.

'What the fuck? Abduction of who?'

'We'll discuss it down at the station.'

'I don't know what you're talking about, this is stupid. You have the wrong person.'

She shrugged. 'If you haven't done anything wrong, why did you run?'

'I didn't know who the hell you were. You could be a pair of insane people for all I know.'

Morgan tugged her lanyard out of her shirt and showed it to him. 'We might be slightly insane but we're definitely police officers.'

Alan looked up at her. 'I want a lawyer.'

Cain was standing next to her and he nodded. 'I bet you do.'

Sirens echoed around the street as a van pulled to a stop behind them and two uniformed officers jumped out. Cain had tight hold of Alan's arm, and he passed him towards them. 'Watch him, he's a runner.'

Alan was shaking his head. 'I'm going to sue the pair of you, chasing me down the street and throwing me to the ground like that for no good reason.'

Cain shrugged. 'If you have nothing to worry about, why would you run? I'm only doing my job.'

Alan began to swear at the top of his voice, and Morgan added, 'I can add a section five public order offence to the list of charges.'

He shut up and glared at her, his blue eyes full of hatred, but she didn't care. He didn't scare her – she'd faced far worse than Alan Cooper.

20

The phone in the hallway began to ring and ring. Paige tutted. Her mum was probably passed out on the sofa. She ran down the stairs and picked it up.

'Hello.'

'Paige, it's Morgan, I just wanted to let you know we have Alan at the station to interview him.'

'Oh, you found him then?'

'Yes, we did. Depending on what happens, if he gets charged, he'll get bail conditions not to contact you or your mum.'

'That's good. Thanks.'

'Take care, Paige.'

The called ended and Paige began to bite her thumbnail. She hadn't expected that and so quickly either. Morgan really was good at her job, probably a little too good.

She went into the lounge where her mum was curled up on the sofa, a second almost empty bottle of wine on the coffee table next to her. Paige leaned over her and shook her shoulder; she didn't even stir. Her mouth open, she was snoring heavily, so Paige pulled the throw off the back of the sofa and covered her up. They may have their differences, but she was her mum, and she loved her.

Paige grabbed a bottle of water out of the fridge and ran back to her bedroom, where her phone was charging on the bed. She picked it up and sent an iMessage to Alisa.

I think we better come clean; this has all gone wrong. They arrested Alan.

She stared at the screen waiting for the three dots to appear to signal she was replying, but nothing happened. She watched it for a minute then pressed the phone button and dialled it. But Alisa didn't answer. Paige felt sick, they should have thought this out better. Why wasn't she answering? They had agreed that she would answer straight away if anything happened. Paige threw the phone down on the bed and crossed to the window. She stared out onto the meadow at the back of the house, across to the treeline, when she felt her blood freeze.

There was someone standing by the trees. She leaned forward squinting her eyes. Was she seeing things? Cupping her hand to shield some of the sunlight, she pressed her face against the glass. There was a blinding flash as the setting sunlight bounced off something they were holding in their hands. The figure stepped back into the trees. They must have realised she had seen them. Surely not, who would be standing there watching her house? And was that a pair of binoculars they'd been holding so they could see straight into her room? That was too creepy, and it wasn't Alan because he was currently at the police station waiting to be questioned.

A cold, crawling sensation made her skin prickle, and she pulled the blinds down so whoever it was couldn't see into her bedroom. Paige had the feeling she had got herself into a mess that wasn't going to be so easy to get back out of, and she ran downstairs to check that the doors and windows were all secure and locked.

Her mum was dead to the world still, and Paige went into every room closing the blinds despite it still being light outside. Someone had been watching her house and she didn't know who. She couldn't get hold of Alisa despite her promising she would answer her straight away, and there had been a murder this morning. What if this was all connected to her and Alisa and it was their fault? Had they started a chain of events that was now out of hand and about to come crashing down onto the both of them with terrible consequences?

21

By the time Ben got back to the mortuary, Declan was in a pair of scrubs along with Amy and Susie. Declan gave him a round of applause as he approached.

'Well, your body turned up at last and aren't you the lucky one that I managed to rearrange my schedule because I love you.' Declan blew him a kiss, and Ben shook his head, but he was smiling. Declan was his best friend and had been for a long time. He had been there when Cindy had died, holding him up, guiding him and making sure he was coping the best that he could when he had no one else around him.

'Thank you, I do appreciate it.'

Declan winked at him. 'Good, I'm glad you do. Come on, do you need to eat something before we get started? Amy brought you a picnic back from the canteen. All that's missing is a blanket for you to sit on and a thermos of coffee.'

He shook his head. 'Thanks, I'll eat after.'

Declan turned to Amy. 'Well, isn't he ungrateful. Come on then, guys, let's get this done and hopefully you can go find the wretched soul who did this to the lovely Melody Carrick.'

When Ben had put on boot covers, an apron and was ready,

they all stood around the steel gurney with the black body bag lying on it. Declan and Susie busied themselves with all the preliminary examinations, while Ben and Amy watched on. Claire and another CSI from Barrow were there ready to record and photograph, and take the samples that needed to be sent away for forensic testing.

When Declan finally cut open the plastic tags on the bag and unzipped it, Ben sucked in a deep breath. He wasn't ready for this again, and he missed having Morgan by his side. They were a great team, both in and out of work. Amy was good too, but it was different with Morgan; they instinctively knew what each other was thinking or about to do.

When all of her clothes had been removed, Ben realised that the harsh lighting made Melody's naked body look even smaller than it was and he wanted to tell Declan to stop and find a blanket to throw over her, and give her some dignity. When all the measurements and samples had been taken, Declan looked around the room.

'Are we ready?'

Everyone except Ben nodded. He didn't think he would ever be ready for this one; the fact that he was a regular at her mum's coffee shop and had been served by Melody on several occasions was hitting harder than usual.

22

Alan Cooper was waiting in the van to be booked into the custody suite. There was a prolific shoplifter who was banned from almost every shop in Kendal and the south Lakes in front of him. Apparently, he had been caught again and was already getting booked in, which gave Morgan and Cain a little time to come up with a plan.

Morgan had tried phoning Ben, but his phone was on silent. She assumed he must be in the post-mortem. She needed some advice, and she didn't have much choice on who to ask. There was Mads or Marc, and technically, because Marc ran her department, it should be him. Cain was at the brew station chatting and searching for biscuits that had been inadvertently left out, which in his opinion meant they were for sharing and anybody's. Morgan went up to Marc's office and wasn't surprised to see it was empty; he was never bloody there when they needed him. She popped her head into the office to see if he was lingering in there, but that was equally as vacant. Going back down to the patrol sergeant's office she supposed it would have to be Mads, but he was nowhere to be seen either. It was as if the place had been evacuated. Cain waved her over and passed her a mug of coffee along with three Rich Tea biscuits, which she took, dunking them into the coffee.

'I thought you couldn't drink instant?'

He shrugged. 'Needs must, I needed something to keep me focused after my heroic sprint. What did the boss say?'

'He's not there.' She pointed to the empty office. 'Neither is he.'

Cain was frowning. 'Where have they snuck off to?'

'I doubt they're together, Cain. I guess we'll have to do this on our own because Ben's not answering.'

'We can do this, no problem; I could have told you that. We want to establish if Cooper has an alibi for this morning, find out where he was at six a.m, and see if he knows who Melody Carrick is. Oh, and if he knows where Alisa is too. Just some straightforward questions. I was always interviewing unsavoury dudes on section. Anyway, by the time his brief gets here Ben or Marc will be back if you're worried about anything.'

'I'm not worried about questioning him. I don't want to mess up that's all. No one seemed that keen on him as a suspect the first time I brought him up.'

'Have a bit of faith, Morgan, we are good to go. We can handle this, we're the A team; it's what we live for.'

She side-eyed him. 'Are you high?'

He managed to spit the mouthful of coffee he'd just taken all over the front of his shirt and had to tear off some kitchen towels to mop it up.

'The chance would be a fine thing, and look what you made me do.'

She ran a dishcloth under the tap and pushed his hands away, blotting at the brown stains. 'Be fine when it dries, you're good.'

He nodded and walked in the direction of the custody suite. She followed behind him, wanting to get this over and hoping that Alan Cooper would give them something decent.

Cooper was just finishing up getting booked in. He'd had his prints, DNA and photographs taken. He was objecting loudly to everything. He glared at both Cain and Morgan.

'Do you want a solicitor? My colleague said you requested one.'

He shook his head. 'No, changed my mind. I just want to get this over with and get out of here.'

Cain nodded. 'Good man, come on then, let's go into that interview room over there.'

He pointed the way, and Cooper, who was still handcuffed, followed. The lights came on automatically. Cain pointed to a chair, and Cooper sat down, his cuffed hands on the table in front of him.

'Are you going to take these off?'

'That depends, are you going to behave yourself?'

He gave a curt nod. 'I'm in police custody, what else am I supposed to do?'

Cain leaned over and unlocked the handcuffs, passing them back to Morgan who tucked them back into her coat pocket. She would clean them with a disinfectant wipe when they'd finished.

'Where do you want to start, Alan? Is it okay if I call you Alan, or do you prefer Mr Cooper?' Cain was polite and professional. Morgan was impressed.

'Alan, is fine.'

'Good, well, Alan, for the benefit of the tape this interview is being recorded.' He pointed to the camera in the corner of the room. 'Keeps everyone safe and there's no discrepancies. I'm Detective Constable Cain Robson and this is Detective Constable Morgan Brookes. Could you state your name, address and date of birth, please.'

'Alan Cooper, seven, twelve, eighty-one; and until a few days ago I was living with my girlfriend at six Meadowfield View in Keswick.'

'Where are you living now?'

'I'm sofa surfing for a couple of nights at a friend's flat; three Co-op Mews.'

Morgan caught the side-eye Cain gave her; she knew he was thinking about how much Alan liked the word Co-op.

'Do you know why you're here, Alan?'

He leaned his elbows on the table. 'I have no idea. You tell me.'

Morgan also leaned a little closer to the table. 'Can you tell me where you were around six a.m. this morning?'

'Asleep, I didn't get up until my alarm went off at seven thirty.'

'Can anyone verify this?'

'Jackie, whose flat I'm staying at, can. She saw me in the kitchen.'

Morgan felt a little deflated at the thought of him having a rock-solid alibi.

'Do you know Alisa Halliday?'

He nodded. 'Of course I do, she's Paige's best friend and always at our house. Well, Susan's house.'

'Have you seen her recently?'

'I don't know, probably the day before I got thrown out. Why?'

'Paige is worried she's missing.'

He rolled his eyes. 'Paige is a lunatic; she's obsessed with true crime. I suppose she put you up to this and you're believing what a fantasy-obsessed seventeen-year-old is telling you. No, I haven't seen her the last couple of days.'

Cain was nodding. 'Do you like young girls, Alan, well, seventeen-year-olds?'

Alan was glaring at Cain; Morgan could feel the tension simmering in the room between them and put her hand on Cain's arm to tell him to wind it back a bit.

'No more than I like anyone else. Why?'

Cain shrugged. 'Just a question, how about teenage girls in general? Do you know Chloe Smith?'

'Never heard of her.'

'Melody Carrick?'

'Means nothing to me, either of them.'

'How about Paige, you must like her?'

'As my partner's daughter yes, but not anything else. What are you suggesting? That I'm some kind of creep?'

'It must have been hard having both Paige and Alisa parading around the house in skimpy clothes. You know what teenagers are like, they all wear tiny crop tops and shorts these days. Paige showed us the pictures of her posing for you. Do you fancy yourself as a bit of an amateur photographer?'

He was shaking his head.

'Come on, you can tell me, man to man. Have you ever had fantasies about hurting—'

Before he could finish the question, Alan Cooper had launched himself out of his chair, across the table towards Cain with his fist pulled back. He punched Cain square in the face, and Morgan jerked at the warm spray of blood that hit her as Cain's nose broke under the force of it with a loud crack of cartilage. Morgan scrambled for the emergency red button on the wall, slamming it with the palm of her hand, setting off alarms ringing throughout the station. Cain was grappling with Alan as the door burst open and in ran at least eight officers into the cramped room. Alan was being dragged away from Cain, who was bleeding all over his chin and shirt. As Alan was taken to a cell, Morgan rushed to get the first aid kit from behind the desk. Jo, the duty custody sergeant came in, took one look at him and said, 'You'll need to soak that shirt in cold water and vinegar ASAP if you want to get the blood out. What the hell happened?'

Morgan had a stack of gauze and was holding it against

Cain's nose, and she couldn't help it. 'At least the blood covers those coffee stains, so you don't need to worry about that now.'

She grinned at him, and he gave her the middle finger as Marc came striding in.

'What is happening? You two get left alone for a couple of hours and all hell breaks loose. You better get him to hospital, Morgan, to get his nose checked out. We don't want to risk spoiling his good looks.'

Morgan nodded. 'Yes, sir.'

Cain stared at Marc. 'Where's my sympathy? I've just been assaulted.'

'Did you ask for it? Why have we got that guy in custody anyway?'

'Charming.' Cain tutted in disgust.

'We went to speak to him, and he did a runner, so we thought we'd bring him in to answer the questions a little more formally. He didn't like that either. I don't think he likes the police full stop.'

It was Marc's turn to roll his eyes. 'Is he a suspect for anything?'

'Not exactly. Maybe. We have his DNA and prints on the system now if forensics bring anything back.'

Marc smiled at her. 'I guess there is a silver lining to this little mess. Get him out of here.' He was pointing to Cain. 'I'll deal with, actually, who is he?'

'Alan Cooper, Paige Evans's mother's creepy ex-boyfriend.'

'Right, that's right, the one that teenager came in to tell us about. I'll sort it out, go.'

He turned around to go and speak to Jo.

Morgan picked up the chair that Cooper had toppled over. 'It could have been worse.'

'How?'

'He could have smacked you over the head with a chair and took your head off.'

'I guess I'm thankful he just broke my nose then.'

She smiled at him. 'Always be thankful for the small things.' She ducked out of the room before he could swear at her.

She thought that Ben was probably going to have a mental breakdown when he got back. Without his supervision for a couple of hours, she'd crashed a car and Cain had got a broken nose. He would be complaining they were more hard work than school children, and she couldn't disagree with him.

23

The custody nurse was walking through the front entrance as they were heading out of the station. 'Are you okay, Cain, is there anything I can do?' she asked.

He nodded. 'Yes, can you take a look at my nose and sort it out?' His voice sounded as if he was stuffed with cold, as he was breathing heavily through his mouth.

'I can, but you still probably better go to hospital.'

'I'd rather not if you can pack it and clean it up.'

'Only because it's you.'

She took hold of his elbow and walked him towards the first aid room, and Morgan felt relieved they weren't going to the hospital or anywhere near to one. She'd had enough of medical emergencies for one day.

Since the moment they'd found Melody Carrick's body she'd been running around finding emergency after emergency. She'd missed the briefing, the autopsy, and she hadn't even had a chance to review the testimonies from the house to house. She had no idea what was happening with the case, and she wanted to get back to it, especially since Alan had an alibi for this morning. She'd have to ask Cain to double check it, but if it was solid, there was no way he could have dumped Melody's body... or let Chloe out of his car at the right moment. Alan Cooper was certainly a creep, an overly confident, odd man, but she didn't think he was their killer. She'd have liked to seize his vehicle so it could be given a thorough search by CSI, but she wasn't sure he would agree to that. All they had was Paige's word that Alan was a creep. Marc might not want to antagonise the guy any more than Cain already had. She guessed he'd be asking for a solicitor now after that outburst; if nothing else, if he was responsible then he couldn't hurt anyone else while he was in custody.

Left to her own devices, Morgan thought maybe it was time to pay Alisa's parents a visit, then remembered she wouldn't be allowed to drive after her earlier accident until she'd filled out all the forms and been approved again by Ben or Mads. She turned around and went back upstairs to the office; unable to drive was the adult version of being grounded. No sooner had she taken a seat at her desk than her phone began to vibrate in her pocket. She expected it to be Ben but didn't recognise the number.

'Brookes.'

'Hi, you phoned me earlier about my daughter, Alisa Halliday.'

'Yes, I did. Is she home?'

'No, we can't get hold of her and normally I wouldn't worry, but I read it on the news about the body this morning and I'm worried it could be her.'

Morgan could have kicked herself for not making it clearer when she spoke to her earlier.

'No, it's not. I can absolutely confirm the victim was not Alisa; they have been identified.'

'Jesus, thank Christ for that.' There was a slight pause.

'Oh, no, obviously I feel terrible for whoever it is and their family, but I've been panicking since I spoke to you. I wasn't

bothered at first and then I saw the headline flash up on my phone ten minutes later and well, my mind went into overdrive. Sorry, I don't know what to do now, should I file a missing persons report, is that how this works?'

Morgan's heart dropped. She was missing...

'Yes, I can take all the details now if you like,' she said quickly. 'I'd come out to see you, but I was involved in a car accident earlier and I can't drive right now.'

'Oh my, are you okay?'

'I'm fine, but the car wasn't. Would you rather I sent an officer to your address to speak to you?'

'I don't mind giving you the details now. Will that save time?'

Morgan looked up at the ancient clock above the whiteboard: it was almost six. If Paige was right, Alisa had been missing for twelve hours.

'Yes, it would. You said her ex-boyfriend has a white car. What's his name?'

'Joe Philips.'

Morgan wrote it down: where did she know that name from? 'How old is Joe?'

'Twenty-two, possibly twenty-three. You might know him, he works at the police station.'

Morgan had been slumped in her chair, but she sat up straight. 'Which department?'

'I think he's a CSI, or he says he is. I'm not sure that he could be, as he seems too young for that. I thought they had to go to uni or somewhere to train.'

Joe, who had got so upset over Melody's body this morning, was also the ex-boyfriend of another missing girl. The tiny hairs on the back of her neck began to stand on end, and the skin on her arms prickled with goosebumps. The thought that he could be involved in this sent a coldness through her that made her shudder. He had been so upset over Melody; she had comforted him the best she could.

'*Morgan, are you there?*'

She realised she had gone silent as she was thinking all of this through. 'Yes, I am. Sorry, I was thinking.'

'*To be honest we didn't really like him, he was a bit cocky, and I know most young men are but he was a little too old for her, and he worked such odd hours; he would turn up at all times when the rest of us were in bed, and it was disrupting her college work. I try not to be a stick in the mud and be as open as I can be, but there's something about him no matter how hard I tried to ignore it I couldn't. He gets under my skin.*'

'You said he was her ex: when did they split up?'

'*A couple of weeks ago. She's been moping around ever since. I'm thinking maybe they got back together and if he picked her up this morning, she could be with him. She was adamant she wasn't coming with us for her brother's birthday treat, maybe that's why she went so early.*'

'I'll check that out, Mrs Halliday, right away.'

'*I don't know his address; she would never tell me where he lived, but I think it's on the outskirts of Kendal in a bedsit.*'

'I can get that information. When was the last time you saw Alisa?'

'*Last night. When she went to bed. As far as I knew she was in her nightwear fast asleep. I've checked her room: her phone, purse, make-up and an overnight bag have gone.*'

'What's her phone number? I need her DOB and anything else you can tell me, please. What pyjamas was she wearing?'

Mrs Halliday began to recite her daughter's number and personal details, describing the bright blue flannel set she had put on that evening. Morgan's stomach was churning.

She thought about Joe. This couldn't be him. But she needed to consider him as a suspect. He could have dumped Melody's body, then returned to the crime scene in uniform. She scribbled *Chloe Smith* underneath all the information that Alisa's mum had given her. What about Chloe? She said it had been an older man, and Joe was working the crime scene when she said she was abducted. If this was all one person, it couldn't have been Joe.

'Thank you, Mrs Halliday. An officer will be around to speak to you at some point, but if it's okay with you I'll get on with tracking Joe down and speaking to him. I'll be in touch as soon as I know something. Please be back in touch if you hear from Alisa at all, or if you think of anything else that might help me.'

'Yes, thank you.'

She hung up and Morgan hoped she hadn't given her false hope. They should have taken Paige's concerns seriously when she reported her friend missing.

She pushed the chair away from her desk and then wheeled it back in. Opening up the Intel system she typed Joe's name into the search bar, just to be sure he didn't have some awful past record that had got overlooked when he'd applied for his job. It had happened before, and it could happen again. If someone misspelled their name on the application form and it wasn't thoroughly checked out, they could literally get away with murder.

24

Morgan dashed to the CSI office to see if Joe was in there, but it was empty; it had been a busy day, and he could be out at either crime scene. He might even have finished work for the day. Wendy sauntered in with a pile of evidence bags.

'Were you looking for me?'

'No, Joe, is he around?'

'He's gone home, hasn't been use nor ornament since he saw that body this morning. He tried to help out at the scene but kept screwing up, so I told him to finish and come back tomorrow with a clear head. Can I help instead?'

Morgan smiled at her friend. 'No, it's Joe I needed to speak to about his ex-girlfriend. It's not important, I'll catch him tomorrow.'

She hated lying to Wendy, but she didn't want to implicate her in anything, especially if Joe was innocent. He may have nothing to do with any of this; she could be jumping to conclusions. What would Ben say to her? *Bring me some evidence.* As she was walking out of the door she turned back to Wendy. 'Do you happen to know where he lives?'

'I think it's a studio, it's on Lound Road but I only know the house and not the number. It's important then, if you need to go to his house?'

Morgan was torn; she hadn't discussed anything with Ben. She hadn't seen him for hours; and she didn't want to get ahead of herself causing trouble for Joe unnecessarily, especially not after the debacle with Cooper.

'I was going to check if he was okay. He seemed pretty shocked and upset earlier but I can catch him tomorrow. I thought he lived in Rydal Falls.'

'Are you going all soft on me, Morgan?'

She smiled at her. 'Maybe, I am.'

She hurried out, back to her office. She would take a quick peek on the system for his address. *Would it hurt if she went in her own car to check if Alisa was there?*

Cain was sitting in the office when she went back in, his nose taped up and the blood cleaned off his face. He'd taken his stained shirt off, changing into one of his old black polo shirts from when he was in uniform.

'Dawn fixed you up then?'

He nodded. 'She couldn't resist my charm; it hurts like a bitch though.' His left eye was turning purple and black underneath; it was a mess.

'Cooper got you good. Lucky for you he didn't hear your bad jokes about the Co-op, or it could have been much worse. He clearly has no sense of humour.'

'Why are you looking so shifty?'

'What do you mean?'

'What's going on? You look like you got caught with your fingers in the cookie jar.'

'I worry about you, Cain, you have a suspicious mind. I just got off the phone with Alisa's mum; she's reporting her as missing.'

'She didn't turn up then?'

Morgan shook her head. 'Guess who her ex-boyfriend is, who she might be stopping with?'

'I don't even want to hazard a guess; I have no desire to unless you say she was seeing Cooper on the side.'

'Joe.'

He shrugged. 'Means nothing to me, Joe who?'

'Our Joe, CSI Joe who was at the crime scene earlier.'

'Well have you spoken to him yet to see if he's hiding her out at his place?'

'You've only been getting your nose cleaned up for the last twenty minutes, I'm not superwoman.'

He released a long, drawn-out sigh. 'I thought you were, don't burst my bubble this way.'

The door was pushed open too hard and it swung inwards with force, slamming into the plaster on the wall, knocking another chunk off, making the dent even bigger. Ben took one look at Cain.

'Do I even want to know?'

Amy followed him in and started to laugh. 'Who punched you? Was it you, Morgan, have you had enough of him already? Do you see what I have to put up with?'

Ben sat down on the corner of Morgan's desk. He looked from Cain to her. Both sporting injuries that had been taped up. 'You two look as if you've been in a boxing ring with each other.' His hand reached out and he gently touched the side of her head. 'Are you okay? I missed all the action. Does it hurt?'

'I'm good, I just banged it a little bit. The car came off a lot worse than I did.'

Ben smiled at her. 'So I heard. Did Mads say you weren't allowed to drive any other vehicles?'

'He was angry, he didn't mean it.'

Ben laughed, then turned to Cain. 'I know about Morgan's injury; what happened to you?'

'We brought Alan Cooper in for questioning, but he

objected very strongly to the line of questions, and he punched me.'

'Alan Cooper, the guy the teenager came in to report?'

Morgan and Cain said, 'Yes,' in unison.

'Okay, so why did you bring him in? Did you have enough to bring him in?'

'We went to have a polite word, and he did a runner from us, made himself look awfully guilty, boss. I used my initiative and brought him in for further questioning. But he has an alibi that Cain is going to check out.'

Morgan was watching Ben's face, and she couldn't tell if he was about to laugh or explode; his eyes and cheeks were twitching a little. Finally, he laughed.

'It's not even funny, but if I don't laugh, I'll give myself a coronary. You know you can't go out in public looking like that, the pair of you. I left you alone for a couple of hours. I don't know who is worse.' He pointed to Morgan then Cain.

'But we do have some leads to follow up on.'

'You do? Please put me out of my misery because the post-mortem was awful and there was very little forensic wise. There were a couple of blond hairs, but Declan and Claire weren't convinced they were human; they looked synthetic.'

'What's that mean? He was wearing a wig?'

'Or they could be from hair extensions. Susie said that Melody had them, but they looked a lot darker than the sample.'

'So, if we searched Alan Cooper's belongings and found a blond wig, we'd have something to compare them to?'

Ben nodded.

'Well, our news is that Chloe said the guy who abducted her lured her into the car by pretending it had broken down. It makes sense that was how Melody was also taken. Also, Alisa's mum has reported her missing. She packed an overnight bag, she also took her phone, charger, purse, make-up. Her mum has flagged an ex she didn't approve of... who just happens to be Joe Philips.'

Ben had a blank expression on his face, as if the name meant nothing to him.

'*Our* Joe Philips, out of CSI, he worked the crime scene this morning, is or was friends with Melody, is the ex-boyfriend of another missing girl.'

'Oh shit.'

'Yes, oh shit.'

'Where is he? Is he in work still?'

'No, Wendy said she sent him home earlier because he was so upset over Melody, but he could be a very good actor, or this could all be some legendary planetary alignment of major, impending doom.'

Cain snorted with laughter. 'Planetary alignment? Are you in full-on witchy woman mood?'

Ben ignored him. 'Where does he live?'

'Lound Road, Kendal.'

He stood up and began pacing in front of the whiteboard, at the same time loosening his tie and undoing the top two buttons on his shirt. Morgan knew he was getting more stressed by the minute.

'Do you need a drink, tea or a coffee?'

He shook his head. 'What I need is to know that a member of our staff isn't involved in any of the cases. It could all be a huge coincidence and unlucky for Joe that he just happened to know both girls. He's a little older than them though, isn't he? He wouldn't have gone to college with them, but he knows them so maybe they have the same friendship group. I'm just thinking out loud; it doesn't mean he's guilty of anything, but we need to go talk to him. And he certainly can't come into work.'

He stopped in front of the whiteboard and uncapped a pen.

He began writing below everything they already knew about Melody and Chloe.

Melody is missing her cross necklace, do we know anything else about her?

Morgan replied, 'Just that she worked in her mum's café every weekend and college holiday. She was popular, had no boyfriend, was lovely and I'm telling you that first hand through my dealings with her in the café. She was always so bubbly and happy, nothing was too much trouble and she was a nice person.'

Joe Philips, Lound Road, Kendal – knows Melody Carrick

'Also, the ex-boyfriend of Alisa. What's her surname?'
'Halliday,' replied Morgan.
He continued writing.

Ex-boyfriend of Alisa Halliday – reported missing.

Paige Evans attended station to report her mother's boyfriend as a potential weirdo and her friend as missing.

Alan Cooper – Paige Evans' mother's partner, friend of Alisa who was picked up at 6am by a man driving a white car. Alibi to be cross-checked.

He stopped writing.
'How does this timeline fit in with Joe? What shift was he on today?'
'I'm assuming an eight to four. Melody's body was discovered around eleven. Apparently, Joe was told to go home at

eleven fifty or noon. Chloe says she was picked up by a guy in a white car in Keswick around ten a.m.'

'How did Joe say he knew Melody? Declan didn't think she'd been deceased long before she was discovered. So, he lives in Kendal and drove to Keswick, say that took him around fifty minutes; the roads are pretty quiet, if he drives fast, he could cut that down even more. He picks Alisa up at six takes her back to his bedsit and then drives the ten minutes to work, to get here on time. That's doable. Hypothetically when did he kill Melody? Before he picked his girlfriend up? Melody is local to us, so he met her, decided to kill her, dumped her body, drove to get his ex-girlfriend and take her back to his flat, then came to work. And where does Chloe Smith fit in? Morgan, you found her at twelve thirty-five – so Joe could have been with her after he left his shift early. Did he decide to do it all over again on his way home because he's on some kind of sicko high? Why did he identify Melody? Why not keep that to himself?'

'I know it's a lot, but it's not impossible. Or each one could be a totally separate incident. He could be involved in abducting Alisa, but not with killing Melody or abducting Chloe.'

Ben ran his hand across his freshly buzzed hair. 'It's a big push. That's some major planetary alignment on his side to help him get away with all of that and only leave two synthetic hairs behind and, forgive me if I'm wrong, but it takes a bit of brute strength to get up close and personal to someone to strangle them with a rope. I don't see it, he's not very tall; Melody is taller than him. I'd say it would have been a struggle.'

Morgan felt deflated and a little relieved, too, because she liked Joe and would be mortified to think he could treat women this way, as if they were dispensable; toss them aside like rubbish.

'We still need to talk to him about Alisa Halliday.'

'Yes, we do. I agree about that, let's go do that and see how it goes. If his wall is covered in photos of the victims then I'm wrong and you're right. We'll bring him in.'

She smiled at Ben, if only it could be so simple.

'Come on, I'm driving. You're on a temporary ban.'

He was standing near to her desk; he leaned over and blew her a kiss. She laughed, but she wasn't sure if she was right, and her stomach was in tight knots at the thought of speaking to Joe about any of this.

25

Ben parked the car on the quiet street where Joe lived just as a girl wearing a black hoodie and leggings turned the corner and scurried along the road towards them with her head down.

'Think that's Alisa?' he asked Morgan, who was thinking that the gait of her walk looked a little familiar. They both slid down in their seats a little, so she didn't notice them; but she didn't even glance in their direction. Instead, she charged up the steps to Joe's studio as if she was on a mission.

Ben opened the car door, but Morgan put her hand on his arm.

'Let's wait and see if she goes in first. He might not be home.'

He didn't step out of the car, and they both watched as she began to hammer on the door. It opened a slither, and Morgan got out of the car and jogged over. She went up the steps and put a hand on the girl's shoulder.

'Alisa?'

The girl froze at her touch. The door opened wide, and Morgan stared into Joe's face. He looked surprised to see her standing there. The girl slowly turned around to face Morgan.

'Paige, what are you doing here?'

Paige looked equally as shocked as Joe did. *Just what is going on?* Morgan thought. Ben joined Morgan and all three stood on the steps, caught up in some awkward silence that dragged on for a long time. It was Joe who broke it.

'Can someone tell me what's going on? Why are you all here?'

Paige was shaking her head at him, but he ignored her and looked to Morgan.

'Joe, we're looking for a missing person. Is she here?'

'Is who here?'

'Alisa Halliday?'

A flash of anger crossed his eyes as he glanced at Paige, then back to Morgan. 'You better come in, all of you. I have no idea what's going on but it's nothing to do with me.'

He stepped back to let them all into the open-plan multi-functional living space with a small kitchen, lounge, bedroom. There was a closed door next to the wall where the bed was and the sound of running water could be heard through it.

Paige was staring at the floor. The door opened and out stepped Alisa Halliday, wrapped in a towel with a turban on her wet hair. Her mouth dropped at the sight of Paige and the two adults standing behind her.

'What's going on, Paige? Who are they?'

Joe's voice echoed Alisa's words. 'What's going on, Paige?'

Paige's voice was full of anger as she pointed a finger at her friend. 'You, that's what's going on. You were supposed to answer the phone, you said you'd answer my messages, so I knew you were okay, and you didn't. I had to come here and check, and they followed me.'

Ben was watching Paige then Alisa, his eyes going from one to the other, a mild look of confusion on his face. 'Can someone tell me what is going on?' he said, his voice loud, clear and a little bit on the aggressive side.

Morgan knew he was annoyed at this whole setup.

It was Joe who spoke, as both Paige and Alisa were too busy glaring at each other.

'Sarge, I don't know what's going on. Well, I'll tell you what I do know. We split up a few weeks ago.' He pointed to Alisa. 'Then she phoned up crying, saying she needed a place to stay for a few nights because she had to get out of her house. So I picked her up and said she could stop until the weekend.'

Morgan welcomed the soft wave of pure relief that loosened her tightly knotted stomach, letting all of the tension flow away.

'Paige came and reported Alisa missing this morning, and her mum also phoned to report her missing less than an hour ago.'

Joe turned to Paige. 'Why? You knew where she was, she told you she was coming here. Why did you do that? Are you trying to get me sacked?'

She shrugged. 'No, I was trying to get that creep Alan arrested and out of our hair.'

Morgan's relief was short-lived with the realisation that Paige had wasted hours of her precious time chasing pointless leads, all to get Alan Cooper in trouble. She could feel a bubble of anger rising up her throat.

'Do you know what you've done, Paige? This is a very serious offence. You have wasted not only my time but my colleague's as well. He has been injured because of your false accusations. Not only that: you took us away from a murder investigation. How are you going to feel if the same guy who killed Melody takes another girl?'

Paige had the decency to lower her glaring gaze to the floor. 'I'm sorry, it just went wrong. I'd feel horrible.'

Ben didn't speak, not because he didn't want to, but Morgan knew it was because he might lose his cool with the two teenage girls and say things he might regret.

'Alisa, phone your mum right now and tell her that you're

safe and there is no need for her to worry. Paige, I'm taking you home to speak to your mum about your behaviour. My boss will decide whether to press charges against you for wasting police time.'

Joe's cheeks were burning so hot Morgan could feel his body heat from where she was standing. He was shaking his head.

'I'm sorry, I really had no idea.'

She looked to Ben, but he shook his head. 'It's not your fault, Joe, we'll take Paige home. Alisa, do you want to go home too?'

Alisa's eyes were filled with tears that were rolling down her cheeks as she nodded.

'Get dressed then and hurry, we don't have time for this.'

'I can take her.'

'It's okay, Joe, I'll need her mum to sign the paperwork so we can close the log.'

He nodded.

Morgan took hold of Paige's arm and turned her to the door. 'We'll wait in the car for you, Alisa.'

She practically pushed Paige down the steps, she was so angry with the girl. When Paige was deposited in the back seat of the car, and she was in the front, she turned to look at her. 'This is serious, you really wasted my time when I should have been looking for a killer.'

'I'm sorry, but he is all those things I told you. He's odd, he's obsessed with killers and murder sites.'

'Enough, I don't want to hear any more about him unless you give me something concrete and of evidential value, Paige, okay?'

Paige stopped speaking and they watched as Ben came down the steps followed by Alisa, who still had the turban wrapped around her wet hair and an overnight bag in her hand. She got in the back of the car next to Paige but didn't speak to her; they were both mad at each other and Morgan wondered if their friendship was going to survive.

Ben turned and spoke to Joe who was shaking his head, but she couldn't hear what he'd just asked him, then he got into the car and drove away, leaving Joe staring down the quiet street after them a look of bewilderment etched across his face.

26

Morgan walked Alisa to the door, and her mum opened it and pulled her in for a hug. 'I don't know what's going on, but don't scare me like that again, love. Why would you disappear like that without telling us?'

Alisa glanced back at Paige in the car, but she was staring out of the other window, purposely not looking at Alisa or her mum. 'I'm sorry, I was really stupid.'

'We'll talk about it later. Get yourself in and get your hair dried; you'll catch pneumonia outside with wet hair.'

They hugged again and Alisa slipped past her mum into the safety of her house.

'Do you want to come in? Are you Morgan?'

'Yes, I am, and I can't, I'm sorry. I just need you to sign my tablet to say Paige is home so I can cancel the misper report.' She held the large phone out towards Mrs Halliday, and she scribbled on it with the stylus.

'Where was she?'

'At Joe's. He didn't know, though, as she hadn't told you where she was going.'

Mrs Halliday glanced at Paige then lowered her voice.

'She's a bad influence. I wish Alisa would find a better friend. I bet she put her up to this. Thank you for finding her so quickly and bringing her home.'

Morgan smiled at her. 'It's my job, I'm glad she's safe. Take care.' She waved at the woman as she strode down the path back to the car. Neither Ben nor Paige were speaking to each other and the energy inside of the car was fraught with tension.

'Let's get you back to your mum, Paige.'

Paige glared at Morgan who ignored her and turned to stare out of the window. She was tired. It was proving to be a long, difficult shift and it didn't look as if they'd be going home anytime soon. She had wasted hours because of Paige, and she wasn't happy about it. She gave Ben the directions to Paige's address.

The lights were blazing from every window at Paige's house, and there was no car on the driveway.

'You can drop me off here. She's gone out. Don't waste any more of your time.'

Morgan shook her head. 'I need to speak to her and please tell me she hasn't driven after the amount of wine she'd consumed this morning.'

'She'll have sobered up and gone looking for Alan. She could drink a case of wine and still be okay to drive; she's used to it.'

Ben looked as if he was hanging on by a thread.

He waited in the car and let Morgan deal with Paige.

'Come on, I'll walk you in and make sure she's not here. If she isn't, I'm going to have to come back to speak to her. You know that, don't you, Paige? You wasted a lot of time today when I should have been doing vitally important things, following up on real leads, and now the person who killed Melody Carrick could be out there looking for their next victim because of that.'

'I'm sorry, I really am, but please don't discount Alan because I messed up.'

Morgan held up the palm of her hand. 'Enough, drop it.'

She left Paige standing in her hallway, looking angry and hurt, and got back in the car. Ben didn't say anything.

'I know I screwed up; you don't need to tell me and I'm sorry. She was so convincing though, I really believed her.'

'The kid has got serious talent; she should be in a drama group or something. At least those two are home safe and we don't have to worry about them.'

Morgan was downcast. Perhaps the Doc Martens had made her want to believe Paige had found a suspect. Did she see herself in the girl?

'You did what you deemed necessary, Morgan,' Ben went on. 'Besides who's to say that Cooper's DNA won't be a match for what little was found at the crime scene? At least we have a comparison sample.'

'That would be a long shot,' Morgan replied, but she appreciated Ben grasping at straws to reassure her. 'Now what are we doing? I've spent hours chasing the wrong leads. We need to find Melody's killer.'

'We are going back to trawl through the house-to-house forms and see if any of our lovely PCSOs flagged potential witnesses or found us some really clear doorbell or dashcam footage of the killer and Melody arriving at the scene.'

She smiled at him, glad he had a plan. She just wished she felt a little bit closer to justice.

27

Morgan had finished going through the questionnaires that had nothing they could follow up on from their side. Three houses had been *no reply*, so Ben had sent Amy and Cain to see if they were home from work yet. Letting out a huge yawn, she tried to cover her mouth, but her hand wasn't big enough.

'Blimey, Brookes, you nearly swallowed me whole.'

She grabbed a pen and launched it in his direction. 'Cheeky, you know I was thinking, and I know this is a bit repetitive.'

'But?'

'Alan Cooper does drive a white four by four like what Chloe Smith reported. I have this feeling that we might be ruling Alan and Joe out because of Paige and Alisa being idiots. They're still our only leads. Alan's behaviour was extremely suspect when we interviewed him.'

'Cain double checked his alibi, it's iron clad,' Ben replied.

'Then why did he run? And I noticed that Joe wasn't particularly distraught when we found Alisa. Didn't he leave the crime scene because he was finding it hard to cope with the loss of his friend? He didn't seem very upset. He was at home with his girlfriend.'

'Have we got photos of either of them?'

'We should have but I don't want to show Jade or Chloe a picture of Joe in his work uniform,' she replied, knowing what Ben was thinking. 'That might cause problems further down the line for him. I can screenshot a couple off Facebook or Instagram.'

'Okay, do that and we'll speak to both Jade and Chloe. I'd ask the family liaison officer to show them to Jade but the FLO will know or might know Joe, and as you so rightly said, we don't want to cause him unnecessary trouble if he's got nothing to do with any of this. We'll have to do it ourselves.'

'Give me a couple of minutes.' She began scrolling through her social media feeds, and Ben left her to it while he went to see if Marc was still around.

———

The light was still on in his office and he was hunched over the desktop computer. Ben knocked, and he waved him in.

'Any decent leads?'

Ben shrugged. 'It depends on what you call decent. Did you see the post-mortem report?'

Marc nodded. 'Maybe he wore a wig to disguise himself.'

'Susie thought they may be hair extensions. Jade told her Melody didn't wear any, so could they have been someone else's? An accomplice? The remnants of another victim in the vehicle he used to move the body?'

'Fuck!' Marc exclaimed, frustrated at the never-ending threads that were appearing before his eyes. They had nothing.

Ben nodded. 'Are we still holding Alan Cooper?'

'He's been bailed for police assault.'

'Any conditions?'

'Not to approach Cain for one, but not really. We have no official complaints about his behaviour, no past record for domestic violence or anything of that nature, so he's free to do what he pleases as long as he does it as far away from this police station as possible.'

'Did you hear about those two teenagers?'

Marc shook his head. 'Enlighten me, but I'm going to hazard a guess that the one who came here to report Cooper was causing trouble.'

'Did you know we found her missing friend at Joe's studio, the crime-scene tech?'

Marc gave one of his epic eye rolls, and Ben was glad Morgan wasn't here to witness it because they wound her up beyond belief.

'Is he involved? I hope not.'

'I don't think so, but Morgan thinks we should speak to the abduction victim from earlier and Melody Carrick's mum to see if either of them recognises Alan or Joe, just to be sure.'

He was nodding. 'That's a good shout, better to get them ruled out or identified if that's the case. I hope that our Joe is not involved; if this goes tits up, we're going to have to get PSD breathing down our necks and we all know what a pain in the arse they are.'

'Yeah, we do.'

As Ben walked out of the door, Marc called after him, 'Thanks for the update, good luck.'

Ben waved at him and went back to the office, where Morgan was cutting up the photocopies of the pictures she'd printed off Facebook. He said, 'The boss thinks you have a point, and after this we're going home because I'm bushed.'

She didn't say what they both knew: that if either man was identified, neither of them would be going home for hours yet.

28

He knew it was risky, he didn't know if it would work, but he had nothing to lose. That girl was causing him nothing but trouble. She had been a nuisance from the beginning, since he'd arrived in Rydal Falls, but after today and her bringing the cops back with her, she was going to have to be silenced and as far as he knew there was only one way to do it. If her drunkard mother got in the way then she would be taken care of too.

He had no feelings towards either of them; he didn't have feelings towards anybody except for maybe himself. He stared in the rear-view mirror. *Would they call the cops on him?* This was blatantly confident. Pulling the baseball cap down low across his eyes, he grabbed the paper bag containing the rope he needed to strangle them off the front seat. He had cable ties in case they got a little out of hand and he needed to restrain them, but he had a sneaking feeling that after her outburst today she would be in her room, headphones on listening to music and writing how much she hated everyone in that small, purple book she carried everywhere with her.

He didn't need to knock – he had a key which came in very handy. He'd watched as Susan had driven like a lunatic into the small cul-de-sac and almost parked her car through her bay window. She'd stumbled out of the car, plastic bag clanging and clinking as the wine bottles she'd bought from the nearest shop all chinked together. She was hammered; how she never got pulled over was always a great wonder to him. He guessed she lived a little too far out of the public view for anyone to notice. He gave her a few minutes to get inside. She wouldn't put the deadbolt on – she was careless like that.

The bag he was holding was from the local Chinese take-away, and he thought he looked like a delivery driver should anyone glance his way. As he stood at the front door he deliber-ated if he should knock instead, but then decided against it. He pressed down on the handle and shook his head when it went all the way down and opened. He hadn't even needed a key. Music was blaring, it was coming from the Alexa in the kitchen, a seventies greatest hits station that Susan listened to all day and night. He locked the front door behind him, pocketing the key just in case either of them tried to run out of it screaming for help. He'd never attempted to kill two in the space of minutes, and it could all go horribly wrong. Placing the bag on the floor he took out the rope, wrapping it around each hand. Susan came out of the kitchen dancing in time to the beat of Earth, Wind & Fire. She looked at him with pure confusion in her eyes.

'Oh, what are you doing here?'

He slipped the rope from one hand and pushed the other behind his back before she glanced down at his hands.

'I thought I'd come and see if Paige was okay, if you were okay and if you needed any help.'

She grinned at him. 'Wow, how kind of you. That's really nice. How did you get in? Did your mother never teach you good manners and tell you to knock on people's doors?'

'I did, but you didn't hear me for the music.' He had a point; it was very loud.

She shrugged and waved the bottle of white wine in his direction, her bracelet jangling against the glass of the bottle. 'Well, I'm depressed and heartbroken. Do you want to help me drown my sorrows and make me feel better?'

He shrugged. 'I wasn't planning on stopping long.'

Susan threw back her head and laughed. 'Since when did that ever stop you before?'

She turned her back on him to go into the lounge. He glanced up the stairs, making sure Paige wasn't around, and then he followed behind her.

As she stood bending over to put the wine bottle on the coffee table, he slipped as close to her as he could get. Hooking the rope over her head, he yanked it as tight as it could go around her neck, dragging her backwards. She managed to hook her fingers underneath it a little and pulled it away enough that she could open her mouth to scream for help. At the same time, she picked up the wine bottle and, throwing her hand back, smashed it into his face, making him release the rope. Susan stumbled forwards, falling full force into the glass-topped coffee table and it smashed into pieces, winding her. She landed on the floor amongst the glass.

He was panicking and bleeding – any minute Paige would come rushing down to see what was happening, and she would be able to run for help. He dived towards Susan, and this time he used his bare hands to choke her until her face turned purple. His palms were slick with sweat, and it was difficult to keep a tight grip. Just as he thought she'd never give in, finally she gargled and took her last breaths. She died with her eyes wide open in shock and horror at what had happened to her.

Perspiration was pouring down his forehead and he was breathing heavily with the exertion. His gaze kept falling on the stairs, but Paige must have her headphones on, or she would have been down here.

Pushing two fingers against Susan's neck to check if she had a pulse, he was satisfied there was nothing, before he clambered from the floor, brushing shards of broken glass off himself. His legs were shaky; it had been harder than he'd expected. He didn't bother to move her, there was no point, he owed her nothing, and he felt no guilt about what he'd just done. He knew she'd cut his cheek with the wine bottle, as he could feel the sticky wetness running down his face and, in a panic, he looked around to see if he'd left splotches of blood all over the place. Luckily for him the collar of the navy polo shirt he was wearing was soaking it up. He stood for a moment, taking deep breaths to steady his nerves. That had been awful – he never would have put Susan Evans down as a fighter.

Earth, Wind & Fire had been replaced with Smokey Robinson and still there was no sign of Paige. Slipping into the kitchen he washed his hands in the sink, drying them on a towel that he discarded. He realised he'd left the rope in the lounge. There was no way he was strangling Paige with his bare hands; it was too difficult, and Susan had been drunk yet she'd still put up a fight. Paige would be like a hellcat, and he knew she would be a challenge. Retrieving the rope he pulled the door shut behind him on Susan's corpse and began to climb the stairs one at a time.

29

Chloe's eyes lingered over Joe a little longer than they did Alan Cooper, making Morgan wonder what she was going to say. She pointed to Joe. 'He's familiar, but he's too young. The guy in the baseball cap seemed older, different hair colour, it was lighter, more dark blond, and I feel as if I know him, but he wasn't the one to drag me into that car.'

She turned her attention back to the photo of Alan Cooper; Morgan didn't know how recent it was. 'I'm not sure about him, he's the same kind of build and height. If he had blond hair and a baseball cap on it might be easier. I'm sorry, I'm not very good, am I?'

Ben smiled at her. 'No, you're doing great. You've had an awful day and now we're here knocking this late, disturbing you again. Thanks, Chloe, we're sorry to disturb you.'

Morgan noticed the way Chloe was staring at Ben, her cheeks a lot pinker than when they'd arrived, and she put her head down to look away. His manner was always so lovely with any victim or with their families, and he looked so ruggedly handsome with his shaved hair and blue eyes that crinkled with genuine warmth. Chloe liked him, a lot, and Morgan couldn't blame her because so did she. They left Chloe with the promise that they'd update her as soon as they knew anything.

Ben talked to the plain-clothed officer sitting in a car on the street near to Chloe's. 'Have you noticed anyone hanging around?'

'Only me, it's not a busy street and there's not a lot of action to be honest. If someone does turn up, they're going to stand out like a sore thumb.'

'Good.'

He tugged the photos out of his pocket, and Morgan waited to see if he would show him Joe's. She didn't know the officer so maybe he was fairly new and wouldn't recognise him.

'If you see either of these guys, stop them and call for backup.'

He passed the printouts through the window, and the officer studied them, nodding his head.

'I can't say I've seen either of them. Are they working together as a team?'

It was a simple enough question, but it was one that blew Morgan's mind, totally. She hadn't even considered that as an option.

Ben glanced her way then looked back at the officer, who was handing the pictures back.

'No, we don't believe so at this moment, but we wouldn't rule it out.'

'No worries.'

'Thank you.'

They walked away, neither of them speaking until they were inside Ben's car.

He turned to look at her. 'We didn't consider that, is it a possibility?'

'It could explain the murder and abduction on the same day.'

Ben was shaking his head. 'We're only showing Joe's photo

as a precaution. We've got nothing else to seriously suggest he was involved. If we did, we would need to ensure he was off duty. We'd have to tell him.'

'Let's go speak to Jade.'

Morgan didn't want to face her again, not tonight, not when she'd had all day alone with her thoughts. If it was Morgan and that had been her daughter, she would be so drunk right now that she wouldn't be able to spell her own name. She pulled up Jade's address from the log and noticed that she lived above the café – there was no escaping it for her – and Morgan felt another piece of her heart tear for the woman who had done nothing to deserve what had happened to her.

Ben was slow to get out of the car, and she leaned back in. 'Do you want to sit this one out?'

'No, it's okay. The FLO should have updated her about the post-mortem. It's just the thought of having to discuss it with her so late. She might be ready to go to bed, and I feel terrible.'

'I think Jade will be grateful that we're working late trying to catch the person who killed her daughter. She won't be all relaxed and having a chilled evening; she'll be on edge and desperate for updates, at least I would be if it was me. I wanted to know every little thing when Stan was killed, and it was the not knowing that drove me insane.'

Morgan closed her eyes and saw Stan's weathered, drunken face smiling at her. He had been the only dad she'd known, and she'd blamed him for her life falling apart when really, he had been the one trying his best to hold it together. She'd never really got the chance to properly thank him for doing that. He'd taken her into his home despite knowing who her real father was; that had taken some doing. She didn't know if she'd be brave enough to take on some killer's kid and all the baggage that came along with it.

She felt wetness on her cheek and realised she was crying. Swiping it away before Ben noticed she blinked a couple of times to clear the tears. Grief, it came at the most random times and hit like a freight train when it did.

Ben was out of the car and already at the side door to the flat, knocking on the door. She joined him but not before glancing up at the sky to see the brightest star twinkling right above her head. Sylvia and Stan had been good people, and she hoped they were together again and happy like they deserved.

The door opened and Caroline, the FLO, was smiling at them. 'Have you got news?' They both shook their heads. 'Oh, that's a shame.'

'How is she?' Morgan asked, knowing full well the answer would be devastated at losing her only daughter.

'She's holding up. I was just about to leave her for the night. She wants to call it a day and go to bed.'

'I don't blame her,' Ben whispered.

Jade was sitting in a big armchair, her legs tucked under her, staring at the television that had no sound on. She glanced at them with a look of hope on her face that made Morgan feel even worse.

'Hey, how are you doing?'

She shrugged. 'Not so good.'

'Can I show you a couple of pictures and you have a look to see if you recognise either of these guys?'

Morgan perched on the arm of the chair next to Jade and passed them over. Jade stared at them for some time before nodding her head.

'Yes, I do.'

Ben, who had been staring at the silent television, turned his attention to Jade. 'You do?'

She nodded, holding up the picture of Cooper. 'He comes into the café once a week, usually with a woman who always smells of stale booze, but she's very pretty and always leaves a good tip.'

'What about the other one?'

'Joe, he comes in probably three times a week. He's friends with Melody and I think he likes her a lot, but I get the impression he's too shy to ask her out which is a shame because I think Melody—' She stopped talking, her hand covering her mouth at the realisation she was talking as if Melody was still here and not lying in a refrigerator in the mortuary.

She let out a sob. 'Oh God, will this ever get any easier? I keep forgetting, I keep expecting her to walk through that door and ask me if I'll make her some cheese on toast.'

Ben approached Jade and knelt down in front of her, taking hold of her hand. 'Eventually it will, but it takes a long time. It's so hard to get your head around that someone you love, who was so full of life the last time you spoke to them, is no longer here and you can't tell them how much you love them or how much you wish you could have been there to help them when they really needed it.'

Morgan knew he was talking about Cindy and felt a lump in her throat. Jade was staring at him. She was squeezing his fingers.

'You lost someone too?'

He nodded. 'My wife took her own life. I know it's much worse that Melody had hers taken from her. Cindy made that choice herself, but it was sudden, and I didn't expect it in a million years. I want you to know that in time you can live with it. You'll never stop thinking about her or loving her, but in time you'll be able to remember the good things and not how she was taken away from you.'

Jade began to cry. 'Thank you, I hope so because all I can see is her face frozen in fear and it's horrible.'

Ben leaned forward and hugged Jade fiercely, making Morgan turn away so they couldn't see the tears streaming down her face. Caroline was openly crying too. Morgan went into the kitchen in search of paper towels, as the tissue box next to Jade was empty. She came back in with a roll and tore sheets off, handing them out to everyone.

Ben was now standing up and he didn't meet her gaze, and she knew he was embarrassed about being so open in front of them all. Morgan put the roll on the coffee table next to Jade.

'Did you have any reason to believe that Melody didn't like Joe?'

Jade shook her head. 'No, quite the opposite. She fancied him like mad and I would tease her, telling her I would ask him out on her behalf, but she'd go crazy with me. Isn't it sad that their chance to have a relationship has been wiped out? Does he know about Melody? He'll be devastated I think.'

'Yes, he does, and he is. What about the other guy? Did he seem to take an interest in Melody? Was she ever working when he was in?'

'I don't think so, I don't think he gave her a second glance. He always had his face glued to his phone. Why? Do you think he might have killed her?'

'No, we're just following up on some information and ruling them out. Their names came up, that's all, and we have to do this.'

Jade was sniffling into her paper towel. 'Okay, do you have any idea who could have done it?'

'I'm sorry, we don't yet but we will. Where was Melody going this morning? When she left the house.'

'College.'

'Did she usually walk past the river?'

'No, she didn't usually walk anywhere and besides, it's in the opposite direction to the college.'

'Did she say if anyone was picking her up today?'

'No, she always gets the bus.'

'Thank you, which college?'

'Sixth form, she's training to be a hairdresser, and they started a new course in partnership with Kendal college; she was going to go to uni but changed her mind so went back again to join the course. I told her it's just because she liked college life so much, she didn't want to leave.'

Morgan smiled at her. 'I can see her as a hairdresser. Her hair was always so pretty and styled so lovely unlike my unruly copper curls.'

Jade shook her head. 'We love your hair. Melody always said how beautiful it is whenever you called in for coffee.'

Morgan felt her cheeks burn a little at the compliment, she was terrible at taking them, but it broke her heart even more to know that Melody knew her enough to think she had pretty hair.

Ben smiled at Jade. 'Thank you, I'm sorry we disturbed you so late.'

'You can disturb me any time you want if it's to do with my daughter. I want the bastard who did this behind bars. I would rather you left me alone in a room with him for five minutes with a baseball bat than go through a court case, but seeing in him prison is the next best thing. Please find him for me, she's all I had, and I don't know how I'll manage without her.'

They both left Jade's flat feeling deflated, their hearts stuffed full of sadness.

Morgan took hold of Ben's hand in the car. 'You were so lovely in there.'

He lowered his head. 'I'm sorry, talking about Cindy like that. I don't normally do that, but it felt right, and it just came out.'

'Don't you ever apologise again, Ben, that was so heartfelt and sad you made me cry for you both; and it was beautiful that you could give that kind of comfort to Jade, she needed it and I think you did too. I'm not some green-eyed, jealous monster who's afraid of you talking about your dead wife. It makes me happy that you can. You've come a long way from keeping your feelings bottled up. I love you so much, Ben Matthews, and I'm so proud of you, you are a good man.'

He pulled her close to him and kissed her. 'I'm not as good of a person as you are, Morgan Brookes, but because of you I'm learning to be, and I love you more than you could ever know.'

They sat in the car in the dark, holding hands in silence for five minutes before Morgan broke it.

'It's so sad that Joe and Melody never got to tell each other how they felt. It's also not much help that both Joe and Cooper were customers at the café, but I'll tell you what is good.'

'What?'

'Melody was going to college, so there is no way on this earth she was walking in the direction of the river. Somebody stopped to give her a lift and that someone drove her there and killed her. Declan confirmed the primary murder site was where Melody's body was found. He also said Melody had no head injury, yet Chloe was hit over the head. I think Melody definitely knew her killer, but Chloe didn't. It would explain why Melody had no head injury, he didn't need to force her. We need to canvas this whole area to see if anyone saw Melody get into a car.'

'And that is why I love you.'

She laughed. 'Do you want to start knocking on doors now?'

He glanced at the clock on the dash. 'No, it's too late. Tomorrow first thing we'll get a whole team together, draft in the PCSOs and get as many officers out on foot in this area as possible until we find someone who saw Melody get into a car.'

30

The blue room was bluer than ever and it was standing-room only, filled with PCSOs all with matching polo shirts on, as Ben talked through everything. He wanted the team to ask anyone who lived on Melody's route to college who might have potentially seen something. Morgan passed out the clipboards with the still warm questionnaires she'd printed out attached to them. At the mention of Alan Cooper's name as a person of interest, she remembered she needed to have a conversation with Susan Evans about Paige wasting their time yesterday. As everybody filed out of the room, she picked up her clipboard.

'Hey, I forgot I need to speak to Paige's mum about her behaviour yesterday. Is it okay if I go there first? Otherwise it's going to get pushed to one side and forgotten about, and I don't think she should be let off that lightly.'

Ben nodded. 'Are you going on your own?'

'If that's okay. I'll go there first then join you after. I won't be long.'

'What if you ring her? Save you the trip.'

'I don't know her number and I have this sneaky suspicion that Paige isn't going to answer.'

'Fine, just don't go in if you think Cooper is there. I don't want you with a matching broken nose to Cain's.'

She smiled at him. 'I won't. I'll get going so I'm not wasting any time.' He blew her a kiss, and she laughed. 'You slept well then?'

He nodded. 'Unbelievably well considering what a crap day we had. Did you?'

'A bit, I woke up and couldn't get back off. All I kept seeing was the flash of Melody's body through those trees.'

'I know, it's hard to block it out sometimes.'

Morgan left him gathering up his papers. She saw Cain walking through the atrium downstairs and getting into the lift carrying a big box, and she waited outside of it to help him. As the doors slid open, she laughed to see he was carrying a coffee machine.

'You were serious then?'

'I was deadly serious, cannot survive on the stuff out of the vending machine. It strips the lining from my stomach – they could use it as paint stripper, it's so vile. This is my contribution to the team. I feel as if I should be promoted for my selfless, thoughtful thinking about you all.'

'I'm not sure about a promotion but maybe a Sainthood.'

'I'll take anything I can get.'

'How's your nose?' Underneath his right eye there were blue and black flowers of bruising that had spread along to his cheekbones; it looked painful.

'Okay if I don't touch it or think about it. How's your head?'

She shrugged. 'Same. I'm nipping to see Paige's mum and let her know what a time waster she was yesterday. Everyone is going to flood the area around Melody's house. We think she got picked up by somebody yesterday because her mum said she was on her way to college, which is nowhere near to the river.'

He nodded. 'Sounds like a good plan. I'll see you soon.'

She had begun to walk down the stairs when he called after

her. 'Is Benno letting you out to play on your own? Are you even allowed to drive?'

She turned to him, lifting a finger to her lips. 'Shush, no one has actually said that I can't, and Mads isn't in today to remind him.'

Cain laughed. 'You are my idol, Brookes. You're such a rebel I sometimes think you're on the wrong side of the law. My lips are sealed. Try not to crash any more cars or we're all going to be using those police pushbikes that are stacked up in the storeroom.'

Morgan nodded. 'I promise.'

She didn't mind riding a bike on a warm day, with a picnic to somewhere not too far away, but she sure as hell wouldn't ride around on one emblazoned with the police logo all over it and look like a complete tit.

She had booked the last div car and was leaving before anyone thought to stop her. Yesterday had not been her fault and at least she'd stopped before she ran Chloe Smith over. It could have been a lot worse – a car was replaceable but a human wasn't.

Meadowfield View was the place to live if you didn't want nosey neighbours or conversation; it was deserted. She thought that the people who lived there might have bought them as second homes which would explain the lack of cars and people on drives, except for Susan Evans's car which was parked so close to the bay window of the house she was amazed she hadn't driven right through it. It could also explain how nobody had reported Susan for drink driving, which she clearly was; she was going to have to pass the information on to the traffic unit. Morgan didn't agree with anyone driving under the influence of drink or drugs because of the catastrophic consequences if they hit someone else.

The blinds were closed, and she looked at her watch; it was early but she thought that Paige would have probably left to go to college or wherever she went by now. She knocked loudly on the door to get Susan's attention then waited, and waited. Lifting her hand she rapped on it even louder. *Maybe Susan is in bed.* She didn't have any time to waste. She couldn't come back here – she needed to speak to her and get this one thing boxed off her list; otherwise it would be there, niggling at the back of her brain all day and night.

Morgan pushed the handle, expecting it to be locked but it went straight down, and the door swung open a little.

'Hello, Susan, are you home?' The smell of something gone off hit her nostrils, and she paused then understood what it was. She knew it all too well. It was the cloying smell of death that filled the hallway, and she felt her blood turn to ice.

She tugged on the last nitrile glove that was lingering in her pocket and pushed the door open wide.

'Susan, Paige.' Her voice was loud and a little shaky. The smell lingered in the hallway, and there was no mistaking the sickly, sweet, putrid smell. *What the hell happened here?* The entrance looked fine. She called out, 'Paige.' As she walked towards the lounge, she let out a small gasp at the sight what greeted her from the open doorway. Lying on the floor, her eyes partly open, staring into space, amongst a puddle of broken glass, was Susan Evans.

Morgan's instincts took over and she rushed to her, bending down to feel if she had a pulse. She most definitely didn't. She was hard to the touch and the sickly, sweet smell was emanating from her dead body.

She stood up and shouted, 'Paige.'

Her heart in her mouth she took the stairs two at a time, blind panic and fear had taken over. The teenage girl was a pain in the arse, but she was just a kid, she didn't deserve this. She ran along the landing not sure which room was hers, throwing the doors open until she reached the room that clearly was Paige's – hair straighteners on the bed, make-up palettes on every flat surface – but there was no sign of her. Morgan checked in the cupboard and under the bed, but she wasn't there. Her radio was in the car, so after completing cursory checks of each room for Paige she went out to the car and called it in. Her phone began to vibrate immediately.

'*What have you got, Morgan?*'

Ben's voice was high-pitched, and she could tell he was a little panicked.

'Susan Evans is dead; Paige is not here.'

'*Christ, any sign of Alan Cooper?*'

'No, do you think it was him?'

'*Who else could it be? Susan threw him out, we arrested him, he was angry and attacked Cain. He could have gone straight there after he was released and took it out on Susan. He might have taken Paige with him. I'm on my way, patrols are too. Secure the scene, Morgan, do not let anyone in until I get there.*'

He hung up, and she looked around. There wasn't a single person peeping out of their windows; it was super creepy. Just to be certain, she knocked on the nearest house but there was no reply. She tried the others – all no reply. She could still see Susan's house from each door she knocked on. The entire area was deserted, and she had never felt more alone in her life.

When the faint sound of sirens echoed around the valley, the relief Morgan felt was palpable. She had never felt so glad to be a part of a team that had your back the way her colleagues in the police service did. Management might be arseholes, but the patrol officers and her friends would risk life and limb to make sure she was safe and in no danger. The first van that screeched to a halt almost at her feet was driven by Cain, with Ben and Amy sitting in the front next to him. They bailed out, and out of the back came an officer who she recognised but had no idea what his name was.

Ben looked her up and down, making sure she wasn't hurt, and the creases on his forehead disappeared with relief. 'You're okay?'

'Yes, shocked because I never expected that but I'm good.' Her voice was drowned out by the arrival of another van and a car both with sirens and lights flashing.

Ben pointed to the other houses. 'What's the score, where are all the neighbours?'

'You tell me, I've knocked on every door and there's no answer. It's weird. It also explains why Susan was getting away with driving over the limit. There are literally no neighbours to report her.'

Ben slowly scanned the area, turning to look at each house before looking back at her.

'Where is Paige? You're sure she's missing?'

'I checked the house, but you're welcome to check again. I didn't go out the back. I don't know about any outbuildings or sheds. Ben, what if he's taken her? We have to find her, this is my fault.'

He nodded.

'I know, we will. We'll throw everything we have at it to find her, Morgan, I promise, and don't be ridiculous, how is this your fault? Did you do this? If anything, you gave her the time of day when most others would have fobbed her off and sent her away.'

She didn't speak, the words were stuck in her throat like the lead ball that was stuck in her stomach.

If they didn't find Paige soon Morgan would blame herself for the rest of her life.

31

Ben's voice was loud as he gave Cain and Amy their orders. He turned to Morgan.

'We need to locate Cooper. Where did you two find him yesterday?'

'At a flat above the Co-op on the main street. Is it wise to send Cain for him after yesterday?'

'Probably not, but I'm struggling for staff here.' He turned to Cain. 'You just track him down, but call it in when you find him and ask for an arrest team.'

'We need to trace Paige's phone. If Marc authorises a cell site analysis it will help narrow down the search area.'

'I don't need his authorisation; I don't even know where he is.' He took out his phone and made a call to put in the request then tucked his phone back into his pocket. 'We need to do a thorough search and check she's not outside somewhere.' He was staring into the wooded area that backed onto the fields behind the houses. 'She could have got scared and ran off into those fields.' He picked up the car radio. 'Control have we got a dog handler on duty?'

'Sarge, I'm already travelling. I was in Penrith but won't be too long. I set off as soon as I heard Morgan's shout for help.'

'Thanks, Cassie, much appreciated.'

Morgan felt a little better. If Paige had run off or, God forbid, been chased into the woodland, Brock the search dog would find her. She hoped her big friendly giant Caesar was in the van, too. She adored the huge Italian mastiff. He had saved her life and saved the day a couple of times. He was a terrifying sight to behold when Cassie released him from his lead and gave him whatever command it was he answered to. The black mountain of pure muscle was fast and whoever he was chasing after never stood a chance; he'd take them down then stand growling, slobbering and scare them to death until an officer could get a pair of handcuffs slapped on them to detain them.

'Are you coming back inside?' Ben's voice broke the trance she was in staring at the trees in the distance.

'Erm, yes. I can do if you need me to.'

He passed her a packet containing paper overalls. 'I think so, I want you to search Paige's room for anything, phone, diary, journal, whatever she might have to give us some clue about what's happened here.'

Morgan ripped the packet open, tugging them on along with the shoe covers, gloves, and pulled the hood up to keep her hair inside. As they reached the front door she paused.

'Ben.'

He was already inside. He didn't hear her and carried on walking towards the room she'd pointed out to him.

'Ben.' This time much louder.

He stopped and turned back to her.

'What if Paige did this? What if she tried to set Cooper up? What if she killed Melody and then snapped last night with her mum?'

His head nodded slowly. 'I don't think she had anything to

do with Melody, but I couldn't say she didn't do this.' He reached the open doorway into the living room and stared at the body on the floor, letting out a low groan. 'What another waste.'

Morgan stayed at the open doorway letting him assess the scene himself; he didn't go too far in.

'Would you two get out of here.' Wendy's voice was stern, startling the pair of them.

'I need Morgan to do a quick search of the missing girl's bedroom then we'll get out.'

Wendy arched an eyebrow at him, then turned to Morgan. 'Have you been upstairs?'

'Yes.'

'What's it like?'

'Clean, this is the primary and only crime scene.'

'Let me document the house and scene then you can go back up.'

'Can you like do it ASAP then, Wendy? Because we have a missing teenager and time is of the essence.'

She pointed to the camera in her hand. Ben retreated from the room, giving Wendy the space she needed, and they both walked outside to wait for the go-ahead from her.

'We were supposed to be canvassing Melody's neighbourhood.'

'I know, the PCSOs are still out there. They will phone if they find somebody who saw something.'

Morgan sighed. 'Melody is continually getting pushed to one side because of Paige.'

Ben's warm fingers gently took hold of her arm. 'She isn't, we have a team down there right now. If anyone can find us somebody it's the PCSOs; they know what they're doing and are shit hot when it comes to house-to-house enquiries.'

'I know, but I feel as if I should be working tirelessly to find the person who took her life as if she was no more important than swatting a fly. I need to do something to make it up to Jade. I promised I'd find her daughter's killer, Ben.'

She knew she was acting irrationally, but it was true: every step of the way, Paige had interrupted whatever she was supposed to be doing, and now she couldn't shake the feeling that there was a lot more to Paige Evans than she had ever considered. She could be involved in everything.

32

Alan Cooper had never felt so rough in his life. He groaned from the back seat of the car where he'd tried to sleep last night, but he was too tall to get comfortable, and his legs were aching from being cramped up all night. He'd gone back to Jackie's flat desperate for a shower and change of clothes, only to find that the safety chain was on, and despite him having the spare key he still couldn't get in. He'd knocked, called out her name, tapped on the window and rang her phone all with no answer. Not wanting to make a fuss and bring any attention to himself, he'd left her with whispered threats called through the narrow gap in the door.

'You fucking bitch, I'll sort you out. I just need a shower and my stuff.'

She hadn't replied, and he thought she was probably sitting on the floor in the dark terrified of what he might do to her. He could kick the door in and go get his stuff, but obviously her nosey neighbours had told her about him running away from the coppers yesterday and getting arrested. They were probably watching him right now, phone in hand, 999 already on speed dial and ready to hit that button should he so much as knock too loud on her crappy door.

Resisting the urge to boot it with his foot, he turned and walked away. He didn't like her that much anyway. She had thrown herself at him the moment they'd met, always wearing low-cut tops with her cleavage on show, which drove Susan insane, and she'd stopped inviting her over. Obviously, he'd told Susan she meant nothing to him, he wasn't interested, and he hadn't been until he had no place else to go and he'd had to come knocking on her door. She wasn't a bad looking woman, and she had a decent pair of breasts which helped, but she whined a lot. Susan complained but she didn't go on for hours unlike Jackie, who would think nothing of spending all evening talking about the same thing, from many different angles. This was a temporary thing. She was nothing more than the means to an end, a place to stay until he could find some other unsus- pecting victim. He had no idea what he was supposed to do now. He didn't have a change of clothes, he didn't have that much money either and now he didn't even have his nan's box that was about the only thing in the world that gave him comfort and reminded him of the good times despite them being few and far between.

He would have to come back when she was at work and get his things. He wasn't letting her keep them. They were precious to him, but to her they were junk.

His car was parked in a lay-by on a quiet road near to the park. It was a bit of a walk from there to Jackie's, but his legs were badly in need of a stretch. There were public toilets nearby too which had been a life saver for him, although he wasn't opposed to peeing in the bushes if he must. He could feel the anger flowing through his veins and was pretty sure the blood had been replaced by a black, sticky liquid that was turning his insides into a swirling mass of oozing fury. At some point it would take over and he might explode; he was scared of the carnage he could do if this fury was unleashed.

He shook his head, bloody Paige had started all of this. She had done nothing but cause trouble from day one and now he was glad he was rid of her. She no longer held any control over him. He was free to do as he pleased, and he would.

33

The streets around Melody Carrick's flat were filled with a swarm of royal blue and bright yellow PCSOs, and despite the warm afternoon sun they were wearing their hats, still knocking on doors and talking to anyone who walked past. They had been drafted in from all over south Cumbria and Westmorland. Sam and Tina had been tasked with Melody's street, the entrance to the flat being on a residential street behind the main street. The door five down from Melody's house was answered by a man with a look of terror etched across his face. Sam's internal radar was going off: something was off with this guy.

'Can I help you, officer?' He moved out onto the top step and saw Tina knocking on the door next to his. 'Is everything okay?'

'Hi, we're doing house-to-house enquiries for a murder that happened yesterday and wanted to ask you some questions. Did you see or hear anything suspicious yesterday morning?'

'Not really, I don't follow, was there somebody killed in this street?' Sam wondered if he was just scared.

'Not on this street, but a teenage girl who lived along here was killed.'

She let that sink in as his eyes flitted along the row of houses on this side. He stopped at the steps up to Melody's then turned his attention back to her.

'I didn't see anything. A teenager you say? I saw Melody Carrick walking that way' – he pointed – 'on her way to college, I assume, like she usually does.'

'What time was that?'

'I was on my way out yesterday morning to collect my news-paper, so it would have been around ten. I always go to the newsagents at that time.'

Sam scribbled this down. 'Was Melody on her own?'

'Well, she was walking like I said, with those big head-phones over her ears. Silly really, how can you hear traffic and such? It's dangerous. Did she get knocked over?'

Sam shook her head. 'No, she didn't.'

'Oh, well actually she stopped to talk to a guy who was having engine trouble. His bloody vehicle was stuck in the middle of the road blocking the whole street, and he had the hood up staring down into the engine.'

Sam tugged on her ear which was burning, her body's way of giving her a small sign that something wasn't right. 'What kind of vehicle?'

He shrugged. 'Looked like a Nissan or maybe a Peugeot. It was white.'

'Did you see him speaking to Melody?'

He nodded. 'They were chatting, so I assume they knew each other because she got in. He slammed the hood down and drove away. Is Melody okay?' His complexion had turned ashen.

'Did you know her well?'

'No, just in passing. She seems, or looks, like a nice young woman.'

'Well your testimony will be very helpful, thank you. Can I take your name?'

'Why?'

'I need it for my records because I've spoken to you and my boss is going to want to speak to you too, about what you saw.'

'Oh, no. I don't know about that. I don't want to get involved or cause trouble for Melody. I don't want her to think I was watching what she was doing, because I wasn't; I was just doing what I do every day.'

'You're not in trouble but you could be a very important witness.'

The guy looked pained. 'Witness to what?'

Sam wanted to say a murder but stopped herself; Ben or Morgan could deal with him. She may have found what they needed.

'Like I say it's just routine, Mr?'

He shook his head. 'Mr Whitehouse.'

'Thank you, Mr Whitehouse, are you going to be in for the next hour?'

He looked as if he wanted to run away, his mouth was downturned, and his eyes were still darting around the street.

'If I have to be, yes, but only for an hour. I have a meeting to go to and I won't be late.'

He closed the door, and Tina, who was leaning on his gatepost, winked at Sam who grinned back at her. Neither of them spoke in case he had cameras; he was super paranoid and there was a good chance he had hidden cameras that his neighbours didn't know about. She'd leave those questions to Ben. When she was as far away from his house as she could be, she jabbed Ben's collar number into her radio handset and dialled.

'*Everything okay, Sam?*'

'You might want to get down here as soon as you can. I just found your star witness but he's shifty and very nervous. He's only going to be in for the next hour, so I wouldn't wait around too long.'

'*You did? You bloody superstar. Thank you.*'

'Yeah, well me and Tina will keep an eye on his house to make sure he doesn't disappear into the night before you get here, and then we're going for our refs. He's at number sixteen.'

'I will buy your refs if this turns out to be a good lead.'

'Fine by me, see you soon.'

She winked at Tina. 'Tea is on Ben, what should we order?'

'Pizza?'

'Yes, I fancy some pizza. Come on, let's make sure he doesn't escape; did you see how he kept looking up and down the street then he stared directly at Melody's house.'

'You think he's the guy?'

Sam shrugged. 'No idea, but how good would that be if it was.'

'Yeah, but we'd still get no thanks for it.'

'Ben's different, he's nice and he's already offered to buy our refs, so that's kind of a thank you.'

They sat on the low wall of an empty house with a *For Sale* sign in the garden directly opposite Mr Whitehouse's and waited for Ben or Morgan to arrive, while Tina ordered their pizza on the Rydal Falls Eats App.

34

Ben took a van and sped along the winding roads from Keswick back to Rydal Falls while Morgan clung on to the handle to stop her flying all over.

'You think he saw the guy hanging around?'

'I hope so, Sam said he was the star witness.'

'Why didn't you ask her what he said? Should I phone her, and see?'

'No, I don't want her talking about him in the street. If he's as shifty as she said he may have cameras watching. God, I hope he does, I hope he has a lovely clear picture of the man who did this to Melody so we can arrest them.'

'Or woman, or teenage girl.'

Ben glanced at her. 'Surely you don't think this is the work of a teenage girl?'

He looked to the road then back at her. 'You think it could have been Paige?'

She shrugged. 'I don't know what I think, Ben, my head is spinning with scenarios and none of them make much sense. I'm just saying that maybe she isn't as innocent as we believed, and I don't want to make a huge mistake by not even considering her.'

'But, Morgan, there is a good chance she's dead. Thirty minutes ago you were feeling bad about that being a possibility and now you're practically accusing her of murder.'

'I know, like I said, I don't seem to be able to get a handle on her. Yes, I'm concerned for her welfare, and I do think that she might have come to some harm or run away from whoever killed her mum, but I also know better than to assume she's innocent. We've been there and done that before, and not with good consequences, Ben.'

He was nodding. 'Yes, we have, and I get where you're coming from so point taken. Let's not assume anything and go from the cold, hard facts and evidence that is put in front of us.'

She couldn't argue with that, it was how they worked, and evidence was key to everything, but still she couldn't shake the feeling that they may be making a big mistake.

They saw Sam and Tina sitting on a wall, and Morgan smiled to herself. Ben parked a little further away from them and both women sauntered down to speak to them. Tina leaning into Morgan's side of the car, Sam into Ben's open window.

'He should still be in there unless he's scaled his back garden hedge and gone through several others to escape. He is very nervy, kept looking up and down, but his eyes kept landing on Melody's house then he came up with the story that she got into someone's broken-down car.'

'Does he know this is a murder investigation?' asked Ben.

'Yes, I told him that, but I didn't tell him whose murder, and he kept referring to Melody in present tense, so he either doesn't know she's dead or he's hiding something.'

'Amazing, well done, Sam. I appreciate this, both of you.'

They got out of the car, and Ben reached in his pocket.

Pulling out a crumpled twenty pound note he passed it to Sam, and she shook her head. 'It's okay, thanks. You keep it.'

'Take it, I promised.'

'No, honestly. Next time you can bring us some cakes and coffee or something nice. I was only joking, Ben.'

He nodded. 'I will, Morgan will remind me.'

'By the way, what's he called?'

'Mr Whitehouse, he was reluctant to give his name. Tina's had a quick search on Intel but couldn't find anything specific to this address.'

'I'm going to draft you two in to work for me, you're wasted working for community.'

They both shook their heads. 'No thanks, we like what we do, and we can't be bothered getting chased by killers. When we're done here, we're going for refs, is that okay?'

He nodded. 'Absolutely.'

Laughing, they walked off to knock on the last two doors, while Morgan and Ben knocked on Mr Whitehouse's.

It opened immediately and the guy stared at them both, eyes wide. He held out his hand.

'ID.'

They both passed him their warrant cards, which he scrutinised before passing them back and letting them into his house. He made them stand in the narrow hallway, his body blocking the corridor so they couldn't go any further inside.

'I don't know what's going on or why you have to be inside my house.'

Morgan didn't take her eyes off him; he was talking to Ben and didn't look in her direction once.

Ben nodded. 'Did my colleague not tell you this is a very serious investigation?'

'Well yes, but not much more than that.'

Morgan didn't like the guy; Sam was right, he was shifty.

'She said you saw Melody getting in a car yesterday morning.'

He nodded. 'And?'

'And whoever's car she got into, we believe they were the last person to see her alive.' Ben's tone was no longer polite or friendly: it was curt and to the point.

The guy let out a gasp and shook his head. 'Melody is the murdered person. Oh no, no, no, no, that can't be true. I don't believe you.'

Morgan glanced at Ben to convey her thoughts, *is this guy for real?* and Ben gave a slight nod as if he silently heard her.

'I'm sorry to say that it is true and what information you have is vitally important to us in finding the person that killed her, so we need you to talk us through it all.'

He turned around and led them into his compact, uncluttered kitchen, pointing at the small breakfast bar with a spider plant on it that had seen better days, and two stools tucked underneath it. 'Please, sit.'

Morgan felt as if she were a school kid and thought that he must be a teacher. He gave off the kind of vibes of someone who was used to dealing with children.

'What do you do for a living, Mr Whitehouse?'

'I'm a supply teacher, but I've been a bit unwell the last couple of weeks so haven't been at work, which is why I saw Melody yesterday.'

He looked sad at the mention of her name, and she continued. 'Where do you teach?'

'Here, there and everywhere. Usually at St George's Primary, but I cover the colleges as well and occasionally the senior schools, but I dislike teaching that age range, so try to avoid it.'

Ben nodded. 'Yeah, they're hard work.'

'What has this got to do with Melody?'

'Nothing, we're just getting to know you and understand how you were around to see Melody yesterday.'

He seemed appeased at that. 'Is she really dead? I don't think my mind can come to terms with it, oh no. Her poor mum, how is Jade? She is such a lovely woman, they're both lovely people.'

'Devastated, she lost her only child to some sick individual.' Morgan watched his facial expressions, but he nodded vehemently.

'She has, the poor woman. She won't get over that. Melody is such a sweet girl, very kind, helpful, friendly.'

'You seem to know her very well.'

'I taught her, then I moved here, and she always speaks, waves, would put my bin out for me last year when I hurt my back.' He looked genuinely sad, and Morgan wasn't sure he was involved despite her initial thoughts that he might be.

'Can I ask what happened to her?'

'We are very limited to what we can tell you. Her body was found by the riverside yesterday morning. Can you talk us through what you saw?'

'Yes, well, like I told your colleagues I was going for my morning newspaper. When I'm not working, I like to leave the house around ten o'clock and walk to the shop. I did this yesterday and saw her talking to a man who was having engine trouble in the front street.'

'Did you recognise him from around here?'

'No, but I didn't really take much notice because they were friendly, and I got the impression that she knew him. I waved and carried on to the shop. They got in and drove away. That's it really, there's nothing more to add. Was it him, did he hurt her?'

'Quite possibly. What kind of vehicle was it?'

'A white Nissan or Peugeot; it didn't look very old which was why I was surprised it had broken down.'

Morgan had her fingers crossed. 'Did you get the number plate?'

'No, as I said there looked to be nothing untoward happening. Melody was chatting to him, and she didn't look as if she felt scared or anything.'

Morgan considered whether he would have done anything if she had. He didn't look the kind of guy who could deal with confrontations very well.

'Do you have any CCTV?'

He shook his head. 'I haven't felt the need. It's a quiet street – there's not much happens.'

The disappointment hit hard. 'Would you recognise him again?'

'No, I wouldn't. I didn't look at him for more than a two-second glance. He had a baseball cap on, dressed in blue shirt and jeans, but apart from that just an average Joe. I wish I could help you, I really do, but that was literally all that I saw. They got into the car, it started and they drove off. Melody didn't look distressed; she looked happy to be sitting there.'

'Thank you, we might need to come back again. Is that okay? We could bring you some mug shots and pictures of vehicles to look at.'

He glared at Morgan. 'You could bring the entire photographic archives from every person on Facebook, I still wouldn't recognise him. I'm sorry, but that would be a waste of your time and mine.'

She bit her tongue. She wanted to tell him to stop being such a dick, but she didn't.

Ben took over. 'Well, we'll be in touch whether you think you could recognise him or not. Melody's body is in a refrigerator in the mortuary, and her mum will never get to talk to her daughter again, so I don't think it would hurt you to look through some photographs.'

Mr Whitehouse opened his mouth to say something then

realised it might be better if he didn't. He gave a curt nod of his head.

'Which shop do you buy your newspaper from?' Morgan asked him with a smile.

'Brockle's News. Why?'

'I just wondered, thank you. I suppose that's it for now then if you have nothing else. I'll leave you a card with my direct contact number on, and if you think of anything or see the vehicle again could you give me a ring anytime, day or night?'

'Yes.'

They stood up, leaving him wringing his fingers and staring down at the floor. Morgan closed the door gently behind her and they walked back to their car, where Sam and Tina were sitting against the bonnet.

Tina looked at Morgan. 'Anything?'

'Now we know where Melody was taken from, and the description of the man matches Chloe's kidnapper. Black baseball cap, tall, dressed in blue shirt and jeans, and driving a white vehicle. But Melody wasn't taken by force, she knew the person, or sympathised with them – offered to help them. So we need to speak to Jade and ask her about anyone with a white car that her daughter would have felt comfortable enough getting a lift from. Sam, before you guys go for your break, would you check the newsagents and see if they have Mr Whitehouse going in like he said he did?'

'Yeah, we're picking up a pizza from Gino's, so it's on the way.'

'Thank you.'

At the mention of Gino's, Morgan's stomach let out a loud groan. It was her favourite pizza place, and she hadn't thought about food until now. When they were in the car Ben reached over to rest his hand on her thigh.

'Smart move.'

'What?'

'Getting Sam to check the CCTV at the newsagents. I don't like Mr Whitehouse, there is definitely something off about him.'

'You felt it too?'

He nodded. 'I did, but being weird doesn't make him a killer or I'd be locking him up now.'

She began to laugh, so hard that her eyes were watering. A sharp knock on her window made her jerk her head towards it to see a dishevelled Jade standing there. Immediately, she felt awful.

Ben started the engine so she could put the window down.

'Jade.'

'Morgan, have you got any news?'

'Not yet, but there is a lot going on so we should have some very soon. Do you need a lift anywhere?'

Ben was looking around for Caroline the FLO, but she wasn't in sight.

'No, I wanted to go for a walk. It's a lovely afternoon and I wanted to clear my head. I wanted to go to the riverside and look at the—' She stopped talking, and Morgan reached out her hand to take hold of Jade's that were trembling as she held on to the side of the car.

'We can take you there, Jade, if that's what you'd like to do.'

'Of course we can, hop in.' Ben smiled at Jade, and Morgan felt her breath catch in the back of her throat. He was so genuinely charming it made it hard to focus.

'If you're sure, I don't want to waste your time.'

'Jade, we were coming to speak to you anyway, so this is perfect timing. How have you been today?'

She got into the back of the car and answered Ben. 'In denial I think is the best way to describe it. I kept thinking that you two were mistaken and that any moment Melody would walk through the door. I lay awake all night listening for her key to turn in the lock, but when it got to five, I must have given up and fallen asleep. When I woke up it was only a couple of hours ago. How did I sleep so well knowing that my daughter was dead?'

Morgan couldn't answer but Ben did.

'It's the exhaustion, the fatigue after such a huge shock; the crying and dealing with everyone takes such an emotional toll on you that you end up sleeping for hours. Or at least I did, once I got that first twenty-four hours over. I don't think you'll sleep like that again for a long time. The nights turn into days when the full extent of how much you are grieving kicks in.'

'Good, because I felt like a traitor, sleeping soundly knowing my baby was in a mortuary. It was morally wrong.'

Morgan considered how to broach the subject of Mr Whitehouse without alarming her. 'We spoke to your neighbour, Mr Whitehouse,' she began.

Jade nodded. 'He's okay, I know he comes across as a bit odd, but he means well. What did Jeff have to say?'

'He said he saw Melody yesterday morning chatting to a guy in a white vehicle that had broken down. He also said she got in and seemed perfectly happy to do so. Jade, I need you to think really hard about this, do either of you know anyone who drives a white Nissan or Peugeot, possibly an SUV?'

She shook her head. 'Not off the top of my head, at least not well enough to remember clearly. That makes it a hundred times worse if Mel knew who he was and she went with him willingly. He took her trust and betrayed it in the worst possible way that he could. Morgan, we have lots of customers, regular customers at the café, and Mel worked every weekend. It could be anyone.'

Morgan squeezed her eyes shut against the tidal wave of tiredness and pain that was beginning to throb inside of her head.

35

Cain pointed to the narrow alley that led to the back of the flats that he'd chased Alan Cooper from yesterday. 'You're going to have go knock on the door and see if he's there.'

'On my own?'

'You're a big girl now, Amy. I think you can handle knocking on a door without me holding your hand.'

'Fuck off, Cain.'

'Well, that's not very nice, is it? I wasn't nasty to you. I meant that you're an adult, you are capable of knocking on a door.'

He didn't get to finish because she punched him in his bicep.

'Ouch, violence is not the answer. Where is this coming from? Has someone upset you? Do you want to talk about it?'

'You, you've upset me and no, I bloody don't want to talk to you about you being an idiot.'

He thought she was a little pale. 'What's wrong?'

'I think I shouldn't be going to face Cooper on my own, that's all.'

'Okay, but if he kicks off when he sees me that might be even worse, and you'll wish that you had.'

She looked down at her hands which were clasped across her tummy. 'I'm pregnant, and I don't want to risk anything.'

Cain looked at her stomach, then at her. 'Congratulations, that's brilliant. I bet Jack is over the moon.'

'Jack told me to get rid of it. He's not happy and now I don't know what to do, but until I make my mind up, I don't want to do anything stupid, and working with you often leads me to make really bad decisions.'

Cain shrugged; he couldn't argue that one with her because between the pair of them they did manage to get into their fair share of scrapes.

'Well, he's an arse. Do you want me to have a friendly word in his ear? Have you told the boss?'

'I haven't told anyone except you and Jack. I don't want to be put on light duties and stuck in the office all day. It would drive me insane. No, I don't want you to mention it to Jack either, but thank you, it's kind of you, but not right at this moment.'

'Amy, it may have escaped your notice, but you work in an office with colleagues who spend more time fighting and what not than doing anything else. It might be a good idea for you to be stuck in that office for the foreseeable future, or at least until you know what you want to do. If you do decide you want me to talk to Jack, just say the word, I'll do it.' He flexed his muscles, and she laughed, but her eyes began to well up.

'I'm going soft, it must be my hormones, but thank you, Cain, that means a lot. Although, I don't think you beating him up will help the situation, do you?'

'Did I say anything of the sort? Right, well you wait here, and I'll go knock. If you hear shouting, call it in, okay? And if Cooper tries to run again, do not get out of this car. He's a piece of work and won't think twice about hurting you if you get in his way.'

'I won't.'

'Good, makes a change you doing as you're told. I don't know who is worse, you or that Morgan.'

'Definitely Morgan.'

He nodded. 'Yeah, I think you're right. Listen out for me though, okay? I'm at a disadvantage today. I can't breathe through my nostrils and therefore I can't run after him if he does, and give chase.'

She put the window down as far as it would go, and Cain strode towards the alley a little more hesitantly than he had yesterday, but that was before Cooper broke his nose and gave him two black eyes that made him look as if he'd been inside the ring with Tyson Fury and lost, badly. He turned back to Amy, giving her a thumbs up before disappearing into the shadows only to come out on the other side of the secret garden, or that's what it felt like. There was a woman with a small hand trowel digging about in one of the flowerbeds. She turned to look at him and her expression hardened.

'Are you lost?'

He shook his head.

'Because we don't allow your sort to hang around here. We don't let anyone drug deal in the close. There are cameras all over, so you best find somewhere else to do your business.'

The silver-haired woman was as feisty as his gran and looked almost as old, and his gran was eighty-two.

'I'm a detective.'

She threw back her head and laughed, such a loud, braying laugh that he couldn't help grinning at her. When she finally composed herself, she said. 'Yeah, right. Is that what you call yourselves these days?'

Cain wasn't sure whether he was insulted because she thought he looked like a thuggish drug dealer or amused. He fished his warrant card out of his pocket and held it out to her.

'Scouts honour, I'm Detective Constable Cain Robson and I'm looking for a guy called Alan Cooper who is living with Jackie. Have you seen him around today?'

She placed the trowel down in the soil and glanced up to the flats.

'That big man, yes, he came back earlier but she didn't let him in, and he stormed off. I don't like him; he has that air about him that he's not to be trusted. I'm sorry I can't be any more help, but Jackie is in. She hasn't left her flat all day.'

'How do you know?'

'I've been out here pottering around all morning. That's Jackie's flat.' She pointed to the one on the second floor.

He nodded. 'Thank you, I appreciate that.'

He moved to go up the stairs, and she called after him. 'So, who broke your nose?'

Cain turned to her and smiled. 'That big man you don't trust got a bit angry with me yesterday when I arrested him.'

She began to laugh again. 'You could have kicked his backside. Why didn't you?'

'He caught me by surprise.'

'Happens, I suppose. I'm Marjorie, by the way, nice to meet you, Detective, and I'm sorry I thought you were a drug dealer.'

Cain shrugged. 'You're forgiven, thank you for your help, Marjorie, and your garden looks beautiful. You keep it lovely.'

He wasn't sure, but he thought he saw a faint blush creep up her neck and cheeks. 'Thank you,' she said and turned away so he couldn't see. He liked her a lot, and he thought he would phone his gran later to see how she was, as it had been too long.

He knocked on Jackie's door, but there was no reply, so he lifted the letter box.

'Jackie, it's the police. Can I talk to you about Alan?'

Movement inside the flat as someone came towards the

front door made him hopeful, and he put his hands together in the prayer position and glanced up at the sky.

'What about him?'

'I need to know where he is or when you last saw him.'

The sound of the door opening with a safety chain on echoed around the space, and he saw one eye peering at him through the gap.

'Who are you? I don't know you.'

Before he could open his mouth, Marjorie shouted loudly, 'It's okay, Jackie, he's legit. I've seen his warrant card; you can talk to him.'

The chain rattled as it was slid open, and the door was thrown back as Jackie peered down at Marjorie. 'Thank you.'

She stared at Cain's bruised face. 'What happened to you?'

'Alan Cooper.'

'Ouch, I don't want him back here. Can you stop him coming back?'

'I can try, but if he turns up ring 999 and we'll do the rest. Are we okay to talk about him, Jackie? Did he ever hurt you?'

She shook her head. 'No, he was okay, but I think that's because he had nowhere else to go when Susan threw him out. She thought we'd slept together, but we hadn't. I mean, we almost did but then she got it in her head that we had and the next thing he's knocking on my door with a holdall full of his clothes and a face like a sad puppy. I let him in and told him he could stay a couple of nights, but not for long because these flats are small. They're not meant for guys his size. No offence, I know you're a big guy. But, when I heard he'd been arrested yesterday I got scared and I don't even know why he got arrested, but I decided to not let him back in. I put his stuff in his bag and left it out on the balcony for him. He came back earlier around eight a.m., but I didn't let him in. I don't want anything to do with him.'

Cain was out of breath for her. She hadn't taken a pause for air the entire conversation.

'Susan Evans was found dead earlier today, and we're trying to locate him.'

Jackie let out a gasp so loud that Marjorie stopped digging and looked up.

'No, she isn't?'

'I'm afraid so. I'm sorry, were you close?'

'We were until Alan got in the way. Oh no, poor Paige, she must be heartbroken.'

'That's the thing, we can't find Paige or Alan. Do you know where he could be? Does he have any other friends, any place he could be stopping? Do you know where Paige could be?'

Cain felt as if he'd returned the favour by bombarding Jackie with multiple questions.

She shook her head. 'I don't know, I don't know Paige's friends, I don't know Alan's either, although Susan always said he was a bit of a loner. If you find Paige, tell her she's welcome to stay here, my door is always open.'

Cain thought that might just be the statement of the century. She'd stolen Alan and now was offering Paige a bed in the same place as her mum's ex.

'I will. If he comes back, we need you to ring 999, Jackie, it's very important.'

'I will, of course I will. Oh no, I don't know what to do. I feel so bad.'

Cain held up his hand to stop her before she continued to talk endlessly. 'There is nothing you can do, leave that to us. All you have to do is keep yourself safe.'

She nodded, and he turned to go back to the car when she called after him. 'I'm not a bad person, it all just got a bit messy.'

He smiled at her, then she ducked back inside her flat, closing the door.

'A bit messy, that's the understatement of the year,' Marjorie muttered. 'He's a killer then?'

'You have good hearing. No, I'm not saying that but he's definitely a person of interest; and the same applies to you, if you see him.'

'I'll ring the police; I don't want anything to do with the creep and yes, my hearing is impeccable. It's my eyes that let me down.'

Cain smiled at her. 'Thank you, take care.'

'You too, I'd learn to duck if I was you and save that pretty face from anymore damage.'

It was his turn to throw back his head and roar with laughter. He walked to the car with a huge grin on his face, back to where Amy was glaring at him, but he smiled at her.

'He's not here.'

'Good, sounded like you were at the comedy club, not investigating a murder.'

He frowned at her. 'Are you hangry, Amy? You know you get mad when you need feeding.'

'No, I just didn't expect to hear so much happiness coming from that direction. I was hanging on to my last nerve waiting for some kind of fight to happen while you were having the time of your life.'

'Some people are funny, some are kind and most are arseholes. I met a funny old lady; she thought I was dealing.'

This made Amy grin. 'You do look like a bad 'un.'

'Yeah, I guessed that when Marjorie accused me, thanks for the support.'

'What are we doing now then?'

'Going to update the boss then go get you something to eat, because I can't deal with you on a good day when you're hungry, never mind when you're hormonal.'

She looked as if she was going to punch him again, but he threw her off tack by leaning over and giving her a gentle squeeze. 'I'm here for you if you need anything, you know that, right?'

Amy nodded, then turned away from him, and Cain marvelled at how much someone's life could change in the blink of an eye. But he would keep his word; he'd be there for her just like he would Ben or Morgan. It was soft, but he knew how lucky he was to work with colleagues who he loved and were his best friends too.

36

Ben stopped the car as near to the crime scene where Melody's body had been found and turned to Jade. 'Are you sure about this?'

'Yes, I need to know and see it with my own eyes.'

His phone began to ring, and he whispered, 'I'm sorry, I have to take this.'

Morgan got out of the car and opened the door for Jade, who nodded at her. As they walked slowly towards the small, wooded area, they came across a row of flowers, teddy bears, candles and cards in plastic bags. Jade stopped to look at them.

'Oh, everyone knew about this place but me.'

Morgan felt bad for her. 'News spreads fast, there were a lot of people who gathered when they realised something terrible had happened. How lovely that they left these tributes though.'

Jade nodded, fresh tears threatening to fall. 'Yes, it is very kind of them. Do you think they knew Mel or felt sorry for her?'

'I'd have to read the cards; I would say both. She was a lovely girl, Jade, and she did not deserve what happened to her, I'm so sorry.'

Those tears that had been making Jade's eyes sparkle finally began to flow down her cheeks as she nodded.

'We can take a moment to read the cards if you feel up to it.'

She shook her head. 'No, I can't do it. It's lovely but it hurts too much, and I feel as if I might never stop crying.'

There were still strands of blue and white crime scene tape strung around the trees, sealing the area off, that should have been taken down and Morgan cursed under her breath at the insensitive officers who had neglected to do this once Ben had released the scene.

'We can go under the tape; in fact, if you give me a minute, I'll take the tape down, as it doesn't need to be there now.'

She charged towards a tree, untying the end, and began to fold it up as she walked to the next and did the same, until she had a huge, messy roll of tape in her hands. Jade was staring into the trees.

'Would you like to go a little further or is this near enough?'

'I need to know the exact place, Morgan; did you see her lying there?'

'Yes, I did.'

Morgan reached out for Jade's hand and led her further into the place she'd first seen the girl's body.

'Did she look scared?'

'No, she didn't, she looked like she was asleep. That's what the guy who phoned it in said, he thought that she was sleeping.'

Jade nodded. 'Good, I'm glad. I hate the thought of her being so scared and alone.'

Morgan squeezed Jade's hand. 'I don't think she knew what was happening. I think it was so fast it took her by surprise.'

'I hope so, I really do.' Jade was staring at the ground, and she turned to Morgan. 'Thank you, I'm good to go now. I couldn't bear the thought of not knowing where she had been found, and I told myself it was better that I didn't, but I kind of feel more at peace now, knowing that she wasn't terrified at her moment of death.'

Morgan didn't know about that, she thought that maybe Melody had been beyond terrified, but she didn't say that to Jade. She needed to take what little comfort she could get from this tragedy, and if this helped, who was she to disagree with her? They walked back to the car, slowly, where Ben was standing waiting for them. Jade didn't speak, but he opened the door for her and made sure she was in and had her seat belt fastened before gently closing it. Morgan felt completely useless. What were they supposed to do to make this better? Ben smiled at her, but it was a sad smile, and she knew how deep Jade's pain was affecting him.

'Are you okay?' she whispered to him.

'Yes, how are you?' She shrugged because she wasn't okay. She was desperate to find the person responsible for this and locate Paige. 'Any news?'

'Cain didn't locate Alan, and Cassie hasn't had any luck tracking Paige. She said her trail ended at the entrance to the cul-de-sac, meaning she had to have got into a car because it stops dead.'

'Let's get Jade home and regroup.'

They got into the car and as Ben set off driving, Jade leaned forward. 'Can you stop the car, please? I think I'll walk back from here.'

He pulled over. 'It's two miles, Jade, are you sure you want to do that?'

'I need to do something; I'm never going to be able to settle at home anyway. I may as well slowly walk back and get some fresh air.' She opened the car door. 'Thank you both, please let me know if you find him.' Then she closed it gently and began to walk back along the riverside.

'Do you think she's okay?'

Ben shrugged. 'Hard to say, but she's an adult and I can't blame her wanting to clear her head a little bit.'

'No, I feel like I could do with that myself. Was that Cain?'

'Yes, no sign of Cooper. He came back around eight this morning and got his stuff that Jackie had kindly packed and left outside for him.'

'Where are we at now then because I literally cannot think straight.'

'Briefing back at the station because neither can I. I'll call the team back.'

Ben had sat at Morgan's desk and between them they had written a list of what needed to be done.

'That's a big list, do you think it's time to call in some help?'

To Morgan's surprise he nodded. 'I think so, I'll call Claire Williams and ask her what to do. I thought she may have offered her services as soon as Susan Evans's murder came in, but I guess if she's not on duty she won't know about it.'

Marc came striding in and Morgan had to admit he looked a little perplexed as he sank onto Amy's chair. His tie was missing, and his top two buttons were undone. She was used to Ben doing this when he was under a lot of stress, but Marc never seemed to lose his cool.

'What's happening?' He spoke directly to Ben.

'A lot, it's a shitshow, boss, that's for sure.'

Marc laughed and all the tension that had been fizzing in the air melted away. 'That's one way to put it. So, what do we think? Are Melody's and Susan's deaths connected? Is Chloe's kidnapping a part of this? And have we found Paige?'

'I can't confirm anything,' Ben replied. 'The vehicle that Chloe was in matches the description we have of the one Melody was seen getting into the morning she died. Melody Carrick is seventeen years old, college student, killed on her way to college, and her body left outside in the open. Susan Evans is a fifty-four-year-old woman, brutally killed inside her own home. Her daughter is still missing.'

Amy and Cain sauntered in. Marc glanced at Cain's face and whistled. 'What a mess, thought you'd have blocked that, big man.'

Cain didn't look amused. 'Yeah, well it caught me by surprise.'

Amy was standing next to Marc, her arms crossed. 'Do you mind?'

He looked at her, realised he was in her seat and got up; instead, sitting on the end of the desk taking up Ben's usual position. Ben stood up clutching the ripped piece of A4 paper that Morgan had torn from the notebook on her desk.

'Should we go through this? Amy, do you want to write it up on the board?'

She shook her head. 'Feel a bit off, can Morgan do it? My head is pounding.'

Morgan glanced at her; she did look paler than usual. Morgan had a pounding headache too, but she stood up and uncapped a marker pen ready to go. Ben nodded.

'Ready.'

She smiled at him.

'Right, well we have found a witness. One Jeff White-house who lives a few doors down from Melody. He saw her talking to a guy with a broken-down car that was in the middle of the road. He said she was chatting to him, didn't look worried or scared and even got in the car with him. We've asked Melody's mother if she can think of anyone else Melody knew, or would have trusted to drive her, and she can't think of a single person. It's likely this was a stranger who asked for Melody's help. Someone unassuming and trustworthy. We need to find this guy like yesterday. So, I need a map of the area, and all the local shops marked off and checked for

CCTV to see if we can capture the car leaving and which direction it went in, even better if they caught the number plate. We did this before, but now we have the exact location of the car, so we can be more accurate.' He waited for Morgan to write it down, then continued. 'We've confirmed Jeff did indeed go straight to the local newsagent for his paper when this happened, so this isn't a story he's concocted to give himself an alibi.'

Ben looked over at Amy, who was shifting in her seat. 'Amy, if you're feeling a bit under the weather do you want to call it a day and get yourself home?'

She shook her head. 'No, boss, I'm good.'

'Well, if you change your mind text me and get off, okay? If you're okay to stay a bit longer, would you do a background check on Whitehouse for me?'

'Yes, boss.'

'Thank you. I'll ask the PCSOs and see if Mads has any spare officers to go check the shops out, then we can hopefully find the car. Next, we still have a missing girl. Paige Evans, Susan's daughter. Priority is to find her. Have we traced her phone? The dog followed her trail to the end of the street then it stopped, so she left in a vehicle. Morgan, can you ring around the local taxi firms to see if they picked her up?'

'Yes, boss,' replied Morgan.

'So, we have Paige's mum, Susan Evans, who was discovered deceased this morning by Morgan and, correct me if I'm wrong, but we have no idea where her ex-partner, Alan Cooper, is, who you arrested yesterday?'

'That's right, boss, he was last seen by the woman whose flat he was staying at around eight a.m. Took his stuff, which she left outside for him, and left the area, also seen by her elderly neighbour Marjorie. Which leads me to the question: did he go back to see if Susan would take him back? They maybe got into a fight, and he killed her. Then drove off in a panic and maybe took Paige with him. Why would she get in a car with him if he'd killed her mum though?'

Morgan turned from the board. 'Maybe he took her by force? Killed her and took her body away?'

Marc, who had kept quiet up to now, shook his head. 'Susan Evans's killer was in a mad rage and left her body in situ, so if he'd killed Paige, too, he would have left her there too. He's already up to his neck in it and looking at a life sentence, so why make life hard and try to move Paige's body yet leave her mum's? It doesn't make sense.'

Ben was nodding. 'So, we're not thinking the murders of Melody and Susan are connected? There are no similarities between them.'

Morgan was shaking her head. 'Melody was on her way to the sixth form college. Does Paige go to the same college?'

Ben was nodding. 'Let's find out.'

'If Paige was right and it is Alan Cooper, then Susan figured it out, they got into an argument, and he killed her to shut her up. He's our only link between all these cases: he's Susan's ex and he's driving a car that matches the description of our POI in Melody's and Chloe's cases.'

'Can we chase up the DNA from Melody Carrick see if there's a hit? Did you get DNA from Cooper when you booked him in, Cain?'

Cain nodded. 'I did, fingerprints, DNA swab, it will all be on his record, so if we get a hit and it's a match we'll know for sure.'

'Do we know what kind of car he drives?' Ben paused. 'Why do we not know what kind of car he drives?'

'I'm on it,' said Amy, who didn't look up from her keyboard, her fingers flying across the keys. 'He has a white Nissan Micra.'

A collective sigh went around the room.

'Hey, it might mean that he's not connected to Melody's murder, we're certainly not ruling him out for Susan or Paige

Evans, don't be despondent. So, we are going to split into three teams. One for Melody, for Susan and for Paige. Morgan, I want you running with Melody's, you have a close connection with her mum, Jade. Is that okay?'

'Of course.'

'Cain, you and Amy take Paige. I will deal with Susan's enquiries. That way we can keep track of what's going on without getting overwhelmed and losing stuff. I'm waiting for a phone call from Claire Williams at HQ. I've requested some help, but she hasn't got back to me yet. Boss, what do you think if we steal a couple of PCSOs to help with enquiries, and they can work with us for the foreseeable?'

'Who are you thinking about?'

'Tina and Sam, they're experienced, they found the witness yesterday and they can be trusted to get out there and do what we ask.'

He shrugged. 'I'm happy to run with that. Do you want me to ask their sergeant if we can have them?'

'Yes, please. I think that until we get a reply from HQ, we're going to need all the help we can get.'

Marc left to go and find whoever was covering the community team.

Morgan reminded Ben, 'They said they didn't want to join us though.'

'They were joking, I think they will.'

Half an hour later the door opened and in walked Tina and Sam. 'Are you giving us shedloads of house to house again, Ben?'

He smiled at them. 'Not as much. Did Marc tell you why I wanted to see you?'

'He said something about us joining your team, but he's always on one so we didn't take any notice.'

Morgan and Cain both sniggered, and Ben ignored them.

'Yeah, he is a bit up and down. I seriously need your help,

ladies, if you could spare yourselves for a couple of days to help
us with our enquiries.'

Tina gave Sam a side-eye, and Sam replied, 'What exactly
does that entail?'

'I need a list of shops visiting for CCTV enquiries, then any
other tasks one of the team pass to you to complete. Are you up
for that?'

'What's in it for us?'

'You can wear your own clothes, work whatever shifts you
want, and I'll provide lunches or teas depending on what shift
you're working.'

They both grinned at him. 'We're ready to start, when do
you want us?'

'Now, please, and thank you. Welcome to the team, be sure
to write your beverage preference on the list stuck to the fridge
door by the kitchen, because Cain makes crap coffee if you
don't tell him how you like it with step by step instructions.'

Cain interrupted. 'Can I just say that I don't, he's just
particular.'

Tina looked at Cain, then Morgan. 'Is a face injury manda-
tory to be a part of this team?'

Ben began to laugh. 'I wouldn't expect either of you to put
yourselves in a position where that might be a possibility. Those
two are the exceptions to the rule.'

'You can say that again,' replied Tina. 'Right then, we'll go
get changed and see you soon. Can we tell Mads you've
promoted us? It will wind him up big time.'

'You can tell him what you want, just don't mention the free
lunches, he might get jealous.' Ben winked at them and left the
room, their laughter echoing down the corridor.

37

It was all too much; it had got out of hand too fast and now he was sitting in a dark room, eyes closed and taking slow, deep breaths to try and think his way out of the mess he was in.

Muffled knocking and shouts from the small room down the hall kept interrupting his thoughts, breaking his concentration, and he was tempted to go down and put her out of her misery. He needed to think, be clear about what he was going to do not just with her but with the trouble he had caused by not being able to ignore the growing pressure inside of his mind that told him he needed to kill.

He shouldn't have taken her; this was reckless and more than a little stupid, but she had headed towards the front gate after walking in the woods that bordered the edge of the houses at the same time he'd walked out of the door, and looked at him as if she knew what he'd done. He'd had no choice. He couldn't kill her here and he couldn't let her go inside the house; some-body could have seen them talking and she would know that he had killed her mum, not that there was anyone around, but he didn't want to risk it. He'd asked what she was up to and she said she was thinking about going to her friends because her mum was drunk again. He'd offered her a lift and she'd accepted, despite the look of fear in her eyes. She had been afraid of saying no, of appearing to be rude when she should have, for saying no would have saved her life, now it was hanging by the balance of whether she would live or die. He hadn't made up his mind yet. She knew him, he knew her, and she knew what he'd done, what he could do. He also knew what she was capable of, and she was a sneaky, trouble-making little shit. But did she deserve to die for it? He guessed it depended on whether he had any other alternative. The banging got louder, and he jumped up off the bed. Striding down the hallway he threw open the door where Paige was hammering on the wall with the small stool that had been tucked under the dresser. She dropped it in fright as he'd thrown the door open.

'For Christ's sake, what are you trying to do?' He strode towards her and swiped the stool off the floor. 'This isn't my house, so don't treat it with such disrespect.'

He towered over her but there was defiance in those green eyes, and she stood her ground, which he grudgingly admired. She was tough, a pain in the arse but a tough one, and he liked that in her. 'You know this, all of this is your fault. If you had kept your nose out of my business, we wouldn't be here, would we? Your stupid, alcoholic mother wouldn't be dead, and I wouldn't have to be babysitting you.'

Was that a look of fear that had crept into those eyes at the mention of her mother's death, and he realised it might not be fear. It might be shock. She didn't know Susan was dead.

'Oops, my bad, I didn't know you weren't aware of that titbit of information, but never mind, that's how that one goes. She was a pain in the arse and now she isn't. I've done you a favour. Moving on, let's get to the problem of you.'

He jabbed a finger in the air at her. 'What do I do with you? Answers on a fucking postcard, please.'

Paige's knees buckled under her, and she slid to the floor, all the fight from moments ago vanished. She didn't look at him and her eyes focused on the vulgar, patterned carpet in front of her.

He knelt down. 'Look, it wasn't supposed to happen like it did, and I am sorry you found out like this, but I need to think and for me to be able to think clearly, I need silence. You hammering on the wall and screaming through that gag are not helping me to do that. It could lead me to making more bad decisions and I seriously don't think you want that.'

He cupped her chin in his hand and tilted her face to look at his. 'I'll get you something to drink in a little bit, but for now can you sit here like a good girl and shut the fuck up?'

Standing up he checked the room for other weapons she could use. He was surprised she hadn't tried to attack him with the stool, but she didn't have much hand movement with the restriction of the rope, and her feet tied together meant she could only shuffle. She couldn't make any quick moves in his direction. Satisfied there was nothing else she could use, he backed out of the door, never taking his eyes off her, and closed it.

He went back to the master bedroom with its plush carpeted floors and rich, cotton bedsheets, where he threw himself back onto the soft mattress that enveloped his whole body like a huge hug. He could get used to this level of luxury if only he could afford it. He picked up the box with the few pieces of jewellery he'd kept for all these years and held it close to his heart, picking up the new addition of the fine, broken chain he'd ripped from Melody's neck then closed his eyes once more. There was only silence from down the hall which was much more pleasing to the ear.

38

Sam and Tina had gone off wearing their own clothes to talk to all the shopkeepers and businesses near where Melody was taken. Amy was waiting for a cell site analysis to come back from Paige's mobile, and Morgan was on her way to the college; she was keen to get further testimonies from anyone who knew Paige and Melody as well as confirming a connection between them. Did Melody know the man driving that car? Could one of her friends or teachers shed light on this as Jade hadn't been able to? Ben hadn't flinched when she'd asked if she could go and speak to the staff and students. How could he, they were understaffed and overworked, and the number of enquiries that needed to be followed up on were extensive.

Her mind kept drifting to Paige and if she was okay. What if Paige had killed Melody and Susan? She was only seventeen, but it didn't mean she wasn't capable. Paige had seemed so genuine when she had talked about Alan the first time they had met, but Morgan had come face to face with more killers than she'd ever thought possible. She'd spoken to them as if they were victims, witnesses... and they'd been hiding a dark side she'd only discovered just in time.

The college was on a treelined street of magnificent oaks, dark and miserable in the winter, dappled in shade in the summer, giving a welcome relief to the students. She had walked here every morning when she attended, as she didn't have a car or a dad who could drop her off. Stan didn't drive, or he hadn't since he'd got arrested for drunk driving after Sylvia's funeral. So, rain or shine she'd made the trek to the sixth form college because she had been determined to get the grades to become a police officer. If there was one thing she had learned from her adoptive mum's suicide, it had been to follow your dreams and work hard towards your goals because you only got one shot at life, and she had desperately wanted to make hers count, and not waste it like those two had.

As Morgan crawled along at a snail's pace scanning all the cars that were parked up, she planned to write down the number plate of every white SUV type car she passed and then get Amy to run the plates on the system. It was better than the nothing they currently had. The majority of cars parked out here were smaller though, Fiat 500s, Minis, Citroens, plenty of white cars but not the model they needed to find.

A car beeped behind her, and she glanced in the rear-view mirror. This was more like it; looked like a bigger white car but not a Nissan or a Peugeot. She realised she was being a pain and driving like an idiot, so she sped up, holding her hand up to apologise. The car followed her into the car park then double parked on the yellow lines. Damn, it wasn't a car. It was more of a truck thing, and it had lawn mowers in the back. Morgan drove up and down the rows looking for a space, but had no luck as they were all full. She realised she should have taken a leaf out of the maintenance guy's books and parked on the double yellows. There was a gap just big enough for her to squeeze this car into, though she didn't even know what kind of car she was driving. Cautiously she managed to manoeuvre it into the space without taking off the bumper. If she damaged another car,

Mads would definitely revoke her licence. He might even make her retake her driving authority test and she didn't have the time for that. It would be three days out of her life she wouldn't get back, three days further away from finding Paige and Melody's killer. The car park had two white SUVs, a Vauxhall and an Audi. Christ, she couldn't be any further away from something useful if she tried. She wrote the registration numbers on the back of her hand anyway then phoned Amy and passed them over to her.

The reception area was full of students passing through on their way to classes, and she waited in line to speak to the receptionist who was on the phone and dealing with enquiries at the same time. After sending a new student in the right direction she smiled at Morgan. It was such a warm smile it made her shoulders relax for the first time in hours.

'Can I help you?'

'I really hope so.' Morgan looked around, not sure she wanted to have this discussion in such a public area. She pointed to the back office at the same time taking out her warrant card to show the smiling woman. 'Could I have a word in private?'

She nodded. 'Yes, of course, go in there and take a seat. I'll get someone to cover for me.'

Morgan walked behind the desk and into the back office, which smelled of fresh coffee, a stark reminder of The Coffee Pot and poor Jade. The woman walked in and closed the door.

'I'm Mary, can I get you a coffee or tea?'

'I'm okay, but thank you. It smells so good in here. I'm Detective Morgan Brookes and we're investigating the murder of Melody Carrick.'

Mary's smile was replaced by a sad expression. 'It's so terrible, Melody was such a lovely young lady. I still can't believe it, that she won't walk in smiling and asking how my weekend was.'

Morgan nodded. 'It must have been a terrible shock for you, for everyone. What I wanted to know was do you have another student who attends, Paige Evans? She's around the same age as Melody.'

Mary's eyes narrowed a little at the mention of Paige's name. 'Yes, we do. Is she in trouble again?'

So they are connected, Morgan thought. 'No, she's missing, and I wondered if the two of them knew each other or were in the same classes.'

'Oh, dear. I didn't mean to sound horrid, it's just Paige is a bit of a handful and spends more time in here annoying me than attending any of her classes. Has she fallen out with her mum again? She's a bit of a drinker and they don't always see eye to eye. I went to school with her mum, and she was even wilder than Paige is, but the drink took over and now she's a bit of a mess. What does Susan have to say about it? Has she reported her missing?'

Morgan didn't see the point in being evasive, although the news of her murder might not have hit social media yet because of the secluded place she lived in, it soon would. Nothing was private for very long anymore when the Facebook police were on one. 'I'm afraid Susan's dead. I found her body this morning.'

Mary let out a gasp so loud it made Morgan jump.

'Oh my God, what is going on? How is she dead? Did she choke on her own vomit or fall down the stairs and hit her head? It wouldn't surprise me.'

'She was murdered.'

Mary cupped a hand across her mouth. 'By whom? Plus Paige doesn't like her mum's boyfriend at all. Have you looked into him? She thinks he's a creep. I asked her if he ever, you know, tried to make a move on her but she said not. Said he was just a weirdo.'

'We're including him in our enquiries.'

Mary nodded, seemingly relieved by this news.

'But we haven't been able to locate Paige. We don't even know if she's aware of her mum's death. Is she in college today?'

Mary began to type onto the keyboard then looked up at her and shook her head. 'She hasn't been in for three days.'

'Damn, did she go to any of the same classes as Melody?'

More frenzied typing. 'Yes, they both study English Lit, that's the only class together.'

'When was Melody last in?'

'I know that because I was chatting to her – it was the day before yesterday.'

'Two days ago?'

Mary nodded. 'The tutor is Adam Hayes, he's in today if you'd like to speak to him.'

'That would be great, thanks. Could you also give me a printout of the students in that class, please?'

'I don't think they were friends, but they obviously knew each other. They are total opposites. Then again, I don't know everything, but Paige never mentioned hanging around with Melody. Her best friend is Alisa Halliday. I live next door but one to her and see the pair of them all the time. Have you spoken with her in case Paige is there?'

Morgan wanted to slap herself – she had completely forgotten about Alisa. She had assumed Paige was kidnapped, but was this another fake disappearance from these two girls? 'I'm going there next.'

'Those two are as thick as thieves, wouldn't surprise me if she's there.'

Morgan wasn't so sure; she didn't think Alisa's mum would be wanting Paige hanging around after the last incident, but still she needed to check it out. 'Where can I find Mr Hayes?'

'I can give him an instant message and ask him to come here. It will save you wandering all over the college; it's a bit of a maze.'

She smiled at Mary and nodded, hoping that Mr Hayes was

going to be a prime suspect, but the man that walked in five minutes later was in his sixties at least, and he had a walking stick that he leaned heavily on. He didn't look as if he was fit enough to kill and carry Melody's body anywhere or fight with Susan Evans, but she knew better than that and it was possible he was fitter than her or Cain. She was judging him by the slow walk, but he looked as if he genuinely needed the stick to support him as he dragged his right leg a little, and not using it to add a touch of drama. He held his hand out, and she shook it.

'I'm so saddened by the tragic death of Melody. She was a lovely, bright, kind student who had so much potential to do great things.'

Morgan nodded. 'It's heartbreaking.'

'Have you caught the killer?'

The question was blunt, and it stung a lot more than it should, coming from this seemingly nice older man.

'I'm afraid we haven't. Did Melody have any problems with any other students or members of staff whilst she was here?'

He shook his head. 'Not that I know about, she was so easy-going, she didn't fall out with her peers or have problems with staff.'

Morgan nodded. 'Thank you, and now Paige Evans is missing, and I discovered her mum dead this morning. I really need to find Paige and tell her the awful news. Do you know where she could be?'

He shook his head. 'I'm sorry, Paige hasn't been in much at all this term. She has potential too, but she's not interested in learning. How awful, the poor girl. I literally have no idea where she could be. You don't think she's come to some kind of harm? I really hope not, that would be terrible.'

Morgan squeezed her eyes shut for a moment then looked at him. 'Truthfully, I don't know. It's a real possibility, but I'm hoping she took off and doesn't realise what's happened.'

Mr Hayes did something so unexpected that it made her

eyes water. He pulled a chair next to her and took hold of her hand. 'I can see you are holding a lot of guilt, worry and sadness inside those eyes, Detective, but I want you to know that whatever is happening, none of it is your fault.'

She was taken aback but she softened, and he carried on. 'You are the one who I suspect is working much longer hours than you should and running off little more than caffeine and snacks to try and stop this evil that is ruling all of our worlds at the moment. I think you should take a moment to reflect on just how amazing you are, and your team. It seems that the police nowadays get nothing but bad press and yes, a lot of it is called for but those few bad apples don't define the rest of you wonderful people who don't get enough credit for the terrible job that you do. I wish I could give you more, but I don't know anything that could help. This is what I do know.'

Morgan had to swallow the lump in her throat at his kind words. His blue eyes crinkled when he smiled at her, and she knew without a doubt that he must be the most wonderful teacher.

'Melody and Paige tolerated each other; they were polite and kind, but they didn't sit together or particularly chat a lot. They had nothing in common, there wasn't anything to draw them together. Paige is a clever girl if she'd only stop being so stubborn, whereas Melody worked hard for her grades, and she got good grades because of her commitment to her classes. However they are both very streetwise and I do not see either of them going off with a stranger. I would imagine that whoever killed Melody knew her, and that makes me even sadder. How could someone want to extinguish such a kind, sparkling light such as Melody? So was it someone she dated, someone who was jealous of her, someone she thought she could trust and paid the price with her life for doing so? I really would not find it surprising to find out that Paige has decided enough was enough with her mum and the boyfriend that she was forever complaining about, or at least I hope she has. It would be very sad for the human race to lose two bright, sparkling beacons of hope for the future to some murderous person full of evil intent.'

'Thank you, that's very insightful,' she said.

She didn't tell him she thought the same, or that she thought he was very kind. He reminded her of her aunt Ettie, and she wondered if he was married; he didn't have a ring on but that meant nothing. The pair of them would get along just fine, she thought. But she squashed these thoughts. He could still be a suspect, and she needed to treat him as such. Were his comments about Melody untoward? He certainly liked her.

He tore one of the Post-it notes from the pad on Mary's desk and wrote his phone number and email address down then passed it to her. 'I am available whenever you need to ask me anything. I had nobody in class who I could point the finger at and say they are a bit shifty. Both girls got on well with the other students, there was nothing to make me feel worried for either of them, but if you have questions about anyone, then phone me.'

He stood up. 'I have to get back. I'm sorry there's nothing useful in what I've told you.'

'Thank you, you've been very helpful.'

He smiled at her. 'Take it easy on yourself, Detective.'

As he walked out, Mary blotted the corner of her eye with her sleeve. 'He's such a lovely man, he's taught here for almost twenty years.'

Then she passed Morgan a sheet of paper with some names on. She scanned the list, not seeing any that stood out, nobody she'd dealt with while working section and nobody that was flagged up on the Intel briefings as persons of interest regarding any drug dealing or crimes.

Morgan agreed he was, but she still had to ask. 'What kind of car does he drive?'

Mary shrugged. 'I think he has a Qashqai, but it's been in the garage all week.'

Morgan felt the hairs on the back of her neck begin to prickle. 'Do you know what colour?'

'It's white, he's forever complaining about how mucky it gets. He often slips the handyman money to power wash it for him. Why did you ask that?'

She smiled at her. 'No reason, I just feel as if I know him and wondered if he lived near to me.'

'I don't know, lovey, but he lives on Victoria Avenue, has done for years. I don't know the number, but he throws the most amazing end of summer party every year. Is that near you?'

'A couple of streets away. Thank you, Mary, I'm sorry to have taken you away from your desk.'

Morgan stood up, as lovely as he was, she was itching to do some Intel checks on him to see if anything interesting came up on Adam Hayes.

Ben was back at Susan Evans's house waiting for Declan to arrive. He began to knock on the neighbouring doors to double check if the houses were as empty as Morgan believed. There were no signs of life from any of them, which was weird. He didn't think that all of them would be second homes. *Would the council allow it?* He would ask Amy to speak to their contact, who could tell them where all the mysterious neighbours had disappeared to. Unless they hadn't been sold yet, but they had no for sale signs, and they all had curtains or blinds at the windows. He peered through one with a small gap in the curtains into a bland, very white room with no furniture. It was all a bit weird if you asked him.

He heard Declan's Audi as it drove into the cul-de-sac and pulled away from the window. Turning, he waved at him.

Declan got out of the car and shouted, 'It's no good, I saw you. There are laws against that you know. I have a friend who could arrest you for being a peeping Tom.'

Ben smiled at him. 'You're an idiot.'

Declan shrugged. 'I'm an eejit, my mammy always said so.'

'A clever one maybe but still an eejit. This street is weird, look at the houses, they are all finished yet no one is home, and that one is empty but there's no for sale signs or anything.'

'Have you looked on the website of the company selling them? Maybe they're under offer or there's a problem with building regulations preventing them from being inhabited.'

Ben shook his head. 'See, you're a clever boy. I didn't think of that.'

'Ah, you're just using flattery, my friend. What have we got this time? Is it something different? All I got on my memo from Susie was deceased woman, possible murder. She took the call. I was giving a tour to some student doctors around the mortuary, and by God do I feel old; they all looked as if they were fresh out of school.'

Ben was at least a couple of years older than his friend, and he flinched. 'You feel old? Try working with Morgan. I feel ancient.'

Declan laughed. 'I bet you don't feel so ancient in the bedroom though. I bet she keeps you on your toes.'

'A gentleman never discusses those kinds of things.' He grinned at him. 'But that's a yes, she does.'

'See, there is life in the old dog yet. So, is it a murder?'

He nodded. 'No doubt about it.'

'Then let's get the official business done, is that why I'm here, just for my professionalism?'

'Yes, I need your help, and I wanted to see your handsome face to brighten my day.'

Declan arched one eyebrow. 'Dear God, you are desperate, aren't you? And if that isn't the nicest thing you've ever said to me. Tell me, Benjamin, you're not feeling the pull towards my side of the bed, are you? Because, don't get me wrong, you have no idea how long I've fantasised about me and you, but I thought you were a full-on one-woman man.'

It was Ben's turn to laugh. 'Right, maybe that was too much flattery.'

'So, you haven't decided to leave Morgan and run away with me?'

He shook his head. 'I would if I was that way inclined, but no I'm hopelessly in love with her and failing miserably at the flattery.'

Declan lightly punched him in the arm. 'Thank God for that, I'm hopelessly in love with Theo, but I would have been tempted even though I've waited a good twenty years for you to give me that kind of attention.'

Declan had dressed himself in protective clothing while they'd been talking, and they began heading towards the house, his heavy case in one hand.

'How is Theo? We missed the quiz this week.'

'He's utterly gorgeous and still in love with God, which is a bit of a pain, but you know better an invisible man crush than a real flesh and blood one. How are you getting on with Melody Carrick's case? Do you think these are connected?'

And with the simplest of ease, they were back in full work mode.

Ben shrugged. 'I'm not sure, I'm thinking maybe this was the work of the victim's ex-partner who by all accounts is a creep, who is into serial killers. He also assaulted Cain and broke his nose when he brought him in for questioning, so he's violent too, but...'

'Ah, there is always a but.'

'But the chance of having two separate killers working at the same time in such a small, remote geographical area kind of goes against the odds.'

The pair of them signed into the crime scene, which was being guarded by Amber who smiled at them both, making Ben do a double take. Amber was usually miserable and full of attitude, but the last few months she seemed to have definitely thawed a little. She looked a lot more approachable smiling than she did with that permanent scowl on her face.

'Thanks, Amber, how are you?'

'I'm good, Ben, yourself?'

'Stressed.'

She nodded. 'I bet you are, this is never-ending.'

He knew she meant well, and she was right. The murders and horrible deaths did seem to be never-ending.

As they went into the house, Declan whispered, 'The ice maiden seems to be thawing out nicely.'

Ben shook his head. 'Maybe she was going through a rough patch.'

'She was going through something, maybe a personality transplant.'

Ben elbowed him. 'Shush, she can hear you.'

Declan turned; she was looking down at her phone. 'It's good, she's distracted.'

Ben let him go first; he didn't need to go in and get so up close and personal to Susan Evans's body this time. Declan let out the little whistle he did through his teeth when a crime scene was particularly bad. 'For the love of God, that is awful.'

Ben nodded, there was no disputing the facts it was awful.

'How did the killer get in? This room is in a state of disarray, yet the front door doesn't look damaged. Did he have a key, or do you think she let them in?'

Ben finished for him. 'She knew her killer, there is no damage or mess anywhere else except for in here, so she led whoever it was into this room without any suspicions about what was about to happen, I'm sure of that. Her seventeen-year-old daughter is also missing.'

Declan tilted his head a little. 'She is? Did she do this, do you think? Although, to be fair it would take some brute strength to throw someone with enough force to smash the table and manually strangle them. Does she look as if she is strong enough to be able to do this?'

He shrugged. 'I can't rule it out, but.'

'But what?'

'Bollocks, I, we, didn't search her room properly. Are you okay down here while I go see if she took any of her personal belongings with her? Wendy chased us out earlier; we didn't get the chance.'

He didn't wait for Declan to answer and bounded up the stairs, checking each room until he found Paige's. He looked at the messy room and wished Morgan was here. She was the expert on searching teenage girls' bedrooms for clues. He crossed to the window and opened it.

'Amber, can you come up here for a minute?'

He heard her running up the stairs. She stood at the door fixing her gaze on him, her eyes staring into his.

'Can you take a look and see if you think anything is missing?'

She glanced at the mess then back at Ben. 'What am I, some kind of expert on messy girls' rooms now?'

The attitude adjustment hadn't lasted very long.

'No, I thought you might be able to figure out if the important stuff was missing. You'll have more of an idea than me.'

She pulled a pair of blue gloves out of her pocket and snapped them on. 'Didn't Morgan do this earlier?'

He shook his head. 'Wendy threw us out and we got sidetracked.'

'Sloppy more like.'

But she stepped into the room, and he swapped places with her, watching from the doorway as she rifled through drawers and the wardrobe. She took her time looking through the Bisley drawers that were at the side of the bed and finally turned to Ben, holding up a purse and a phone.

'I'm not the expert, obviously I'm just section, but if you ask me, no teenager would go anywhere without their phone. The purse maybe because everyone has Apple Pay these days and you don't necessarily need cash, but I can't see her leaving her phone here. Also, I have no idea how much make-up she wore but there is a lot of it on the dresser and there are no gaps; there's foundation, mascara, eyeliner, lip gloss, those are the basics, even if you're sleeping at you friend's house you tend to take the basics with you.'

She pointed to a big frame on the wall above the dresser full of photos. 'She is wearing make-up on all of these; I don't see her going out without it.'

'You don't think she walked out of here with the intention of running away?'

'Not unless she was terrified and running for her life maybe, even then, surely she'd take her phone to ring us?'

'Thanks, Amber.'

She shrugged. 'Anytime, if you're a bit short and need another pair of hands I could help out for a few days in CID, if you asked Mads.'

She was standing a little too close to him with a smile on her face that, to put it bluntly, terrified him.

'I mean, I'm just as useful as Amy or Morgan, maybe even more. I don't seem to get myself in trouble like either of those two do. I'd be such an asset to your team, Ben, and I'd love to work with you. I've always wanted to be in CID. We could make a great team.'

She was standing so close to him he could smell her perfume; it was too strong and was making his eyes water. He took a step back.

'Ah, I've just seconded Tina and Sam to help out, I don't think Mads will release you as well. His team is almost as short-staffed as we are.'

A glint of fury crossed her eyes, then left as quickly as it came, and for a second he wondered if he'd misread her, but her voice was so cold when she spoke, he felt the chill in the air.

'You asked two PCSOs to help you guys out? When you could have asked me? Sorry, but what are they going to do?

Chase your killer and use harsh language to detain him?' She let out a cruel laugh, and Ben discovered that Amber hadn't changed much at all, she was still as mean as ever.

'Actually, I have no intention of letting them chase anyone. I requested them because of their dedication to the job, their experience and the fact that they are brilliant at any enquiries they are given. I didn't know you were interested in working on our team, Amber, but should the chance come up again I'll bear you in mind.'

He turned away from her. She was in his personal space, and he felt awkward; he wanted to get as far away from her as possible. He could feel her gaze glaring into the back of his neck as he made his way downstairs back to Declan, and imagined her eyes glowing red like some robot trying to burn his brains out.

Declan was standing over Susan Evans's body, but he glanced at Ben as if to say he'd heard everything. Amber thundered down the stairs to take up her place on the front step, and Ben mimed wiping his brow with the back of his hand.

Declan whispered, 'What was that about?'

Ben shrugged; his voice as low as he could get it. 'Whatever it was I haven't got the time for it.'

'Nobody has. I thought she was trying to seduce you up there, and I'm sorry but if anyone is going to get you to cheat on your good woman, please God let it be me.'

Ben began to chuckle and had to put his arm across him mouth to muffle the laughter. He didn't want to make Amber any angrier than she already was, but Declan was too funny and that was exactly why he loved his best friend, because of his terrible sense of humour.

40

Morgan hammered on Alisa's front door as hard as her heart was hammering in her chest. Alisa opened it and stared at her as she pointed her finger in her direction.

'Is Paige here? And don't lie for her. I need to know. This is vitally important.'

'No, I haven't seen her. I'm grounded even though I'm too old to be grounded.' She raised her voice so her mum could hear. 'Why do you want her? Have you been to her house?'

Morgan was sick of these two and their attitude, enough was enough. 'Yes, this morning I was there, and I found the dead body of her mum and no Paige, so if you know where she is you better tell me.'

'Susan is dead?' All the colour drained from Alisa's face.

Morgan nodded slowly. 'Yes, she is, and I'm worried about Paige. When did you last speak to her?'

'Oh God, I haven't spoken to her since you took us home. I was so mad at her, is she okay? Did she do it, did she kill her mum?' Her eyes as wide as saucers as she asked this last question.

Morgan shrugged. 'I don't know who did it, but I need to

find her. Do you have her on Snapchat? Can you do that location thing to find out where she is?'

'Yes, I can.' Alisa pulled her phone out of her pocket and opened Snapchat. A few swipes of her finger and she turned the screen around to show her. 'She's at home or her phone is.'

'Thanks. Look, if you hear from her, you must tell me. Does she have any other friends' houses I can check to see if she's there?'

'Not really, well there's Joe, but I doubt she's gone there again. Not after you so spectacularly made the two of us look like idiotic kids. He won't want anything to do with either of us, and I can't blame him.'

'I didn't have to do anything, you both acted like idiotic kids. That was on the pair of you not me.'

She turned to go back to her car, not even feeling bad for being so mean to the girl. Anger was raging through her bloodstream she was so frustrated. Alisa had caused nothing but trouble, her and Paige. Between the pair of them they had wasted her precious time and now it had come around to bite them on the backside. She didn't know if she could believe anything Alisa said.

She phoned Ben, glad to hear his voice even though it sounded as strained as hers was.

'Hey, did you check Paige's bedroom out? We didn't get the chance to, and Alisa has just tried to locate her on Snapchat. It's showing that she's either at home or her phone is.'

'Her phone's here. I asked Amber to search her room for me, and she found that, her purse and reckons that her make-up is all there too.'

'So, she didn't run away? Damn, we're no nearer to finding her, Ben. Amy is waiting for a cell site analysis that's a complete waste of time if her phone's at home.'

'I know. How did it go at the college?'

'Melody and Paige have the same English Lit tutor. He was

very nice, an older guy, but he drives a white car that is apparently at the garage.'

'Did you ask him which garage or get the reg?'

'No, because I didn't want him to think I was looking at him as a suspect.'

'Morgan, he is a suspect; anyone who drives a white car that matches the description Chloe Smith gave is a suspect.'

She paused and then said, 'He doesn't match the description. He's old. I'm going back to the station to run some checks on him anyway, and I'll check the DVLA database.'

'I'll meet you back there. Declan has almost finished up here.'

'Okay, see you soon.'

She slammed the palms of her hands against the steering wheel in frustration and set off back to the station to tell Amy to cancel the cell site. It had been some time since she'd felt this fiery, and she hoped to God that no one in the station tried to wind her up in case she lost her cool and did something stupid she would regret.

41

Morgan rushed back into the office. Cain was out, and Amy was staring out of the window.

'Hey, are you okay?'

Amy turned to her and nodded. 'Yeah, I'm fine. I got your message about Paige's phone, what a disappointment that was. I asked Ben to bring it back with him just in case there's any messages on there or clues where she could be. It's not looking good for her though, is it?'

'Not particularly but fingers crossed she's okay. I wonder if Joe is around today? It might be worth checking if he's seen her.'

Amy stood up and stretched. 'I'll go see who's in their office. Do you want anything to eat from the canteen?'

Morgan was starving but not enough to eat a shrivelled up tuna sandwich. 'I'm good thanks, we might get a takeaway when the others get back if we're working late. Hey, did you find anything on Jeff Whitehouse?'

Amy nodded. 'He's our typical nosey neighbour, complains about anything and everything from the people who deliver leaflets for the local takeaways to kids playing football in the street. There are more than thirty emails from him on the system. No criminal record though; he just sounds like a complete pain in the arse.'

With that she walked out. Morgan began to search the system for Adam Hayes, but nothing came back. She hadn't really expected it would. He wouldn't be doing his job if he had a criminal record, although plenty of other creeps managed to slip through the system. Look at Ian Huntley, he had lied and fooled everyone before there were DBS checks. She didn't get the creepy vibes from Adam Hayes, though, not the same ones that Huntley had given off from the moment he was on camera.

Picking up the phone she dialled the PNC bureau.

'Good afternoon, it's Morgan Brookes from Rydal Falls CID. If I give you a name and street could you look up if they have a vehicle for me?'

'Good afternoon to you too, Morgan Brookes from Rydal Falls CID. It's Beccy, I knew it was you, your picture flashed in the bottom of my screen.'

Morgan laughed as she stared at the picture of Beccy in the bottom corner of her screen. She'd worked with Beccy on section for a while before Beccy moved to PNC. 'I forgot about that.'

'Fire away.'

'Adam Hayes, lives in Victoria Avenue, Rydal Falls.'

'Reason for asking?'

'Intel.'

'Uhuh, it's thinking about it. God, this computer is slower than ever today. Ah, here it is. He drives a white Qashqai 2008, clean licence no points or fines and it's registered to one Victoria Avenue.'

'Thank you, Beccy, that's very helpful.'

'It's what I'm here for, you have a good afternoon, Morgan Brookes, and don't leave it so long next time.'

She ended the call to Beccy's laughter. Beccy had always been a comedian on shift. She was one of those people who automatically made you feel at ease. Staring down at the notepad on her desk where she'd written the car details, she googled the car, wondering if the interiors of these cars had anything memorable about them. If she showed Chloe some pictures of the different makes and models their suspects drove, would it help her to narrow down their list? Chloe had said it was an SUV, though. She went through her notes: *Adam Hayes drove a Qashqai 2008, etc., etc.*

Chloe's house was a small terraced in a busy street with not one parking space in sight. Morgan had to drive around a couple of times before finding one a couple of streets away in a ten-minute parking spot. She hoped the parking attendants weren't around because she didn't want to get a parking ticket. Then she remembered that Paige's life could be hanging in the balance; a twenty-five quid fine was nothing compared to that. Morgan had no idea if Chloe was home, she was running on hope and a prayer that she was. As she knocked on the door, she held her breath until the door opened and Chloe was standing in front of her looking confused.

'Hi, is this a good time?'

She nodded. 'Come in.'

Morgan followed her inside the beautiful vintage-themed house and fell in love with it straight away. It was furnished with stripped pine furniture, candles, throws, floral wallpapers and lots of little antique knick-knacks. 'Your home is beautiful.'

Chloe laughed, though it seemed strained, and Morgan wondered again how she was coping.

'My mum's home. She has an antique shop in Kendal and ends up bringing home more stuff than she sells.'

'I love it all, it's so cosy.'

Chloe sat on an oversized orange velvet armchair, behind her was an entire wall of bookshelves. As Morgan sat on the matching sofa, she sighed. 'This is literally my idea of heaven; do you love reading?'

She nodded. 'We both do. Luckily, me and Mum have similar taste in books so we can share them; occasionally we buy the same one and have to donate it to the charity shop but yeah, books are our life.'

Morgan smiled. 'Mine too, I've just read *The Maiden* by Kate Foster, and it was so good.'

Chloe was nodding. She pointed to the shelves where Morgan saw a copy of the same book. 'We loved it so much we're planning a trip to Edinburgh to see the guillotine on exhibition in the Museum of Scotland.'

'Amazing.' Morgan thought how much she would love that; she would go with them if she could. 'I'm sorry, I got distracted. I'm afraid I'm not here to talk books although I'd very much like to. I'm here to show you a couple of pictures to see if you recognise the interior of the vehicle when you were abducted, or some of the people we have on our suspects list. I'm not saying either of these were the guy who took you, but I'm trying to rule them out of my investigations. Is that okay with you?'

'Yes, of course.'

Morgan passed her the pictures of the interiors of the cars, and Chloe shook her head. 'It doesn't look like any of those. I'm sorry, I was thinking it might have been but it's more like a pickup kind of thing. It had a big back seat, but it also had an open back on it with tools in it.'

'You're sure about that?'

'Yes, sorry, should I have told you that before?'

'No, that's good, at least we know now. How about these guys, do you recognise either of them?' She passed the picture of Cooper over, and Chloe shook her head.

'No idea, I've never seen him before.'

'What about him?' Morgan handed her phone to Chloe with the picture of Adam Hayes on the screen.

'That's Mr Hayes, my English teacher. It wasn't him, I'd have known if it was him. He was younger than him by at least twenty years I'd say.'

Frustration mixed with relief flooded through Morgan's veins. She was glad the tutor wasn't involved, but she was annoyed that it hadn't been Cooper because it meant she had nothing.

'Sorry.'

'It's okay, could you have a look at some pickups now on your phone and see if you can find one similar while I'm here?'

Chloe leaned forward and picked an iPad up off the table. She began to google *white pickups UK*, and Morgan moved to sit next to her and then it hit her: all three of them had at some point been in the same English class at the same college.

'Do you know Paige Evans?'

'Know who she is, she never really speaks to me. She never really comes to class anymore either. She's always hanging around the canteen, or the office.'

'What about Melody Carrick?'

'I know Melody, I can't believe she's dead. That was such a shock when I found out. She is one of the nicest girls I know... or was.'

Chloe was looking at Morgan, her eyes opened wide with realisation. 'Oh God, do you think her killer was the one who tried to take me?'

Morgan saw no point in trying to hide it. 'Yes, I do. I think he targeted Melody, then you and now Paige.'

Chloe let out a sob. 'Is Paige dead too?'

'No, she's missing.'

She looked at the rows of books, there were thrillers, lots of historical fiction and a row of true crime. Chloe wasn't stupid, she deserved to know the truth.

'Paige is missing, but her mum is dead and I'm very worried for her.'

'Is there anything I can do to help?'

She reached out and patted Chloe's hand, which was icy to the touch.

'You've been very helpful, but there's nothing more you can do except keep yourself safe. Please don't go out on your own or let anyone inside your house you don't know.'

Big wet tears began to roll down her cheeks as she whispered, 'It's my fault Paige is missing, isn't it? If he hadn't let me go, he wouldn't have taken her.'

Morgan shook her head and gently squeezed her fingers. 'It's not your fault, it wasn't Melody's or Paige's either so please don't blame yourself. This is way beyond your control, and I'm just glad that, for whatever reason, he let you go. You were very lucky, Chloe, don't waste this second chance on feeling bad about things that have nothing to do with you. Now, let's look at these pickups and see if you can identify the one that you were in.'

Chloe nodded, and they both stared at the thumbnails of trucks that had loaded onto the screen. She pointed to a couple of them, enlarged them then shook her head and began to chew her thumbnail at the same time. Eventually she let out a sob. 'I don't know, I'm sorry, Morgan, I can't say which one it looks like, they all look the same.'

'It's okay, it was worth trying, please don't feel bad about it. It was definitely something like this?'

'Yes, I remember there was a lawn mower in the back. Well, I do now. I didn't at the time. All I could think of was what they taught us at Junior Citizen when we did stranger danger at junior school. They said we should get a description. And it was white car, white guy, blond hair, blue eyes – I said it over and over to myself in the car. I was so fucking scared I was going to die, it was like my whole brain shut down.'

A coldness gave Morgan full body chills. There had been a guy cutting the grass outside a house a few doors down from

Paige's the first time she had driven to her home. There had been a white pickup parked on the kerb, and the guy who followed her into the college car park had a lawn mower in the back of his white truck. Everything was spinning around her head; she had seen him not once but twice and hadn't given him a second glance. She needed to find the gardener from the college, she was sure it was him, but first she wanted to speak to the owner of that house. If he was their gardener, surely they could give her a name.

42

Cain had a shopping basket with cakes, biscuits and a box of cereal inside of it as he wandered around the Co-op. He was trying to imagine what a pregnant woman might be craving; well, he'd heard they had cravings, but he didn't know what of because he'd never had the chance to have children with his wife before she'd upped and left him. It broke his heart at the time and shocked him too; he never saw it coming at all, but then again how many coppers had failed marriages behind their backs? It was more common to be divorced than it was to stay with someone until they got old, which was what he'd hoped him and Catherine would do. He no longer wished she'd fall under a bus; he was getting better at accepting it. His phone rang and he smiled to see Angela's number.

'I wondered if you fancied a bit of supper when you finish work?'

'I would love some, it's been a day.'

'I imagine it has, I've seen all the crap over Facebook. There is a conspiracy theory that the girl's murder and the attempted abduction are all part of a trafficking ring that's gone wrong.'

'Jesus,' he muttered. 'We haven't looked at that angle

because what good is killing the person you're trying to traffic straight away and releasing the other girl? It wouldn't make any sense.'

Angela laughed.

'*I know, I'm just updating you on the rumours. You sound a little stressed.*'

'I'm a lot stressed. Should I pick up some wine? I'm in the shop now. Do you need anything else?'

'*Just you, I have everything we could need so don't worry. Do what you can and then turn up when you can get away. I'll be waiting for you and, Cain, be careful. One broken nose is enough for this week.*'

He laughed. 'You haven't seen the state of my face yet, you might not want to stare at it.'

Angela paused.

'*I would stare at your face no matter what. I can also kiss it better. See you later.*'

She hung up, leaving him staring at the bags of crisps and wondering what he had done to deserve finding a woman so kind and caring who didn't mind that he worked long, strange hours. He swallowed a lump in his throat. He was getting soft in his old age, and it hit him that Angela was older than him, she wouldn't want children at her age or at least he didn't think she would. He would have to accept that it wasn't meant to be. He'd rather have the company and love of someone who cared for him, and besides, he could be a great uncle to Amy's kid and fill any longings he had with looking after them. His phone rang again.

'*Just what the hell are you doing, Cain? I asked for a bar of chocolate. I didn't tell you to go do your weekly shop at Sainsbury's in Kendal. I'm starving, like now.*'

'If you're desperate, go to the vending machine in the canteen.'

'*Already done that in case I died of malnutrition while you were out. It's broken.*'

He laughed. 'You really are a bitch when you're hungry.'

'*You ain't seen nothing yet. Please could you get me a sandwich while you're there and I promise not to bite your head off again.*'

'You better pinky promise because I'm feeling all sensitive, and you being mean to me is not helping.'

'*Are you pregnant too, Cain?*'

He hung up. The woman behind the counter was listening in; she probably thought he was cheating on his wife after having those two completely different conversations. He paid for the shopping and went back to the car. Throwing the bag of food in the boot he saw a guy hurry past him, head down, trying not to stand out too much. But he recognised him.

'Cooper,' he whispered to himself.

He watched him from around the boot of the car and saw him get into a car parked further down the street. Amy was going to have to starve a little longer. He wasn't letting him get away again. He had a bone to pick with the guy, and how nice would it be if he returned to the station with their prime suspect as well as Amy's food? Maybe they could all get an early finish, and he could spend the rest of the evening with Angela and a bottle of red wine.

43

As Morgan drove into the cul-de-sac, she expected there to still be some activity outside Paige's house and was surprised at how eerily still it was. There was no sign of Ben, no van parked outside of it and no scene guard. She parked her car out front and got out, looking around the houses. The only thing signifying the heinous crime that had happened here was the flapping of the blue and white police tape that had been tied to the gate posts to warn people not to enter. Morgan ducked under it. Was someone inside the house? Maybe they were short of cars, especially after she wrote that one off the other day.

As she knocked on the front door it echoed around the house. She lifted the flap of the letter box. 'Hello.' Her voice fell flat. It had been the only sound to have cut through the silence. Straightening up she walked away, no one was home. She must have missed the updates about the undertaker arriving to transport the body to the mortuary.

Taking her radio out of her pocket, she found why she had missed them: it was dead. The battery was flat, and she had been so preoccupied she hadn't even heard the beeps it gave off to warn that the battery needed changing – Damn. She stared at the houses in the cul-de-sac to see which had a freshly cut lawn. They all did. The company that built them must employ the gardener. She was sure it had been the house three doors down from Paige's. The radio was as heavy as a brick and as much use as one when it wasn't working, and she threw it onto the front passenger seat of the car. She didn't bother locking the car; it wasn't as if there was anyone around to steal it.

This area was so perfect it reminded her of *The Stepford Wives*. She couldn't live here, it was too remote and too in each other's face despite the distance between the houses. The shape of them, in a semi-circle, meant even if you weren't a nosey neighbour, you couldn't help but see what everyone was up to. It was a little bit too freaky for her liking. Opening the gate to the garden she looked around and decided to hammer on the door. It was worth trying to get an answer. Hollow, it sounded, as if she was knocking on an empty wooden box, not a house and definitely not someone's home. There was a small wooden bench under the bay window, and she sat down. Her phone had one bar of signal, another reason she wouldn't consider living somewhere like this, crap signal.

She rang Cain hoping it got through.

'*Cain's crumpets.*'

'What?'

His laughter filled her ear.

'*Sorry, I was just trying it out, you know, in case I decide to leave this shithole and open a bakery.*'

'Well, it's a crap name so don't bother. Are you at the station?'

'*Not far, I'm on a snack run for ungrateful Amy, which is her new nickname by the way.*'

It was Morgan's turn to laugh. 'Is she giving you a hard time?'

'*When isn't she? I feel like she's the nagging wife who should be at home, not in my office. What did you want anyway?*'

'Aw, poor you. I might not want anything; I might have just wanted to hear your voice.'

'But you do want something.'

'Yes, I do. Sorry, do we know who owns these houses at Meadowfield View?'

'Where is that?'

'Susan and Paige Evans's address.'

'Oh, sorry, erm – that's a no. Why?'

'Someone must be maintaining the front gardens; they are all neatly cut and there isn't a weed in sight. I need to find out who that is because I think they're our number one person of interest and we should check them out.'

'Okay, that's good.'

She could barely hear him, his voice kept dropping out. 'Sorry, Cain, the signal is crap here. I'll see you back at the station.'

She had no idea if he'd heard her and hung up.

44

Ben arrived in the rear yard of the station at the same time as Cain, who was carrying a plastic bag and had a huge box of Coco Pops under his arm, which did not surprise Ben in the least. He glanced at the box. 'Hungry?'

Cain nodded. 'Starving, are we ordering food at some point?'

'What, you don't fancy Coco Pops now?'

Cain laughed. 'I never fancied them.' He lowered his voice. 'These are for Amy because she's been in a foul mood, and I thought she needed some carbs or something.'

Ben didn't waste his time replying and telling him that there was a good chance Amy was likely to smash the box of cereal over his head, but his heart was in the right place.

'Oh, Morgan rang, she wants to know who owns Susan Evans's house, do you know?'

'I thought Susan Evans did.'

'I think she means the other houses. Maybe the company that built them.'

'No idea, but you can find out for her.'

'I will after I've fed ungrateful Amy.' Cain said that a little too loud as Ben pushed the door to the office open.

'Ungrateful Amy?' said Amy, staring at Cain.

Ben laughed. 'I don't know why you two aren't married, you're like an old married couple.'

Both Cain and Amy gave him the V's, then Cain thrust the box of cereal in her direction.

'Peace offering.'

She stared at the box, a look of horror on her face, then at him, nodding in Ben's direction. Cain shook his head furiously and she mouthed. 'Thank you,' to him.

Ben left them to it, going into his office, no idea what was going on with the pair of them and too stressed to even ask. He needed time to gather his thoughts. He still wasn't over Amber's attitude.

His peace didn't last long as Marc came bounding in full of too much life after being at work all day.

'What's happening with the scene of Susan's murder?' Marc asked.

'Evening, boss.'

'Oh, yes, hello.'

'It's so secluded and section are really short-staffed, so I've taken officers off scene guard and released them. I waited until Susan Evans's body had been removed and taken to the mortuary before I locked up. I'll give the keys to the duty sergeant when we finish. There was no point tying staff up when they're needed elsewhere. I checked the other houses before I left, door knocking, there's still no cars or signs of people around.'

'I suppose that makes sense. Have we any updates to ease my heartburn even a little bit?'

'Morgan wants to know which company owns the properties, but we're not going to get hold of anyone now. It's too late.

We can get a list off them first thing and find out if they've been sold or what's happening with them.'

'Yes, that makes sense, but have we not already checked?'

'Apparently not, it has been a bit full-on.'

Marc sat on the seat opposite Ben's, leaned back, putting his feet up on the edge of his desk and said, 'So, what are we eating because I'm not a fan of cereal and whoever brought those Coco Pops in can keep them.'

Ben laughed. It was so out of the blue and an un-Marc like conversation that he felt himself thawing a little more towards him. He almost sounded like one of them and that could only be a good thing, maybe he was finally losing his big city, tough guy edge and realising that none of them were out to get him; they just wanted a boss they could trust and work with.

45

Morgan stretched out her legs and yawned. It was such a warm evening despite the setting sun, and she relished the little bit of heat on her face. Sunset was her favourite time of the day, when the darkness came creeping in, taking over the sky; she loved it. She had always been drawn to the dark, the moon and stars.

A muffled thud broke her daydream, and she stilled, her ears pricking to attention. She looked around, but couldn't see anything that had made the noise. It happened again and she turned more slowly, relieved she wasn't sitting in Susan Evans's front garden. One haunted house investigation had been enough for her as she saw an image of Margery Lancaster's dilapidated, lonely cottage in her mind. She didn't call out or make a sound, but turned and pressed her face to the window to see if anyone was inside the front room. There was a tiny crack in the curtains, but she couldn't see anything inside that room. It was empty. But it happened again, and it sounded as if it was coming from the back of the house. She moved to try the gate latch, but it didn't budge. It was locked.

Stepping back, she surveyed the fence. It wasn't that high, she could climb it if she dragged the bench over to stand on. So she did just that. She peered over the other side, it was a bit of a drop, and she had a dodgy ankle, but she had clearly heard two thuds from inside the empty house, so she swung her legs over and dropped onto the grass which was thankfully longer out here and hadn't been maintained like the front. It cushioned her feet as they landed with a thud. Amazed she hadn't fallen onto her arse, she walked to the back window to peer in. The kitchen was new and unused. It was also as empty as the front of the house, so what was making the banging? Taking a few steps back she stared up at the bedroom window just as something hit it with such force that it splintered into hundreds of pieces. Morgan ducked instinctively putting her hands on top of her head to protect herself as she was showered in glass.

The noise had masked the sound of the man creeping up on her and before she even understood what was happening, he grabbed her from behind.

They began to tussle, but he had a vicelike hold of her arms. Lifting her foot she rammed her boot into his shin with such force he yelled loud and threw her to the ground.

She looked up at him. *Who was he?* Whoever he was, she knew he was going to hurt her, and she wished with all her heart that she still had her brick of a radio to smash him over the head with. She began frantically searching for something she could use as a weapon. But there was nothing.

She jumped up and began to run. If she could get to the car, she could call for help and lock the doors. Morgan looked at the fence and took a run at it, no idea if she could get herself high enough to scrabble over it. Her fingers gripped the rough-cut wood, and she felt pain like hot needles as they scraped over it, embedding splinters in her fingertips. He was up now and running at her. She tried to pull herself up, but he was too fast, and he grabbed her ankles, dragging her down, her hands gathering more splinters as she felt herself falling. Morgan hit the ground with an 'ugh.'

He leaned over her; she'd managed to knock the baseball cap and saw the ashen blond wig he was wearing. It had been thrown off-kilter. It was the guy who had been mowing the lawn the first time she'd been here. There was a look of pure rage in his eyes, but she didn't care. As he leaned down to grab her, she threw a left hook with everything she had and caught him on the jaw with a loud crunch; but it wasn't as loud as the crunch when he lifted his work boot and slammed it down into her head with such force, she was knocked unconscious.

Ben opened his drawer and pulled out a plastic document holder with a list of menus from the local takeaways and passed it to Marc.

'You choose, I'll eat whatever at this point and I think Cain will too. I'm sure Amy is full of the cereal he kindly bought her.'

Marc rolled his eyes. 'Has he got a death wish?'

Ben grinned and nodded. 'Apparently so, let me ring Morgan and see what she wants.'

He hadn't even thought about her being out on her own so long when everyone else was back at the office. But as her phone began to ring out, that cold, prickling sensation of fear began to creep along his skin, leaving goosebumps on his arms, and he felt a cold shiver cross the back of his neck and shoulders as it went to voicemail.

'Hey, it's me, where are you? We're ordering food. Ring me back ASAP and let me know you're okay and what you want.'

Marc was studying the menus. He didn't even glance at Ben as he stood up and went to talk to Cain.

'Where did you say Morgan was last time you talked to her?'

'She never said, boss, she just asked who owned the houses. She did say she had a crap signal though, and I could barely hear her so I wouldn't worry too much.'

Ben nodded, that would explain her not answering, but why wasn't she back here? He'd waited nearly an hour for the undertakers to arrive then driven back to the station. She'd only gone out on a couple of enquiries. He grabbed Cain's radio off the desk and punched her collar number into the keypad, then jabbed the green *call* button. It didn't even ring. Lifting it to his mouth he spoke into it. 'Morgan, this is Ben, are you receiving?'

Nothing. After a few seconds the control room inspector spoke.

'Is everything okay, Ben?'

'Do you have the last location for Morgan, ma'am?'

Cain was standing up, a look of panic on his face. He tried ringing her, but it rang out. He looked at Ben. 'I think we should go to Susan Evans's house; she was asking about it. Maybe she's there and got no signal?'

'Give us a couple of minutes. We're just reloading the GPS tracking system, Ben.'

Ben nodded to Cain, and they rushed out of the office, leaving Marc none the wiser and still deciding over what to order for his supper. Amy wanted to go with them but knew if Morgan was in trouble, then there was a good chance that she would drag the others into it with her, and because of her predicament she stayed where she was, feeling torn but not sure she should get herself involved in anything violent. She silently prayed that this was a false alarm and that she was on her way back. Ben and Cain were panicking for nothing, but a little niggle in her stomach told her life wasn't this simple and something was wrong.

46

Through the haze of pain, she could hear someone faintly moaning, but she couldn't open her eyes or move her hands to see who it was. Morgan didn't need anyone else to tell her she was in deep shit because the pain in the side of her face and head was so intense. She knew it. She was on a soft floor, at least there was that. She tried to open her left eye a tiny bit, but it wouldn't open; it was swollen shut. She managed to see a big king size bed in the middle of the room with her other eye. There was somebody with her, they were in the shadows but it didn't sound like the guy who had attacked her. Turning her head the slightest in the direction of the sound sent a wave of nausea rushing up her throat that she had to choke back down, and the acid burned her throat as she pushed it back and gulped. She didn't want him to know she was conscious enough to vomit all over herself; she wouldn't give him the pleasure.

Could she see Paige? Or was she hallucinating? It was hard to tell with the head wound she had.

'Paige.' Her voice barely audible enough to be heard. The girl was nodding violently, and Morgan thought *well at least I've solved that puzzle* before closing her eyes for a second to try and stop the sickness that was threatening to come back up. What was she going to do? Paige was alive, that was good. Morgan was too which was a bonus, but the pain in her head was a huge problem. No one knew anything about the gardener yet. They'd have no idea to look for her here. She lay there listening for sounds of movement In the room or outside of it, but there weren't any.

'Is he here?' She looked at Paige through her one eye, and she shook her head. She wondered why Paige didn't speak then saw the material that he'd gagged her with biting into the soft flesh of her mouth.

'Are you hurt?'

Another violent shake of the head this time.

'Good, that's good, but you can't move or scream?'

Another shake.

Morgan lay there taking deep breaths in through her nose and out through her mouth. Why hadn't he gagged her? Maybe he was panicking and not thinking straight, that was good. Although it wasn't as if anyone could hear her scream. She was like Ripley off *Aliens*, alone on a foreign planet with no one to hear her scream, well, except for Paige and that didn't count because she was being held captive too. They could make as much noise as they wanted and the only person to hear them was the psychopathic killer who had taken the pair of them. She tried to move her hands. They were tied together but there was movement in the rope.

'Paige, can you untie me if I shuffle towards you?'

She shrugged, and Morgan pushed both of her feet into the soft, plush carpet, moving her body a little bit and sending shockwaves of pain straight to her brain. Gritting her teeth she ignored them, even though she could only move an inch at a time. She kept on wondering if she was leaving a trail of her brain matter behind like a giant slug, and would it repair itself or was she slowly killing herself? She had to keep going because she knew she would rather risk killing herself than letting whoever this bastard was do it.

Her head touched something soft, and she realised it was Paige's thigh. A silent tear fell from her good eye, and she felt soft fingers stroke her forehead. She lifted her hands towards Paige and felt the girl's cold fingers begin to work at the ropes. Neither of them had much movement but there was enough to try and jiggle them loose for Morgan to slip her hands out and untie Paige. As Paige struggled to loosen the ropes, Morgan strained her ears, listening out for any noise. A car engine started outside, and she hoped he was driving away. She didn't care if he left them here for days, between them they could get loose. If she could untie Paige the girl could run for help. She was younger and didn't have the disadvantage of a head wound. And then Paige would survive.

Finally, she felt the rope lose its grip and managed to slip her hands through. She began to do the same to Paige, gritting her teeth at the pain in her fingertips from those bloody splinters off that fence, although Paige's ropes were a lot tighter. He'd obviously panicked when he'd realised who Morgan was. He must have been through her pockets and found her warrant card. Good, she didn't care. They would find him eventually, let him run away. She felt the rope give and Paige slipped her hands out. Pulling down the gag she gasped and sucked in deep breaths of air.

'Oh my God, Morgan, I thought you were dead. He carried you in here like you were a sack of shit. You were thrown over his shoulder and then he just dropped you and you let out a small grunt. I was so relieved.'

'Do you know him, who is he?'

'He does the garden, he cuts the lawn for Mum.' She stopped at the mention of her mum's name. 'He said he'd killed her.' A sob filled the room. 'Is she dead?'

'Yes, I'm sorry, but unless we figure out a way to get out of here it won't matter because he'll kill us too. I need you to be brave, Paige. I can hardly move my head, so I want you to be my eyes. I need you to find me something that I can use to hurt him when he comes back. Can you do that? Anything that's heavy, hard or sharp.'

Paige pulled herself up and began to look around frantically. But there was nothing in here except the small wooden stool she had used to break the window. She picked it up and took it to Morgan, who looked at it and thought that she would need to be able to swing it hard to make a difference to him if he came back. It was no good, it was too clumsy as a weapon.

'Can you get a pillowcase off the bed and rip it, then tie it around the wound in my head? If you tie it tight enough, I might be able to move it and stop feeling like I'm on the deck of the *Titanic*.'

Paige did that, rapidly tugging off one of the soft cotton pillowcases. She managed to tear it in half and wrapped it around Morgan's head, knotting it as tight as she could. Then watched as Morgan managed to slide herself up so she was leaning against the wall.

The room was spinning, and Morgan felt as if she had the worst hangover of her life, but she stayed upright, breathing deeply through her nose and exhaling through her mouth with the pain, waiting for the dizziness to subside enough for her to get to her feet. Paige helped her up and even though she was swaying and unsteady she managed to keep upright.

'So far so good, we need to get out of here before he comes back.'

'What if he comes back?'

'I'll distract him, and you run like fuck, Paige. I mean it, you run as hard and fast as you can because if you don't, we're both dead. Even if he's getting the better of me you run, you don't stop to help, you'll get yourself killed. You run to my car; can you drive?'

'Sort of.'

Morgan felt in her pocket for her keys. They'd gone; he'd taken her car.

'It doesn't matter he's got my keys. Where's his car?'

'In the garage, he's been renting this house. He keeps it in there.'

'Plan B, we get out. You run to the woods; do you know how to get to the nearest houses through those woods?'

'Yes.'

'Then you have to do that.'

A loud bang as the door slammed shut downstairs filled them both with fear. Fresh tears shone in Paige's eyes.

Morgan picked up the stool and whispered, 'You hide behind the door. When he comes in, I'll get his attention, and you do what I said.'

'I can't leave you.'

'You better had; I mean it.'

But he didn't come upstairs right away. They could hear him moving around downstairs, and Paige tiptoed into the en suite to look for something to use against him. She came out empty-handed or at least it looked that way, and Morgan closed her eye in frustration. *How had it come to this?* She had been enjoying the sunset and minutes later fighting for her life. She hoped that Ben had noticed she wasn't around and came looking for her, but she didn't have the time to rely on Ben or Cain to save her. This was on her. She gripped the stool as tight as she could, and they both waited to hear his footsteps climbing the stairs.

47

Ben let Cain drive, he was better at driving vans than Ben; had been a response officer a lot longer than he'd been a detective. It was the other way around for Ben and the last time he'd driven at speed he'd taken the wing mirrors off the car. His heart was pounding inside his chest. He knew they were panicking but something was wrong. Morgan knew how much he worried about her; she wouldn't ignore his calls unless her phone had died, but she'd head back to the station if that was the case.

'Ben, we've located her radio in the area of Meadowfield View, Keswick.'

'Thanks, urgent assistance to that area, please. I'd rather be safe than sorry.'

The inspector called out.

'All patrols to head for Meadowfield View, who's nearest?'

Ben heard Amber's voice

'Twenty minutes away, Inspector.'

As much as he didn't want to face her, he needed her assistance. 'We're en route, we'll meet you there. Is there no patrol nearer than that?'

'Ben, they're all around twenty minutes away. How far are you?'

'Ten,' replied Cain.

Marc's voice filled the van.

'What's going on? I'm on my way.'

Cain rolled his eyes. 'Oh good, that makes everything better, doesn't it?'

Ben couldn't answer. He was furious that Morgan might be in trouble and hadn't called for backup, but at least they had a location. She would be the one who was furious when they all turned up and she was sitting in her car having a breather. God, he hoped that was exactly what she was doing. The alternative was too scary to think about.

———

Finally, he stopped doing whatever it was he'd been doing downstairs as it went quiet.

Morgan looked at Paige. 'You run, promise?'

Paige was nodding, but Morgan didn't trust the girl. She hadn't given her much hope with her previous track record of doing exactly the opposite of what she was told. Morgan counted the footsteps as he came up. It got to eighteen and then he paused. Could he sense something had changed? Had they made a noise? Did they smell of fear and perspiration with all the effort it had taken for them to free themselves? Her heart was racing, her vision was blurry, and she had to blink several times to clear it enough so that she could see straight. She didn't want to try to smash him with the stool and miss completely because she was seeing double.

The door handle turned, and she held her breath. He threw the door open hard and it hit Paige, but she never made a sound. The kid was a lot tougher than she looked. He searched the floor where he'd thrown Morgan, a look of confusion on his face, then he looked to where Paige had been. *Closer, come in the room, you prick.*

Morgan waited and then he stepped in and looked at her with such puzzlement he just stood there. She didn't hesitate and swung the stool towards him as hard as she could. It cracked against the side of his head, making him stumble forwards. She saw Paige run from behind the door and out of the room, making her feel a tiny bit better. Not giving him time to recover she hit him again and again until he was on his knees. His leg shot out as he kicked backwards, repaying the favour from earlier, and she felt her knees give way as she stumbled towards him. Too dizzy to stop herself from falling she landed on the floor with a heavy bang.

He began to laugh, a loud braying sound that chilled her to the bones, and then he was grabbing her and on top of her. They were wrestling, he was grabbing her wrists as she tried to shrug him off. He let go and punched the side of her head, but she managed to move so that it didn't make direct contact and only grazed the open wound, though that was enough to make her grimace. He pulled his fist back again, and she steeled herself for another blow, when he stopped mid-air, a look of surprise on his face as he began to topple towards her. Unable to move, Morgan was pinned down by his dead weight. Paige was above her, wielding a kettlebell in both hands and a grin on her face.

'Should I hit him again? They never do in the movies, and then they get up and stab them all to death.'

Morgan lifted a hand to his neck to feel for a pulse, it was there but his eyes were closed, and she could feel the warmth as his blood gushed out of the wound on the back of his head which was even deeper than hers.

'No, but if he moves you can. Help me get him off.'

Paige put the kettlebell down far enough away so he couldn't reach it, but in distance so she could use it again if she had to. She grabbed hold of his arms and dragged him off Morgan the best she could, then helped Morgan to extricate herself from under the unconscious man. Paige helped Morgan to her feet and towards the door, but she couldn't help herself and turned back to kick him hard in the kidneys with her Dr Marten boot. 'That's for Melody, you fucker.' Paige ran back and did the same to his other side. 'And that's for my mum.'

Morgan grinned at her as Paige wrapped her arm around her and helped her out onto the landing, then down the stairs. They let themselves out of the front door and out into the darkness, Paige still holding on to the heavy weight in one hand. Morgan pointed to the bench and the pair of them sank onto it, exhausted, in pain but alive, and she would take that any day over the alternative.

They heard the sirens and saw the bright blue lights as they swept into the cul-de-sac, where the police van screeched to a halt, the halogen headlights blinding them both so much they had to lift their hands to cover their eyes. Morgan heard Ben calling her name and she had never felt so glad to hear his voice.

'Morgan, oh my God.'

He sank to his knees in front of her, his hands cupping the sides of her head gently.

'Paige did great, he's upstairs. I'd say I wished he was dead, but he isn't so I'm not wasting my breath.'

Ben turned to Paige. 'Are you hurt?'

'No, but Morgan's head is a mess.' She pointed and Ben's face dropped. 'Maybe not as much of a mess as his. Are you going to arrest me?'

Cain shook his head. 'No, we are not, it was self-defence. You did great, Paige.'

Taking out his handcuffs he gave an update over the radio and asked for two ambulances.

Ben stood up. 'I can't let him go in there alone. Are you okay if I go with him?'

'Yes, go.' She couldn't nod, it hurt her head too much.

Morgan closed her one open eye and let her head press against the coolness of the window behind her. There was no way she would get away with asking for this to be taped up and sent on her way. Maybe she should give in and let them take her, as long as she didn't have to look at his face. She realised she didn't even know his name and didn't really care. That would all come out soon enough. More sirens in the distance sounded like music to her ears. Say what you want about the police, when you needed them, they were there. It was a crappy job at times, but she was glad to be a part of it.

48

Ben helped her out of the car, and she let him. He was cut up enough about her getting hurt, and she wasn't going to make out she didn't need him because she did. Maybe she didn't need him to save her, she was pretty good at saving herself, but she needed him in her life. His love, compassion and company were the most amazing things she never knew she needed. As she walked into the house, she heard the gentle Irish lilt of Declan's voice and Theo's low throaty laugh. Ben led her to the kitchen where her two favourite people were standing next to Cain and Amy. She smiled at them all.

'What is this, a homecoming party?'

Declan stepped forward and pulled her into his arms, rocking her gently from side to side. 'It's a thank God that Brookes woman has a head harder than granite party. You know, considering what it's been through, you would think you'd be punch drunk and unable to talk without slurring.'

Both Ben's and Theo's mouths dropped wide open in horror, but she began to laugh. It hurt her head, but it felt so good. Declan released her and he was replaced by Theo, who hugged her much softer than Declan had. 'If he carries on it will be a wake for the insensitive Doctor Donnelly party. I'm glad you're home, Morgan. We were terribly worried about you.'

She smiled at him. 'Thanks, Theo.'

Amy, who didn't do hugging, gave her a brief one then stepped away, leaving Cain gazing at her.

'Do you need a bear hug?'

She nodded, and he swept her into his arms, lifting her off the floor and making her squeal with laughter until Ben slapped his arm.

'Oops, the boss is getting all jealous.' He put her down, and she let out a sigh.

'I never knew just how lucky I was to have you all in my life, but thank God that I do.'

Declan smiled at her. 'We have a couple more surprises for you, my little sweet potato.'

'You do?'

She heard someone walking in behind her and turned to see Marc carrying what was the biggest birthday cake she'd ever seen.

'Whose birthday is it?'

'It's more of a we're glad you didn't die cake, but Costco didn't have time to write that on it, and they said it was offensive. I nipped back to Manchester especially to buy this.'

Morgan giggled. 'You took notice of the cake advice. That's good, I like that, boss, well done.'

He grinned at her. 'I'm getting better at not being a dick, at least that was what Cain said when I arrived at the scene.'

Cain nodded at Amy. 'Amy has something to tell you all, don't you?'

Her cheeks burned red, but she nodded. 'I'm pregnant, and no, Cain is not the father no matter what he tells you. Jack is, but we've split up so it's a bit of a mess. However, Cain has offered to be my birthing partner, so what more could I ask for?'

Cain was grinning. 'She's fibbing, I am so.'

'No, you are not.'

'Well, I'll be a surrogate dad. What more could you ask for? Isn't this great, she actually has a reason to be a mean and moody mare now. Who'd have thought it?'

Morgan thought that her cheeks might crack she was smiling so much as everyone congratulated Amy, even Marc.

'Right then, let's eat cake. What a grand afternoon this has turned out to be.' Declan was waving a huge kitchen knife around. 'Should I do the honours? I'm an expert at slicing and dicing.'

Theo let out a groan. 'Your sense of humour is terrible.'

'I know, but that's why you find me irresistible.' He winked at Theo, and he passed the huge cake box over to him.

Morgan watched her friends; she was no longer the lonely, moody girl who had locked herself away when she was fifteen, afraid to have friends after losing Brad in a terrible accident. Life was better when you had laughter and friendship, there was no doubt about that.

EPILOGUE
TWO WEEKS LATER

Morgan and Amy were both office bound, there had been no ifs and buts about it. Amy was on light duties and Marc had specified to Morgan that under no circumstances was she allowed out on active duty until she had a clear bill of health. She hadn't argued with him. She was happy to be sorting through the evidence from the house where Harry Thomas had been squatting and hiding out.

She bent down to pull one of the plastic evidence bags out of the container they'd been placed in and examined the small wooden box. She could just read the inscription on it: *Sarah*. She was wearing a pair of blue nitrile gloves, but she needed to see what was inside the box, managing to open it without ripping the bag or her gloves and ruining the chain of evidence. She stared in wonder at the odd earrings, broken crucifix and bent silver bangle. She counted the pieces of jewellery, there were three pairs of earrings, the necklace and a bracelet, all completely different, and felt a cold chill settle across her shoulders. Five pieces of broken jewellery: the crucifix she knew was Melody's because Jade had given her a picture of it when she'd realised it was missing; Paige had told her that her gran's silver bangle was missing off her mum's arm when she'd gone to visit her, and she hadn't been able to find it anywhere in the house. That left three odd earrings, three different shapes, styles and sizes. She swallowed the lump in her throat. He had taken these from other women that he'd killed, she had no doubt about that. Now, she would make sure she tracked their families down and found out who they were, even if it took her the rest of her career. She would make sure she found any other victims that had been killed by Harry Thomas.

Cain walked in and stared at the bag. 'You know I found Cooper, don't you?'

She nodded. 'Yeah, I interviewed him. He was living out of his car and had all his worldly possessions in the boot, including a blue box bigger than that, but it belonged to his gran after all. He showed me pictures of his gran wearing the stuff that was in it. Paige was a little off track with that one, but she meant well I suppose. Actually, I don't know if she did. She was trying to get rid of him because she knew he was cheating on her mum with Jackie, so she came up with an elaborate plan to set him up. It was her bad luck to be living a few doors down from a real killer. Honestly, one day we should write about this stuff, people would love it. The truth is far worse than what those writers you're always raving about come up with.'

This made Morgan smile. 'Yeah, who'd figure that out?'

'Well, us, we're shit hot detectives, it's what we do.'

She couldn't argue with him on that point, it was what they did, and she was glad to be a part of it.

A LETTER FROM HELEN

I want to say a huge thank you for choosing to read *Two Broken Girls*. If you did enjoy it, and want to keep up-to-date with all my latest releases, just sign up at the following link. Your email address will never be shared, and you can unsubscribe at any time.

www.bookouture.com/helen-phifer

Thank you so much for reading this instalment in the Morgan Brookes series!

I hope you loved *Two Broken Girls* and if you did I would be very grateful if you could write a review. I'd love to hear what you think, and it makes such a difference helping new readers to discover one of my books for the first time.

I love hearing from my readers – you can get in touch through my social media or my website.

Thanks,

Helen

www.helenphifer.com

ACKNOWLEDGEMENTS

As always, the biggest thank you goes to my wonderful editor Jennifer Hunt who works so hard to make these stories so enjoyable. I love working with you, Jennifer, you're the best.

Another big thank you to Jeanette Curry for her skilful copy editing. A massive thank you to Shirley Khan for doing such a great job with the proofread.

Many thanks to Jen Shannon and the rest of the amazing team at Bookouture for everything you do, I can't remember my kids names most days so I'm really happy you will have your own page after this. Well done, everyone, teamwork is the dream work and the whole team at Bookouture are amazing.

A massive thank you to Kim Nash for making my Theakston's Crime dreams come true this year. I had the best time hosting a table at the author dinner and if you love crime stories, I highly recommend going to the crime festival in Harrogate. It's a wonderful weekend and I walked around like I do every year, starstruck at all my favourite authors. So for me to be there in a professional capacity was the highlight of my year, actually it's the highlight of my entire writing life.

A huge thank you as always to my publication day and cover reveal day wing gal Noelle Holten, always there to make sure it all goes smoothly, and I can't thank you enough.

Thank you to Jenny Geras, the youngest looking woman I know. I'm never getting over it!

Also thank you to Peta Nightingale for the German translations, and the lovely Levke Kluge, my German editor, for all your hard work and the regular updates. It makes me so happy to know that Morgan Brookes is now international.

I'd like to thank all the wonderful, amazing reading groups that choose my books and recommend them to the other members, it is such an honour to see my name mentioned in your wonderful groups. Especially The Friendly Book Community, UK Crime Book Club, Fiction Addicts @ Socially Distanced Book Club, Novels N Latte Book Club and the fabulous Lisa Reagan Reader Lounge.

Special thanks to Maureen Downey, Beverley Ann Hopper, Teresa Nikolic, Sarah Kingsnorth, Trina Dixon, Dawn @ Hampshire Book Lover, Mel @Melanie's_Reads73, Jen @Books in Jens Library for all of your support, I really appreciate the publication day love you always show me and if I've missed anyone please let me know, I'm sure I have missed lots of you but not on purpose, I truly love and appreciate you all.

A huge thank you to all of the wonderful book bloggers too, how you find the time to read so many books and share the love with everyone is just amazing and so very much appreciated.

The biggest thank you goes to you, the person reading this book. You have no idea how much I love and appreciate your support. You are the reason I get to carry on writing and doing what I love every day. I'm so honoured that you choose to read my stories and, if I could hug you, I would give you the biggest squeeze ever!

Thank you to Sam Thomas and Tina Sykes, my coffee gals, porn star martini support group and best friends. You never fail to make me laugh and are always there when I need to rage rant about something. We have shared some good and bad times over the years as well as lots of laughter. I love you both!

Thanks to Krog Crosthwaite for the unofficial therapy coffee chats too and the laughter.

A special thank you to everyone in book club; we have such

a great time and now Joanne has taken charge we might even read the books.

A huge thank you to the amazing Selena, Dan and Jenny for letting Jaimea into your home and lives so much that he'd live there if he could. You're his second family and I can never thank you enough for taking such good care of him so that I can write these books, go on research trips and occasionally drink porn star martinis.

Thank you to the wonderful staff at Mill Lane Day Care Centre too, you are all Saints and Jaimea loves his time with you all.

Where would I be without my amazing, wonderful, crazy family! I'm so blessed to have such wonderful grown-up children, who have such amazing partners and who have given me the best grandkids a Nanna could ask for. Jess, Josh, Juju, Jeorgia, Jaimea, Danielle, Deji, Gracie, Donny, Lolly, Tilda, Sonny, Sienna and Bonnie. You make my heart so full that some days I think it might burst with love and pride. We recently spent a morning feeding Alpaca's at the brilliant Bardsea Alpacas and Llamas, and it was an amazing sight to see you all with your beautiful children having fun. Family days out have drastically improved from your younger days, I didn't have to blackmail any of you to come. 😉

Lastly thank you to my husband Steve, the best bag carrier, research companion and cheerleader I could ask for. I love you all so much. Xxx

PUBLISHING TEAM

Turning a manuscript into a book requires the efforts of many people. The publishing team at Bookouture would like to acknowledge everyone who contributed to this publication.

Audio
Alba Proko
Sinead O'Connor
Melissa Tran

Commercial
Lauren Morrissette
Hannah Richmond
Imogen Allport

Cover design
The Brewster Project

Data and analysis
Mark Alder
Mohamed Bussuri

Editorial
Jennifer Hunt
Sinead O'Connor

Made in United States
Troutdale, OR
10/24/2024

24076789R00163